PRAISE FOR *HEART LIKE AN OCEAN*

From page one, Christine Steendam had me hooked and caring about what happened to Senona, a character that I could identify with even though we are separated by centuries. Christine does an awesome job of showing how human emotion and desire flows as one across the expanse of time ... and oceans. I don't want to give any spoilers, but rest assured that you'll feel the roll of every tide right along with Senona and the ending is not one that you'll be able to guess! Can't wait for more from this awesome author!
– Sara Barnard Bestselling author of *An Everlasting Heart* series

I didn't consider myself a historical romance reader- but this book has proven that I simply didn't give the genre a chance. I'm definitely a fan! Eloquent and passionate- this book is a must read.
– C. Elizabeth Vescio author of *Uncontrollably Wasted*

I will be looking out for more books by this author and look forward to her next offering with excitement!
– Lisa J Hobman Bestselling author of *Bridge Over the Atlantic*

I highly recommend this book- it has action, adventure, great characters and, much like it's main character, exceeds the limits of what it's been labelled; this book isn't a good historical romance novel, it is a GREAT BOOK.
– Andrew Lorenz Creator of *Legacy* and *New Guard.*

PRAISE FOR *UNFORGIVING PLAINS*

This is a great book! Get your pajamas on, grab your favorite blanket, get a diet coke and curl up in your favorite chair and enjoy this sweet book.
-Stephanie Lasley, from The Kindle Book Review

It is a great book to curl up with on a cold night with a cup of cocoa to escape into a beautifully portrayed landscape with characters that you will root for…or possibly, thump on the forehead.
– CaSondra Poulson author of *Calling Me Home*

Romance and building suspense come together to make Unforgiving Plains a very enjoyable contemporary western. Ms. Steendam has a writing style that is easy to read. I would recommend this book to readers of romantic suspense and contemporary westerns.
–Denise Moncrief author of *Crisis of Identity*

Overall, a wonderful story, plausible, heartfelt and with endings that bring you back to earth gently.
– Barb Fenwick

Christine Steendam is clearly a very versatile writer and the shift from historical to contemporary romance was done effortlessly. I would certainly like to read more contemporary romances from this author.
-Lisa J Hobman bestselling author of *The Girl Before Eve*

This is tale worth reading, as readers enjoy the push and pull of opposites against the beauty of the great white north!
– Ind'tale Magazine

Betrayed by the Ocean

Christine Steendam

ISBN: 978-0-9939259-2-4

This is a fictional work. The names, characters, incidents, places, and locations are solely the concepts and products of the author's imagination or are used to create a fictitious story and should not be construed as real.

Hazelridge Press

PO Box 21 Group 37 RR3
Dugald, MB R0E 0K0
 www.christinesteendam.com

ISBN 978-0-9939259-2-4
Betrayed by the Ocean
Christine Steendam
Copyright Christine Steendam 2015
Published by Hazelridge Press

Photo Credit: Viola Estrella
Author Photo: Prairie and Pine Studio

First Edition/First Printing January 2015 Printed U.S.A.

HAZELRIDGE PRESS.

To Kyle: Who taught me what it is like to be found.

CHRISTINE STEENDAM

CONTENTS

ACKNOWLEDGMENTS

I am so very blessed to be sitting here writing acknowledgements for yet another book. When I first started writing I never thought it would come to this point. Being published was a pipe dream. One that I didn't really think would ever come to fruition. I've never been more thankful to be wrong.

Thank you to Kyle, my husband, my best friend, my partner in life. Your support and encouragement is everything to me.

Thank you to my parents, Wendy and Henry. I'm fairly certain you're my biggest fans, and have been since the day I was born. When I doubted I could make a career out of writing, you were the ones who always believed in me.

Thank you to Jasper and Deacon, you're the best sons I could ask for. Someday you'll understand why I spend so much time clicking away on the keyboard.

Thank you to Heather for being my beta reader yet again, for hating Brant so that I had to work that much harder to make you like him (did I succeed?), and for always pushing me to make my story the best in can be.

Thank you to Elissa also, for beta reading, and for getting as passionate about the story as I do.

Thank you to Carmen. Without your insistence, encouragement, and letting me bounce ideas off of you, I probably wouldn't have written this story. Thank you for being yet another pair of eyes to read and give feedback.

As a blanket thank you to my beta readers and advance readers—your input, feedback, and time dedicated to this book is invaluable to me. Thank you.

Thank you, Ellen. I don't know what I'd do without you.

Thank you to Viola, my cover designer. As always you created the perfect image to accompany the story.

Thank you to the entire team of people that brought this book from its first word, to publication. It takes an author to write a book, but it takes an army of supporters to release it.

And thank *you*, the reader. This book is for you and I want to thank you from the bottom of my heart for picking it up. I hope you enjoy it.

Christine Steendam.

CHAPTER ONE

Spain- 1671

Brant stared at Catherine, her words not quite sinking in. His ears buzzed as if they were in the aftershock of a cannon firing. "What do you mean you're leaving?"

Catherine's eyes welled up with tears. "I got a letter from my parents. They're worried about the unrest between Spain and England and they want me to bring Johnny home. We leave tomorrow, and I won't be coming back."

Brant walked away, unable to look at Catherine. He looked out the window of the house he had built for her. It had been completed a month ago. She'd just moved in, and she had spent hundreds of doubloons on furnishing and decorating the house that was supposed to be their home.

He'd promised her the wedding she'd been asking for this coming spring. He'd given her everything she'd ever asked for, and now she was leaving.

"I don't understand," he said, still looking out the window. Unable to look at her tear streaked face—the sorrow that mocked him and his pain.

"This past year with you has been… an experience. We've been through a lot, and we've done our fair share of hurting each other—"

"And we moved past that, stronger than ever."

"No, we forgave and tried to forget, but didn't fix anything."

"I gave up my life for you!"

"I know."

"Everything you could ever ask for, it's here."

"Except you. I've ruined you, Brant. You're living life half asleep."

Now he turned to face her. He knew his eyes burned with anger, accusing and violent. He didn't care how much it hurt or scared her—it was her fault. "You wanted this. You wanted me to live a legitimate life."

"I know," she replied, her face falling, guilt written all over. "Brant, have you ever thought that maybe we just aren't meant to be together? You fought so hard for Senona, why didn't you fight like that for me?"

"You're bringing up Senona? We moved past this a long time ago. And I thought we moved past this sacrifice you think I'm making. I feel like we're stuck in a loop. I *love* you, Catherine. Why can't that be enough?"

She shook her head, tears streaming down her face, her eyes red and swollen. But she remained stalwart in her decision. "Johnny and I will be leaving tomorrow morning. I'd appreciate it if you didn't make this any harder than it already is."

Brant couldn't bring himself to say anything in return. He pressed his lips together tightly in an attempt to keep the tears that were burning his eyes and the back of his throat at bay.

Walking out of the house, he found his horse in the stables and saddled him quickly, all the while hoping that Catherine would change her mind, that she would run after him and tell him that she had made a mistake, she'd had a momentary lapse of judgment, and she loved him. That she'd bring Johnny home and return as soon as possible to *finally* marry him.

But no one came. The stable remained silent and empty apart from the four-legged animals confined to their stalls.

Mounting his horse, Brant rode away from his house and his life with Catherine.

In Barcelona, he stopped at the first tavern he saw and dismounted, tying his horse to a post outside. Walking in, he slammed a doubloon on the counter and took a seat.

"Rum, and keep them coming until the doubloon runs out."

The barkeep nodded and snatched up the dirty coin, simultaneously pouring the golden liquid into a foggy glass.

The second the liquid stopped pouring, Brant grabbed the glass, shooting the burning liquid back.

Placing the glass back down, it was quickly refilled. With the initial pain purged by the quick shot, he sipped at this drink. The tears he had been fighting earlier were gone now, and all he felt was anger and bitterness.

He'd given up so much for her, everything, and this was how she repaid him?

With each drink he finished, his anger increased. A doxy draped herself over his shoulder and whispered something in his ear, but he didn't hear. He pushed her off roughly.

"What's your problem?" she asked. Somehow she sounded less pathetic than her English counterparts, speaking in lilting Spanish.

"I'm not here for that."

"You're here for something, and it sure ain't cards. Who you drinking away? I can make it better."

Brant chuckled, but it sounded bitter even in his ears. "You can't make anything better. The only thing a woman is good for is ruining men. Go take your business elsewhere and leave me be."

The woman huffed and flounced away to find her next victim. The minute she was gone she was out of Brant's mind. But his thoughts returned to Catherine, and Senona; he'd only ever been betrayed by the women he had trusted. He'd been land bound too long. He needed to return to his first love, his mistress, the only thing that had never betrayed him; the ocean and his ship. They were the only constants in his life, and he had so foolishly put them aside, for what? For a chance at a normal life? To settle down and have a family? He should have known better, should have known he could never have those things.

Downing a few more drinks, Brant's vision began to swim and he leaned down on the bar top. He just needed to rest.

"Hey, you can't sleep here!" shouted the barkeep, shaking him roughly.

Brant blinked at him a few times before the words sunk in, and he nodded. Getting up, he walked unsteadily across the room, bumping into a few tables and chairs. He received angry glares and exclamations as he went, and then finally stumbled through the door and out into the street.

Unsure of where he was going, his feet moved aimlessly through the streets of Barcelona. He had no idea how far he walked. He briefly thought about his horse, and frowned, pausing in his stumbling walk. Where had he left that animal? He shrugged, unsure of what he was concerned about, and continued on his way. Somehow, he found himself in a familiar area of the merchant quarter, and he wove down the street towards the townhouse that Caton kept.

Making his way up the steps, he rang the bell and sat down with his back against the door. Then everything went black.

* * *

Brant woke up the next day with a pounding head and a churning stomach. He sat up slowly in the plush bed and looked around. How had he arrived at Caton's house, and in his own bed? Rubbing his eyes, he looked around. All he could remember was the dirty bar near the docks the night before, and way too many drinks.

Slowly climbing out of bed, he sat on the edge and waited for the room to stop spinning before he attempted to stand. He didn't bother searching for his boots, just walked out of his room in stocking feet in search of someone who could tell him what had happened.

"Good morning, Captain Foxton," came a much too familiar, feminine and mocking voice. She shouldn't be here. She never came into the city. This house was for Caton when he worked in the city and for Brant when he was in port.

"Senona, I didn't expect to see you here."

She smiled and held up a cup of steaming coffee in invitation from where she sat at the dining room table.

Brant walked over and sat down, accepting the coffee. "You going to tell me what happened last night?"

Brant shook his head and groaned. "Don't really want to talk about it."

"Then maybe you want to explain to me why Catherine stopped by this morning and asked me to check on you. The servants told me they found you passed out on the front step sometime after midnight, and had to drag you up to your bed." Her expression was that of disapproval, but was contradicted by her amused tone and dancing eyes.

Brant groaned again and sipped at his coffee. "I don't even remember leaving the tavern."

Senona reached for his hand, but he flinched and pulled away from her touch. He didn't want to open up to her, but there was something about Senona that had always made him feel at home, comfortable, despite the feelings that he still harbored for her—or maybe it was because of those feelings.

"She left me," he said. The words still didn't seem real.

"I don't understand. I know she left. But—"

"Neither do I. I thought we were in a good place, now suddenly she's leaving for England and not coming back."

"She didn't explain?"

"She said she was ruining me."

Senona's eyes no longer danced in amusement. Instead, they held pity, which only made him angry. She reached for his hand again, squeezing it in sympathy. "You haven't been yourself lately. Caton and I have noticed it as well."

"You're the one that told me I needed to be a better person. She did that for me."

Senona said nothing. Getting up slowly from her chair, she embraced her round, pregnant belly, and walked over to the window. She was six months along now, and the sight of her starting her family with Caton had Brant's chest tightening in painful jealousy. This was what he wanted. He was supposed to be starting his life with Catherine, starting a family. She wasn't supposed to walk away, not after everything they'd been through.

"Her ship left an hour ago," Senona said, staring out the window, refusing to meet his eyes.

Brant sighed. "So she's gone. I won't see her again." But he could. All he had to do was collect his crew and sail after her. She'd said that he had never fought for her— maybe that was her begging him to make some grand gesture.

Brant stood up, the realization bringing with it hope. "I have to go."

"Don't." Her tone told him she knew without him saying anything what he was going to do. "Let her go. These ups and downs have gone on too long with you two. You need to move on. It would have been easier for her to stay than to return home to all the questions and whispers. Don't you think if she had any hope, if she saw a future with you, she would have stayed? Don't you think the fact that you were willing to give up everything was gesture enough?"

She was right, and he hated it. He'd lost Senona and now he'd lost Catherine. It was as if the world was telling him he would always be alone, that there was no place for women in his life. He didn't deserve happiness.

He nodded slowly and sat back down. "I think I need something stronger than this."

Senona smiled slightly, but it was patronizing and not amused. "The last thing you need is more alcohol. And besides that, it's ten in the morning."

"What do I need then? You tell me, because right now I don't know. I don't think I've known what I needed for the last two years."

"Where were you the last time you were happy and at peace?"

"Sailing; I was my own master and answered to no one. I was a free man."

"What are you now?"

Brant sighed. "Trapped. I feel trapped by this business. I spend too much time on land, and when I'm at sea, I'm controlled by deadlines and destinations. I want to sail again just for the love of it."

Senona nodded. "Then do that."

"I have a business—"

"You have a partner. I'll talk to Caton. He'll contract another ship and you can leave for as long as you need."

"What about James?"

"He is happy here. You aren't his only family anymore, Brant. Caton and I are happy to step in. You need time to find yourself. You've been raising James since you were barely a man yourself."

"What's that supposed to mean?"

"It's supposed to mean that you have too much on your shoulders."

Senona was his constant, his rock, and she was right; he needed to get away. But not just from Spain. He needed to get away from her. If he needed to let Catherine go, he needed to let her go as well. Too long he'd been living in the past, holding onto something that wasn't there.

"Talk to Caton. I'm going to leave next week."

* * *

Brant stood on deck of the *BlackFox* as Matt, his quartermaster, shouted orders to the crew. He watched the activity around him and smiled. For the first time in a year, he felt good. This time he was sailing for himself. There were no deadlines. There was no destination. Brant was heading out to sea because he loved it. He had pulled out his letter of Marque, collecting dust in his cabin safe and read it over, reminding himself of the life he had once had—the life he was trying to get back to.

He'd talked with Caton a lot over the past week. They hadn't said anything to Senona, but they both knew that Brant didn't plan on returning. This life wasn't for him. And if he chose to return to his life as a privateer for the crown, there was no safe return to Spain.

He had transferred ownership of his house to James. Caton would act as his guardian until he turned eighteen next year, when he would receive the remainder of his inheritance and take over Brant's shares in the Amador-Foxton shipping company.

Brant smiled and placed his hat on his head. Looking towards the dock, he saw the approaching figure of a pregnant woman in breeches and a billowy white shirt that she'd left untucked. So, she'd come to bid him goodbye. He wondered when she'd make an appearance. She'd kept her distance ever since their initial talk, as if she knew he couldn't handle being around her. However, she had never missed a launching, and apparently, she wasn't about to break her tradition.

She waddled up the gangway, and Brant chuckled at the sight, trotting over to offer his arm.

"You shouldn't be here. This is no place for a lady, especially one in your condition."

He knew that she wouldn't appreciate the comment. She was a capable woman, as capable as any man on his crew, and she knew it. She hadn't taken kindly to her reduced capability through pregnancy, but she smiled graciously and seemed to accept that it was for the greater good.

"My condition? Give me a cutlass and I'll show you just how capable I am, Brant Foxton. If I were you, I'd keep your tongue tied if you don't wish to be shown up by a woman expecting a child."

Brant laughed, "Wouldn't that be a sight. Now, what brings you here this fine morning?"

"You didn't think I'd miss a launch, did you?"

Brant shook his head. "I guess not." But he had hoped. Goodbye wasn't something he was good at, especially when it came to saying goodbye to someone he loved as dearly as Senona.

"Take a turn around deck with me. We're almost ready to cast off."

Senona grasped his arm tightly as she moved beside him. She was slower than she used to be. Not nearly as steady or strong physically, but emotionally she was still an immobile rock.

"Where will you go?" she asked.

"I'll sail the high seas like I did before, and stay out as long as I can. I'll only make port long enough to repair and restock."

"The good old days have returned, then."

"I hope so."

"Will you be making any visits to Port Royale?"

"Sam?"

Senona nodded.

"I hope so. But that is no longer my home, and I don't want to intrude."

"You think Sam and Julie would consider your presence an intrusion? You are their friend."

"Senona…" he trailed off, unsure of how to appropriately put to words what he felt.

"You're cutting us out," she said, stopping and turning to face him.

"Senona…" he trailed off again. He didn't know how to confirm it when her eyes held so much pain and hurt just at the thought.

"You aren't just going back to the good old days. You're going back to when you had no friends, no family, and no ties to anyone but yourself and this ship."

It wasn't a question. She saw right through him. He should have known that she would. She always had been able to, which was why he had been avoiding her, and why he had hoped she wouldn't show up today. It would have been easier just to disappear and she could think that he was lost at sea, or dead. He never would have had to look in those wide, sad eyes and realize he was letting her down… again. Instead, she saw the truth of it; he was abandoning the people who loved him and called him family.

"I didn't know how to tell you."

"You could have just said it, Brant. You could have just said you'd be leaving and you weren't going to come back."

He nodded.

"Caton knows?"

He nodded again.

"That's why you've been avoiding me? That's why he has been skirting my questions all week?"

"I'm sorry."

Senona grabbed his hand and squeezed it tightly. "Do what you must, Brant Foxton. Sail away into the horizon and never return if that's what will make you happy. But know that there are people who love you and care about you. You've impacted our lives and you can't just erase yourself, even if you can erase us."

"Senona, please. I just need time to find myself again."
She nodded. "I know, and I understand. But that doesn't have to mean forever and I don't have to be happy about it."

Dropping his hand, she embraced him. Then she reached up, balancing on her toes, and planted a kiss on his cheek. She didn't say goodbye; she didn't say another word. She strode off the ship and didn't look back once.

Brant watched her until she was out of sight, and then turned back to his crew. Matt was standing nearby, evidently waiting for orders.

"Cast off," said Brant, walking towards the bow of the ship where he watched the open sea welcoming him home.

CHAPTER TWO

Brant walked the deck of his ship, feeling the refreshing ocean breeze caressing him like a long lost lover. They'd been at sea for two days, and had just sailed through the strait of Gibraltar into open water. He felt like he could breathe again for the first time in over a year.

Somewhere along the line, his life had strayed from the plan. He'd expected to privateer until the day he died. Instead, he'd become a knight in shining armor; first to Catherine, and then to Senona.

If it had just been Senona, he could have been happy. They were kindred souls, both looking for the same things out of life, but looking for it in different places. That was why they never would have worked. She would have been a chapter in his life, nothing more. But Senona had made him want more out of life, and Catherine had offered that to him. Too bad she couldn't live with him. Too bad they were like oil and water.

Brant sighed and picked up a tangled pile of rope and began coiling it.

He'd been thinking too much about Catherine. He hadn't stopped in the two weeks since she'd left. But he was back at home. That was a start. The rest would just take time, and he had plenty of that. Really, he had nothing but time. He was only twenty-seven. He'd been the captain of his own ship for eight years. He'd made his fortune many times over.

Eleven years ago he'd left everything he knew, everyone he cared about, to find the life he was meant to live. The years that followed hadn't been easy, but they had been good. It was time to get back to that, and the only way Brant knew how to do that was to leave everything behind, and cut all ties.

"Sir, we're in the clear, should I give the order?" asked Matt, interrupting Brant's thoughts.

"Yes, unfurl the last sail."

Matt turned and shouted the order, then turned back to Brant. "Sir, I'd like to go over the course with you, if I could."

Brant nodded and dropped the rope he'd finished coiling into a neat pile, leading the way to his cabin.

Matt and Brant split the responsibilities of sailing master ever since Matt had been promoted to quartermaster after Karl's death. Brant could have promoted someone else to the position, but he missed the work, and between the two of them they kept things running smoothly.

Pulling out a chart, Brant spread it across his desk and weighed down the edges with various items. "I think if we head this way, towards Port Royale, we'll be able to take a few ships before making port," he said as he traced a route along the worn paper.

Matt nodded, but Brant saw apprehension in his face. It was no secret that the young quartermaster preferred the life of a merchant. He'd fallen into this life by chance, and had just never left.

"Sir—"

"Matthew, how many times do I have to tell you to call me Brant?" he said, changing the subject.

"You're cap'n, Sir. That deserves respect."

"Karl never called me sir."

"Karl ain't me."

A silence fell over the two men, but Brant nodded and returned to the map, having successfully diverted Matt from his discomfort.

"Wind seems a bit quiet."

"Aye, won't make much headway today."

Brant nodded again and removed the weights from the chart, rolling it back up. "It's good to be back out, though. It's been too long since this girl has really been able to stretch her legs."

"The crew seems to be in good spirits. They haven't taken too kindly to the quiet life."

Brant chuckled and grabbed his hat from its hook, placing it on his head before following Matt back out on deck. "The quiet life isn't for any of us, probably why we took to sailing in the first place. We need a little more freedom and a little less law."

* * *

Matt was right, spirits were high among the crew. That night they pulled out their various instruments; guitars, harmonicas, hand organs, and played. Brant pulled out bottles of rum and port for the men, eager for a celebration himself. The deck was awash in light from lanterns. A circle of men played a game of dice, while another group sat with cards in hand.

Brant walked over to the card players, sitting in an empty spot. "Deal me in," he said in response to the questioning looks from his men.

"Don't go bettin' us outta all our gold, Cap'n."

"I wouldn't dream of it, Harold. Not until you got a little more to take. I'm told you went and spent it all on a pretty girl."

"Not so pretty," teased another sailor.

Harold guffawed and dealt out the cards. "Prettier than any lass you ever took home."

Brant smiled, enjoying the banter as the circle of men laughed uproariously. He'd missed this; camaraderie with the crew. It wasn't often he immersed himself in their world. As captain it was important that he remained in a role of respect, but every once in a while he made an exception to his rule and joined in the fun. It never hurt to remind the men that even though he was the law out here, he was human.

He'd abandoned cards and gambling long ago, but tonight he played a few hands, won some gold, lost some gold, and probably came out even in the end. At first the men had been cautious and subdued, but soon enough they forgot their inhibitions, or the alcohol allowed them to, and they embraced him as one of them.

After a couple rounds it was time to return to reality. Brant took his leave from the game and found Matt sitting near the mast playing his guitar.

"Have you been drinking?"

Matt shook his head, still picking at the strings.

"You take first watch then, I'll take second."

Brant didn't wait for his reply, there was no reason to. When he gave an order it was followed, no questions asked. Matt was good at that. Karl, his predecessor, had always questioned, always pushed Brant to be a stronger and better leader. He missed that, then again he missed a lot of things.

Pulling off his boots and falling into bed, still fully clothed, Brant sighed. Why couldn't he get them out of his head? Ghosts of his past, dead and alive, haunted him. He didn't do guilt. He was supposed to live in the present, never making plans, never looking backwards. This voyage was supposed to fix him, supposed to bring him back to who he was. And yet, he couldn't seem to find that.

It was as if his beloved ocean was punishing him for turning his back on her. But how do you beg for forgiveness when the one spurned is a much prouder being than any human that ever walked the earth?

Brant should have been sleeping, he had watch in three hours, but he tossed and turned, plagued with thoughts of Senona's smiling face, her hair blowing in the wind as she stood on deck. Why couldn't Catherine have been more like her? Why couldn't she have embraced his life? Instead, when he tried to meet her halfway, she turned and ran, scared of what she was turning him into. He wished his heart would stop hurting, would stop pining for women he could never have.

Three in the morning came too quickly. Brant hadn't slept a wink since he'd fallen into bed three hours earlier. Getting up, he pulled on his boots and sleepily made his way down to the galley to pour himself a mug of coffee, likely hours old being kept warm on a smoldering stove.

Tasting the bitter liquid, he grimaced. It tasted burnt, but it did the trick. Walking back out on deck, now abandoned by the earlier festivities, apart from one of the younger sailors who lay passed out where the dice game had occurred earlier. Matt was walking around the deck, slapping his arms in an attempt to keep his blood pumping and his mind aware.

"Go turn in," said Brant, walking up to his quartermaster.

Matt nodded, too tired to speak, and walked past Brant down to the hold.

Brant strolled around the deck alone. It was the first time he'd taken a watch in a long time, and he embraced the silence and serenity. The only sound was the flapping sails and the slapping waves against the ship's hull. Brant ran his hands lovingly along the rail of the *BlackFox*.

"What did I do wrong?" he asked the passing wind. "Have I sinned so much that I don't deserve any happiness?"

Tears streamed down his face that he had been holding in for the last week. The pain of Catherine leaving ripped through him and found its release. "Why?" he screamed out, thankful that he was alone, that his men weren't around to witness his breakdown. *Everyone has abandoned me*, he thought.

Brant laughed through his sobs, and swiped angrily at his tears. He was a joke. He played at being a rough and tough pirate, a man beyond the law, but reality is he was a fraud. He was half a pirate, falling into the safety net of a privateer. He claimed no man was his master, yet he paid tax to the king, bowed and scraped where necessary, then took back to the high seas. He had never been a pirate. He had always been held back by inhibitions, by fear of death, and he allowed women to reduce him to tears.

He'd never truly let go of his old life; the life of privilege and standing. The fact that he had chased Catherine was proof of that. He had held onto his father's estate in Port Royale for years, playing at nobility when he wasn't on a ship.

Walking over to the mast, Brant grabbed the lowest rung and climbed up the ladder to the crow's nest. Up top, he doused the lantern and waited a few minutes for his night vision to return before pulling out his glass and slowly scanning the water around. They were alone, the water as smooth as glass, barely a breeze in the air. It was calm. The ocean seemed completely ignorant of the turmoil he felt.

Climbing back down, he strode into his cabin. Walking straight to the wall safe, he turned the dial and forcefully pulled the handle. Inside was tidy; a bag of doubloons, his ship's log, and a single piece of parchment.

Reaching in, he pulled out the paper and scanned it. It had been his safety net, his life line for the last eleven years. It had kept him living a half-life, somewhere in limbo between legitimate and free. This paper was what had been holding him back from the start. Not Senona, not Catherine, not even his father. It was this simple piece of paper with the signet of the King stamped on the bottom.

Clutching it in his hand, wrinkling the once pristinely smooth parchment, he left his cabin and climbed the stairs to the upper deck. He stared out at the wake left by the ship. If he did this, there was no turning back.

The deck was too dark to see what was written on the paper, but Brant knew it by heart, and knew what it meant. This simple piece of paper was a prison. Taking one last look at it he let his hand fall loose. The paper was picked up by the slight breeze and it left Brant's hand, floating down softly and resting on the surface of the water for just a moment before sinking out of sight.

It was done. It was as if the shackles that had been imprisoning Brant fell from his wrists and ankles, and left him a free man. He no longer belonged to the King. He was his own ruler, and this ship was his domain. There would be no women or laws to hold him back, to dictate who he should be, how he should act, or what he should do. No, as of right now, the *BlackFox* was on its own, a free agent.

It was as if a weight had been lifted off his shoulders. Brant continued his watch, walking the length of the deck every half hour. As the horizon began to turn pink with the rising sun, he was relieved of his watch. He climbed into bed exhausted and ready for a couple hours of sleep before the day began.

Unlike last night, his mind was calm and at ease. Lying in bed, he went over what he would tell his men, then closed his eyes and let blissful sleep take over. Just before his mind entered that state of complete relaxation and rest, he realized that he hadn't thought of Catherine even once since he'd dropped his letter of Marque into the ocean.

Maybe his mistress hadn't welcomed him back, but it seemed she still cared. Tonight she washed away his troubles, and carried his prison to her deepest depths. Nothing returned from there. Given time, she would embrace Brant again. Last night had been the first step to forgiveness. The sunrise had risen on a new man and a new ship. The sea had no idea what had been unleashed.

* * *

Brant awoke to the sun beating down through the large window at the back of his cabin. He took his time getting dressed and freshening up. Despite the short night, he felt surprisingly rested.

The deck was quiet, even though all hands were present and going about their various jobs. It seemed many of the men hadn't rested as well as Brant, and the festivities from the night before left them quiet and subdued this morning.

Walking down to the galley, Brant dumped the old coffee, likely still the same he'd drank from last night, and stoked up the fire under the stove to brew a new pot. He waited in the hot galley until the water boiled then soaked the coffee grinds. The aromatic smell filled the room, bringing Brant's senses to life, and he poured himself a cup before heading back out on deck.

The Caribbean sun was beating down mercilessly. It was easily midday, but no one questioned their Captain's late appearance on deck.

Brant went over to where Matt bent over a table, studying some charts and making calculations.

"How is our course?"

Matt looked up. "Good, Sir. The wind has picked up today and seems to be in our favor."

"I want you to make some changes, and get us on the busiest trading routes. There has been a change of plans."

Matt nodded, but his face betrayed his concern. "I'll make the changes right away."

"Good. I'll be dining with the crew tonight. I want to go over the new plans and purpose of the ship."

"Purpose, Sir?"

"We're no longer going to privateer for the King," he replied, grinning wildly.

"Sir, are you sure that's wise?"

"Wise? No." He didn't elaborate, but Matt's confused expression had him laughing as he walked away.

* * *

As the crew ate supper that night, Brant found himself a place on the steps leading up to the deck, and cleared his throat.

"I've decided on some changes. From now on every single doubloon we earn will belong to us. There will be no more paying tax to the King."

He was greeted with a loud eruption of cheers, but he couldn't help but notice Matt's lack of enthusiasm.

"If any of you are not okay with the increased risk this new life carries with it, you can disembark at the next port."

"Boo to that. Any man coward enough to leave this ship ain't a man at all," exclaimed Joseph.

Brant chuckled. "That is true, but far be it from me to stand in the way of any cowards. There is no room on this ship for them." Brant looked pointedly at Matt, who wore a look of disapproval.

Turning on the step, Brant walked back up on deck. It didn't take long for Matt to follow.

"Sir, may I talk to you?"

Brant stopped and turned to face the crewmember that was second only to him on this ship. "Of course, Matthew. What's on your mind?"

"This change, I don't think it's for the best. A letter of Marque is not easy to come by and it gives you the freedom to live the life you want without risk."

Brant smiled. "I like that you're speaking up, Matthew, but I also need you to trust me in this decision. Are you with me?"

"You're my cap'n, Sir. I don't have much choice."

"You always have a choice. Just because we're going beyond the law doesn't mean the way I treat my crew will change."

"Everything will change. You take away law and you will have to get ruthless to retain control. Are you ready for that?"

"Ruthless? I've had to be ruthless in the past, and it wasn't because there was no law." Brant sighed. "Join me for a drink, we need to talk."

Brant walked towards his cabin, Matt following silently, taking the offered seat next to Brant's desk. He went over to a cabinet and pulled out a bottle of port, pouring two glasses of the burgundy liquid.

"When I was nineteen, I served on this ship under Captain LaFleur. I had been serving under him since I was sixteen, and had moved up in his crew quickly, much like you. But mutiny changed everything, took Captain LaFleur's life, and left us with a leader who knew nothing of how to run a crew. He tore the crew apart, dividing their loyalties and sacrificing their lives to bad decisions.

"Karl and I could feel the unease growing, and we feared a second mutiny, so we had to make a tough decision. That decision landed me in a position of power. This was only shortly before I found you.

"It hasn't been easy being a captain. I know you don't agree with every decision I make, but I appreciate that you don't question me in front of the crew."

"Sir, it ain't my place to question you."

Brant nodded and sipped at his port. "Karl questioned me. In private he always challenged me, always forced me to make the best decision. I don't have that anymore, and I'd appreciate it if you'd take on that role."

"Sir, I'm not comfortable—"

"Matt, it isn't good for a man to be infallible, or to think he is. I'm asking you to help me be a good captain. I can't do that alone. Besides, you just did it out there on the deck."

"Sir, if you want me to be honest, I already told you I think you're makin' a mistake. Going rogue don't bode well with me."

"I know."

"That won't change yer mind though."

Brant shook his head. "No."

Matt got up, finished his glass of port and put it down. "Then what's the point? Why should I speak up?"

"Because, if you don't no one will."

Matt nodded. "Sir, you know how I feel. You do with that what you see fit. Yer story, you becomin' captain, that's touchin' and all. No one on this crew doubts that you've done yer due, me least of all. I seen you live through some hard times, and I can't help but think this is just another hard time, and you're dealing with it wrong."

Brant nodded, remaining silent to allow Matt to continue.

"This sudden change; cuttin' ties with the Amadors, with Senona—I heard you talkin' with her when we left. She said we weren't going back. Never thought you'd leave her… no matter what happened with Miss Catherine."

Brant nodded.

"You're lookin' for a way to make it all better. Fine. You do that. But if you land yourself in the gallows I ain't gonna help. You're on yer own."

Brant chuckled. "You sound just like Karl."

"Yeah?" He seemed pleased.

Brant chuckled and topped up Matt's glass. "Sit down. Stay a while."

He sat back down, leaning comfortably into his chair and lifting the full glass. "You do realize that you've unleashed the kraken, invitin' me to speak my mind."

Brant shrugged. "I felt alone without someone smarting off to me. No James, Johnny, Senona, Karl… It can get awful lonely up here at the top."

"Sir—"

"Brant."

"Brant, I'll be yer friend, if that's what you're lookin' for. But you realize that there are people who are yer friends, and you just sailed away from them, and told the one who loves you most that you ain't comin' back."

Brant's brow furrowed. "I'll deal with that when I'm ready. So this means you'll stick around? You won't leave at the next port?"

"Were you worried that I would?"

"My quartermaster is the only man not happy with how I'm running my ship. I had my concerns."

"I'll stay for now. But if things don't sit well, I can't guarantee I'll stay. I need to make peace with my conscience."

"We're wicked men."

"Aye, Cap'n, we are. But it's the little things that make living day to day bearable. You take that away, and you're left with emptiness."

Brant nodded. Matt could have taken the words right out of his mouth. But right now, it wasn't wicked deeds that made him feel empty. It was betrayal, and love, and heartache that he wished would just go away.

CHAPTER THREE

Things were looking up on the *BlackFox;* the weather was in their favor and the men were in good spirits, creating an environment that Brant could feel at ease in. Things between Matt and Brant were still tense, and although they acted at being friends, knowing that Matt disapproved of his choices made things anything but easy. But despite their differences, things were slowly becoming the way they should be.

"You look awfully chipper today," said Matt, walking up with a cup of coffee.

Brant accepted the hot beverage. "It's a good day. I can feel it in my bones."

"Sure that ain't just the old age creepin' up?"

Brant chuckled, looking out at the white capped waves. "Nope, pretty sure we're in the ocean's favor today."

Matt shook his head and muttered something about "no such thing as favor and luck" as he walked away. Brant just smiled to himself. Think what he will, the ocean had a personality all her own, and she could turn on you in just a moment. It was best to enjoy her while she was in a good mood.

The only problem was that it was too quiet. It had been two days since decisions had been made, but they had yet to come across another ship, and Brant was eager for some action. It was coming on a year now since he'd had a good raid.

Walking away from the rail, Brant sipped at his coffee and went about checking on the work his men were doing. They weren't all busy. It had been smooth sailing so far, and the *BlackFox* was in good repair. Most of the men were working leisurely, sharpening blades or cleaning their guns. A small group played dice, and occasionally shouted expletives of disappointment or victory erupted from the circle. The wind gently caressed the ship, causing the sails to flap with an audible snap. From high above in the crow's nest, Brant could hear the music of a harmonica drift down. Yes, life was good. No one was complaining about the leisure, but it wouldn't be long before that too became old. Boredom was quick to come at sea when things were going too well.

Walking back into his cabin, Brant retrieved a book from his shelf and went back out on deck to enjoy the quiet morning. He'd find something for the men to do this afternoon to stave off boredom.

Brant read all morning. Catherine had bought the book for him before one of his voyages, but it had sat forgotten on a shelf, collecting dust until now. *Paradise Lost* it was called, written by some poet in England called Milton. It dealt with all kinds of religious things, which wasn't really Brant's cup of tea, but the title resonated with him. Maybe this had been Catherine's way of preaching to him, of trying to bring him to some kind of faith or trust in God. But to Brant, it was all fiction, an epic story of love, betrayal, and punishment put to pretty words and sensationalized deities. It was reminiscent of Greek or Roman epic poetry, like *The Odyssey* or *Aeneid*, books he had been forced to read during his time in boarding school.

Brant smiled to himself, looking away from the book. He had assigned James to read those same books, not really knowing how else to expand his literary horizons. He would have considered it a boring assignment, but his brother—so opposite himself in personality—had embraced the books and requested more. He'd have to send this one to him once he was done with it.

"Sail ho!" came a shout from above.

Without a second thought, Brant tossed the book aside and trotted over to the rail, pulling out his glass. He searched the surrounding waters and was greeted with the sight of a pretty looking Spanish merchant ship. He scanned over to the bow where he read the name, and a sigh of relief escaped him upon discovering it wasn't one of Caton's ships.

If it had been, Brant would like to think he'd sail by, but he was happy to not have to make that choice.

"Okay, men, we got us a merchant ship ripe for the picking!"

Cheers erupted, and where the deck had once been quiet and serene, men were jumping up, pocketing dice and gold, putting guns back together, and preparing for the sanguine meeting that was about to happen between the two ships.

"Run up the colors!" shouted Matt. "Stow away those ropes!"

Brant walked back to where he had been seated earlier, and picked up the book he had carelessly tossed aside. It was no worse for wear, and he carried it back into his cabin where it would be waiting for the next time he had a quiet hour or two.

Retrieving his cutlass and brace of pistols from where they were slung over the back of his chair, Brant returned to the deck. His heart thundered deafeningly in his ears. The nerves never did go away, no matter how many raids he experienced. His heart still pounded, his hands began to shake, and the sweat began to bead on his forehead. You just never get used to facing death; every time is just as terrifying as the first. And although Brant had grown adept at shutting the danger and fear out of his mind, his body still betrayed him.

Waiting was the worst part. Brant walked up and down the ship, checking his glass every few moments to keep an eye on the activity on the other ship. They were scrambling to roll out their guns. The captain looked angry, and Brant chuckled at how red his face was turning. But the crew looked frightened and unorganized.

Brant lowered his glass and signaled to Matt to give the order.

"Roll out the nines!" he shouted.

The ship rumbled and rolled with the force and weight of thirty-six cannons being rolled forward. Each cannon weighed close to 1600 pounds, and took a crew of three or four men to roll just one forward and successfully load and prep it for firing. It was time consuming and hard work, leaving much of Brant's crew below deck, busy with the heavy artillery.

He no longer needed his glass to see the crew on the opposing ship. They feverishly worked at their own guns, rolling them forward and preparing them to fire.

Brant looked over at Matt and nodded.

"Fire!"

A few cannons shot off iron balls, while others shot off two balls connected by a chain. These were aimed higher, at the masts and at the crew in an attempt to cripple the ship before boarding. The balls ripped through the air, a destructive force that could not be stopped. Wood splinters flew into the air and a chained ball found its mark on one of the forward masts, ripping through the thick wood like it was nothing more than a dry, dead twig.

A cheer erupted among his men, and Brant smiled. Slowly his nerves calmed. Things were going his way.

It took a good three minutes to reload the cannons, but their prey was already floundering, weakened by the initial volley.

Brant nodded again, and Matt called for a second attack.

Once again thunder erupted, and splinters flew like lightning. They were closing in on the ship, and the crew was scrambling for cover.

"Fire!" shouted Brant to the boarding crew. The smaller artillery; pistols, and blunderbuss discharged, and powder flasks flew through the air. Some exploded harmlessly above, while others found their marks, wreaking havoc.

The crew abandoned the cannons and joined the others on deck, ready to board when Matt and Brant gave the orders. Picks were drawn and ropes were clutched in eager hands.

"Today we take the ship for ourselves. Not for the king or anyone else!" shouted Brant as he walked up and down the ranks of his men, some stepping from foot to foot, others shaking their arms in attempts to shake off their nerves. They were all eager and ready for action, but the nerves never left. Never.

"Prepare to board!" called out Matt as the ships drew alongside each other. He didn't need Brant to give him the nod, he knew what to do.

The ships lined up and Matt shouted, "Board!"

Even as the words were still leaving his mouth, men scrambled across the expanse between the ships by various means. Some threw grappling hooks, lashing the two ships together. Others threw down planks, while some men swung across on ropes, occupying the crew while the ship was tethered to the force bent on destroying it.

Brant grabbed a free rope and swung across, cutlass drawn, joining in the foray. He knew this wouldn't take long; the deck was already slick with spilled blood. Men fought individual battles all around him—with each man that fell, with each battle won, there were less and less opponents.

A sailor, covered in blood and grinning, ran at Brant. He could tell this one was more experienced. No fear was in his eyes. Their swords clashed as they met, but Brant parried the sailor easily, running him through within seconds. He watched as first disbelief, and then fear entered his eyes. There was no more confidence, only the bleak realization that his life was over.

As the man fell away to draw his last breath in a pool of his own blood, Brant stepped over him and continued the trek towards his goal; the captain.

The captain, from what Brant could tell, was a worthy opponent. He fought bravely and calmly, not blinded by arrogance or fear.

Brant's men backed off when he reached the man, allowing him the fight he wanted. His sword met his opponent's, and their dance started, but Brant was already disappointed. The captain was aging, and he wasn't as energetic as he might have been in the past. Brant could see the exhaustion taking over as he saw his men falling all around, and the despair he felt was beginning to show in his face.

"Surrender," offered Brant.

The captain shook his head. "I shall never surrender my ship to pirate scum," he spat out.

Brant shrugged, ignoring the insult. "Have it your way."

He had to admit, the captain put up a valiant effort. He was breathing heavily, and sweat dripped from his brow, but he didn't give up. Brant could have beaten him long ago, but he chose to keep the fight going, allowing the man to see his crew fall one by one.

Yet even when he was the only one left fighting, his crew either dying, dead or surrendered, he didn't give in.

Brant realized that he would have to kill the man for this to end.

Sighing, he disarmed the proud man and held his blade against his neck.

"Do it, kill me," uttered the captain through clenched teeth.

Brant shook his head. "I will not kill you. You will go down with your ship, like a captain should, not by the hand of *pirate scum*."

Brant turned away as his men rushed forward to detain the captain. "Take anything of value. Tie the survivors up."

* * *

That evening, the crew of the *BlackFox* ate well. Stores of food had been confiscated from the merchant ship, including fruit, potatoes, herbs and cheese; to name only a few things. Not to mention the fresh bread the cook had baked with the barrel of flour they had found.

Though there hadn't been much gold to be had, the wares they had taken were worth their weight. Matt had divided it up for use and for trade at their next port. They would eat well for at least the next week, and that meant happy men.

After supper, the celebration turned from food to liquid form. Brant excused himself, climbing up to the crow's nest for some much needed silence.

While his crewmembers preferred to get raucous and revelrous after a raid, Brant usually needed some time alone; to think, to plan, to recall the dying faces of every man he killed that day, and give them a few moments of respect before erasing them from his memory. It was a tradition he had carried on since his first kill. He liked to think it kept him human; better than some, worse than others.

He carried with him a bottle of port, and for each face he recalled, he took a drink. He used to say a prayer, something to follow their souls up to wherever they were headed, but had long ago abandoned that practice. He didn't believe in a god, so why should he say empty words? Leave the prayers to their loved ones.

From below, sounds of music, dancing, and drunken shouting drifted up. But it was distant; as if belonging to another world. What they did below didn't affect Brant, and no one knew what he did on his own up here. Here, as the sun set on a successful day, Brant was alone in his sanctuary. Up here, even the ocean couldn't touch him. She was far below, her waves slapping harmlessly on the ship's hull.

Brant looked behind, where they had left the merchant ship burning. He could just barely make out the faint glow of the wreck that would soon sink to the bottom of the ocean. He hadn't been completely heartless, though. He'd ushered the handful of surviving sailors onto a lifeboat and sent them adrift with a few supplies. If they were smart about it, it would get them to a port alive.

The captain, however, in his pride, had refused a spot on the longboat. Brant granted him his last wish, and left him aboard his ship to be buried with her. Brant smiled wryly as he thought of the man. A proud fool, some of his sailors had said, but Brant didn't agree. Proud? Yes. Fool? Maybe. But he knew he would have done the same thing. When you love your ship, you don't abandon her. You die with her, and you take your eternal rest with her. That was the way of the sea—the cruel siren that she was.

Brant lit the oil lamp he had carried up with him and opened his book to where he had left off earlier that day. He was reading about the fall of man and being cast from the garden. It felt similar to his own fall; a fall from grace with Catherine, and being cast from his legitimate life to one of crime and danger. The difference was, he liked it here.

Brant's reading was serenaded by the festivities below—distracting him. Eventually, after re-reading a page for the fifth time, he gave up and set the book aside. He had no interest in joining his crew's celebration. He'd spent too many nights in the bottle because of Catherine and he was done letting her control his life.

Pulling out a cigar from his shirt pocket, he bit the end off. He spit it away, and lit the other end, puffing the sweet tasting smoke. He'd long ago given up smoking, and had never been attracted to a pipe, but every once in a while he liked to indulge in a good cigar.

This one was from a box that Johnny had bought him for his birthday last year. There weren't many left now. Every time he smoked one, he thought of the boy who was quickly turning into a man. Johnny was so much like Brant and had a promising future in sailing. He hadn't really thought of him since he had left with Catherine, he had been preoccupied with the collapse of his personal life. Now, however, his thoughts turned to the boy that loved the ocean nearly as much as Brant did.

It must be killing him that he had to return to England. Johnny was so different from his sister Catherine. He was a younger, less bitter version of Brant. He had all the promise, all the natural skill needed to be a great captain someday. He wanted to join the King's Royal Navy. Would he get that opportunity once back in England? Was he being summoned back to do that, having had enough time and discipline on a merchant ship?

Brant puffed on his cigar. He hoped Johnny wasn't expected to fulfill his duties to the family in the court of the king, or some such nonsense. Anyone with as much natural skill as Johnny, deserved to be at sea; but some people didn't see that. Even Calvin Foxton, Brant's father, who was a man of the sea himself, hadn't seen it in his own son. Maybe that was why Brant felt so akin to Johnny.

Puffing away the last of his cigar, Brant ground it out and tossed it away, into the sea. It was dark, and the noise from below had died down. The festivities of the day had come to a close, the sun had set on their first independent raid. Brant smiled, but the joy he wanted to feel, convinced himself he should feel, wasn't there. And the smile was somewhat forced. Instead he felt a little sick. Once upon a time he would have sent a prayer up for the souls he had taken today. Now, all he could bring himself to do was stare out at the faint glow in the distance, and tell himself it was all just part of life.

CHAPTER FOUR

Brant lowered his arm and shouted as the cannons shot off, rocking the *BlackFox* back and forth in the water. With each raid, the ship sat heavier and lower in the water, but the powerful nine guns could still rock her from side to side as well as any storm of nature.

It was a rush, the moment that all hell broke loose and there was nothing but beautiful chaos. But this raid was different. This was no Spanish galleon or Dutch merchant. This was a British ship; the forbidden fruit. Something he hadn't been able to touch in all the years he'd been sailing was right there, in his grasp. He could almost taste the sweetness that she held in her hold.

The ship wasn't a beauty. She was an old, small, merchant ship. One volley from the nines and she was looking precarious. But that didn't take away from the thrill of the raid. Brant shook in anticipation. It was more than just nerves this time. It was pure excitement and adrenaline coursing through his veins.

Matt, at the helm, maneuvered the *BlackFox* expertly through the roiling waters as another volley was let free. Thirty-three iron balls flew through the air, some going wide, some falling short, others hitting with devastating accuracy. Brant felt like laughing as he watched a ball crash into the main mast, sending a shower of splinters through the air and an ear splitting crack as the great wooden post first leaned, then slowly fell across the deck, tearing down sails with it. The British flag that had once been flying high and proud on this sad little ship dragged in the water, a testament to the defeat they were about to succumb to at the hands of Brant's men.

Matt brought the *BlackFox* around next to the ship, close enough for the grappling hooks to be thrown, securing the two ships together. Planks crashed down across the two ships, spanning the water beneath. Men ran across, cutlasses drawn and war cries pouring from their lips.

Many of the sailors on the merchant ship dove over the rail and into the water below, swimming to a safe distance where they could escape the carnage that was unfolding. Brant's men let them go. Let the cowards flee. If they could swim long enough to make their way back to the ship when all was said and done, then perhaps they would survive and be picked up by a much more well-meaning vessel than his own.

The fight lasted mere seconds. After the sailors too afraid to fight had jumped ship, Brant's crew was left with an underwhelming number of brave men who quickly saw that no amount of bravado was going to save them. The surrender came quickly from the captain, who hobbled forward and offered his gun and cutlass.

Brant crossed over to the ship, which sank lower in the water from what was likely a heavy leak below deck.

"Take anything of value," instructed Brant. It was something he said at every raid, but it was a command that the men waited for.

He walked the deck, looking each defeated sailor in the eye. There weren't many dead. A few that hadn't been lucky enough to avoid bullets or falling debris from the cannon volleys, but none from hand-to-hand combat.

"You call yourselves merchants of the crown?" scoffed Brant, stopping at the captain. "You are a sorry mess. You couldn't even give your lives for your ship or cargo."

The captain's eyes were tired and sad. "Is my life worth a few barrels of gun powder and bolts of cloth? I'll surrender to live another day."

Brant scowled, greatly disappointed in this British captain, after the raid on the Spanish ship had left him with admiration for a man that would not leave his beloved vessel. This man likely didn't even own this ship. He was probably an employee of a larger company. The state of the vessel spoke to little pride being taken in his livelihood. Was this nothing more than a means to put bread on the table for a family in England? He searched the captain's eyes for answers, but there was a quiet acceptance, not the fear or defiance Brant was used to seeing.

Brant wanted something, anything from this man who didn't deserve the name captain. His blood boiled in anger and he drew his knife, holding it against the man's throat.

"Do you even care?" he seethed. "Your cargo, this ship, sailing, does it mean anything to you?"

"There is more to life than sailing and money. I will do what I must to make it home safely to my family," the captain answered calmly.

Brant shook his head, pressing the knife harder. "No. If you're a captain, you love your ship and you go down with her. That's the way it works."

"I pity you, my friend, if a ship is the most precious thing in your life."

Brant blinked and released the pressure on the man's neck, taking a few steps back as the shock of the captain's words rolled over him. This man did not spit at him or mock as so many did. He did not call him names, did not stare at him in disgust. No, he looked at him, perfectly calm, and called him friend. What kind of man did that? What kind of man so graciously accepted his fate as to call the person who could have him killed, 'my friend'?

Brant looked at Matt, who had joined him to foresee the transfer of goods. He shrugged, a look of confusion on his face.

"Take the captain to the brig," said Brant finally. "Leave the others here. The sea will decide their fate."

Matt nodded and moved forward to walk the captain across to the *BlackFox* and lock him in the brig below deck.

Brant never took prisoners, but he wanted to know what made this man think and speak the way he did, and he needed more than the few minutes he had before this ship floundered.

Brant walked along the deck, cutting the ropes that held the longboats in place. The ship was going down quickly, but there was no need to drag the smaller vessels under with it. He would leave them free to float, and the sailors might have a chance of survival, if the elements didn't kill them before a ship came by.

With all the boats cut free, Brant walked across to his ship and waited for the rest of his crew to join him.

They relieved the ship of the cargo they could use; gunpowder, ammunition, and food stores. Much of the hold was filled with cheap bolts of fabric and thread. Brant had no use for those, nor did he want to try and unload them, so they were left behind to rest at the bottom of the ocean with the sad ship that carried them.

With the last of the useful cargo transferred, Brant and Harold went along unhooking grappling hooks and pulling in planks. Already the ropes that tethered the ships together were stretched tightly, and pulling the *BlackFox* down on an angle to the starboard side as the merchant ship sunk low in the water.

A few men went by, cutting the ropes and letting the sinking ship free. With the *BlackFox* no longer acting as buoy, the ship sunk even lower, leaving nothing more than the deck and scattered debris above water. They quickly left the ship in their wake as the wind carried the *BlackFox* away. Matt stood at the helm, correcting their course, and steering them away from the crimes they had committed.

Brant watched from the stern of his vessel through his eyeglass at what was supposed to be his sweet, delicious, forbidden fruit bobbing so unsatisfyingly in the water, and then disappearing beneath the ocean waves.

He watched the sailors who hadn't drowned swim for the boats that he had cut free and left for them. Where was the satisfaction? Where was the sweet taste of victory and rebellion? Instead, the captain's words had left Brant's victory feeling empty and hollow. He wanted to kill the captain, to watch his life bleed out on his deck, to watch the fear of mortality dawn in the man's eyes. He wanted to wipe that calm acceptance off the captain's face, and steal the taste from the apple that he so desired. If Adam and Eve could have their taste from the tree of knowledge of good and evil, why couldn't he?

After so many years of serving a king that didn't even know his name, of bowing and scraping to a society that laughed behind his back as he acted the part of the rogue, he wanted nothing more than to tell the King he no longer owned him. But instead he felt more lost than ever.

* * *

Brant took supper in the small dining room with Matt and the captured captain that night. It wasn't a lavish spread; the same foods as the men were eating below in the mess hall just in the privacy of an intimate dining cabin.

The air was tense, as Matt looked from Brant to the captain and back again. Brant could see the question on his face; what would happen next? Why had he taken this man prisoner? The brig was reserved for malcontents on the crew, and rarely used.

As the food was served, the captain looked up at his captor and smiled. "May I say grace?"

Brant stared, his spoon frozen in midair, half way to his mouth. Of course he'd managed to find a religious man among all this soul searching that he was doing. "Do what you must, just keep it to yourself," he replied, bringing the spoon the rest of the way to his mouth and chewing defiantly on his food.

The captain didn't seem fazed at all, just bowed his head and boldly said his few words of thanks. But what struck Brant the most was not the prayer, but the fact that he was giving thanks at all. The man had lost his ship, his crew, and his cargo today, and yet here he was thanking his God for bringing him safely through the day, and for sparing his life in the face of trials and hardships.

The man ate in silence, and Brant did his best to ignore him. He was quickly regretting bringing this captain aboard. He should have killed him, or left him on his ship. He would learn nothing from this man.

"Sir, can I ask why you pray in thanks?" asked Matt, voicing the question that Brant had only thought.

The man smiled graciously at Matt, and finished chewing his food before speaking. "The good Lord chose to work in your captain's heart to spare me today. I think I have lots to be thankful for."

"But your ship, your cargo—"

"Nothing but earthly possessions. I'm living to see another sunset, maybe even another sunrise, and that gets me closer to my wife and children. There is always something to be thankful for."

"I never said I'm going to let you go," said Brant, looking to break the man's hope.

"No, you didn't. But I have faith you'll do the right thing. You didn't murder my men either, and you cut free the life boats to give them a chance. You aren't as hard as you'd like others to think."

Brant grimaced and returned to his food.

"Where do you make your home?" asked Matt.

Brant wished he would just be quiet so that they could get through supper and throw the captain back into the brig.

"Port Royale, but I'm at sea most of the time. My trade route brings me with cotton and tobacco to England, and then back with fabric and various other niceties."

"You've been sailing long, Sir?"

"All my life, and please, my name is Nathan. The only sir around here be your captain."

"You've been sailing all your life and you don't even have the decency to go down with your ship?" asked Brant, his voice laced in bitterness and resentment.

"I do believe that a captain going down with his ship was more the sentiment that he put his crew before himself, and would be the last to take a seat on a lifeboat, not needlessly throw his life away for the sake of a vessel made by the hands of man."

"And what? Your life is made by the hands of God?" he scoffed.

Nathan nodded. "And should be treated as a temple."

Brant choked back a laugh. A temple? This coming from a man with crooked yellow teeth and dirty clothes. Finishing his food,

Brant pushed back his chair and stood up. He didn't want to spend any more time with this Nathan, who spouted religion and contentment in God. He didn't care that others believed it, but he didn't want it. He'd come to terms long ago that if God existed, he wasn't going to be passing through any pearly gates, so there was no point in trying to please Him now.

"Matt, lock the good captain back in the brig once he's eaten his fill."

Matt nodded, but the look on his face betrayed his displeasure. Brant didn't really care. If Matt wanted to come speak to him about how holding Nathan prisoner didn't sit well with his conscience, then fine. It would do no good.

Brant walked about the ship, checking any damage that may have been caused on the deck, then below. There was nothing much. The merchant ship hadn't been equipped with many guns, and the couple of cannon balls that had found their mark had done little damage. There was a slight leak in the hold that Harold would have to see to, but it wasn't anything the pumps couldn't keep up with until he managed to patch and pitch it.

Inspection done, and a mental list made of what needed to be accomplished in the next few days, Brant returned to his cabin. Lighting an oil lamp, he sat down at his desk with a sigh, and opened his ship's log. Before he could even dip his quill into the inkwell, a knock sounded on his door.

"Come in."

Matt entered and walked over, pulling a chair up to the opposite side of the desk and sitting down.

"Sir, about Nathan."

"What about him?"

"Why is he here? You've never taken a prisoner before."

Brant sighed and closed the log, sliding it to the side in an attempt to stall long enough to get his thoughts straight. But the truth was, he had no idea why he was here.

"Something about him intrigued me."

"So you decided to take him prisoner?"

"I made a mistake. I'll be getting rid of him."

"How?"

"Figure we can set him adrift, like I should have done originally."

Matt shook his head and set his hands on the desk. "You can't do that."

"I can't?" he asked, raising his eyebrows. "I'm pretty sure I can, if that's what I decide."

"The man don't mean you any harm. The least you can do is drop him at the next port."

"And have him run straight to the officials reporting me for piracy? I think not."

Matt sighed. "You can't just set him adrift. You know his chances of survival—"

"And my chances of survival if he runs straight to the authorities and reports me are slimmer than his."

"Because you attacked a British ship, which you shouldn't have. You knew just from lookin' at her that she wasn't anything worth takin'. You attacked her cause she was British and you had something to prove."

Brant stared at Matt, shocked at how blunt he was being. "Thank you for that input, Matthew. Now if you would excuse me, I have some work to do before I call it a night."

Matt stood up, a frown on his face, but he didn't argue.

"Oh, and set watches of two tonight. There is a leak that'll need pumping until Harold can fix it."

"Yes sir," said Matt, leaving the cabin.

The door slammed shut and Brant looked up. Had it just been the wind? Or was Matt really that upset? It wasn't like his quartermaster to show such outward signs of unhappiness with a decision that he made. But things weren't decided. Brant still hesitated to set Nathan adrift. He still wondered about the man and the calm he presented. If he was completely honest with himself, Nathan reminded him of Karl.

CHAPTER FIVE

Brant didn't send Nathan adrift. In fact, to Matt's urging, he allowed the man time to wander the deck during the day. Matt seemed to have taken a liking to the old captain. They spent hours together, working and conversing. Brant watched from a distance, curious about Nathan, but unwilling to subject himself to the preaching that seemed to accompany the man. Matt, however, seemed eager to soak it all in: the gospel and message of forgiveness.

"Nathan says it's never too late," said Matt, one evening as they walked the deck. "Jesus forgave the thief on the cross in his last moments before death."

"Don't tell me you're swallowing this stuff."

"What's to swallow? It's the truth."

"Truth that the crown and the church have been shoving down our throats for centuries. Don't forget that they like to change their religion with every ruler as well. Catholic, Protestant, they're always fighting, always struggling for power. That's all it is; power. You're going to give that to them?"

Matt shrugged. "I don't think that's what it is supposed to be. Look how content Nathan is. Why can't we have that?"

"When I'm at sea, I am happy. I don't need God or religion to give that to me."

Matt smirked but didn't respond.

"What?"

"The sea ain't offering you that peace this time around, is she?"

"I've been absent, she's just letting me stew," muttered Brant. "You want to find your peace in religion and empty promises, fine. But, like you said, I have until my deathbed to find forgiveness, so I'd rather just keep living the way I have been."

Brant walked away, but he could see Matt shaking his head out of the corner of his eye. His quartermaster had been pestering him about religion and Nathan since the old man had come aboard, and quite frankly, he was getting sick of it. Nights weren't leaving him rested anymore. He tossed and turned, his dreams haunted by his father, Catherine, Senona, and James. His father would tell him that this was no life for a Foxton, that he had let down the family name and dragged it through the dirt, a diatribe he had heard countless times growing up. Catherine would look at him with tears in her eyes, asking through sobs why she couldn't be enough for him. Why he had to hurt her over and over, and made her feel like she was holding him back instead of fulfilling him. And Senona, she would stand there with a baby in her arms and smile. "If this is what you want, you have to be willing to make sacrifices," she would say, and then walk into Caton's waiting arms.

All the people he'd let down, disappointed, and abandoned over the years. But the worst was James. Brant only ever saw his back. No words were ever spoken, but his brother's posture was enough. He'd betrayed him, abandoned him after promising to be his family.

Brant would wake up from his dreams in the early hours of the morning, blankets tossed about from his restless sleep, and sweat soaking his clothes. He'd lie in bed until the sun began to rise, staring at the ceiling of his cabin and waiting. Waiting for the day's distraction, for the distance to become great enough to erase the memories, for the blood that soaked his hands to scare away the ghosts of the people who tried to make him a better person.

"I'm not a good person," Brant muttered, getting up at the first sign of light and walking outside to the water barrel, where he washed away some of the sticky sweat that clung to him—a bitter reminder of the night's horrors.

Matt came up shortly after. He climbed straight to the stern of the ship, where he went to measure the knots. Nathan followed close behind.

Brant grimaced. That man was like Matt's shadow and he'd had enough. "Matt!" Brant shouted. "I want the prisoner in the brig where he belongs."

Brant could see Matt's frown from where he stood, but he didn't care. An order was an order, and his quartermaster would follow it.

Sure enough, Matt dropped the rope he had been measuring and motioned for Nathan to follow him, heading below deck without a word to Brant, just a questioning glance.

When he returned, he didn't go back to the job he had been working on. He walked straight to Brant. "Why is he being confined to the brig?"

"He's a prisoner; I can't have him wandering my ship. He can have an hour a day supervised on deck, that's it. And he'll eat in the brig."

"Sir—"

"That's my decision, Matthew."

Matt's face went blank. "Yes sir," he uttered, and then walked back to the stern of the ship.

Brant didn't really care if he'd upset Matt. Nathan was a prisoner, and a prisoner belonged in the brig, where he could keep his preaching to himself and stop trying to corrupt his men.

* * *

Brant shouted orders as his men prepared to board. His sword drawn, he rushed across the planks and into the heart of the foray. As they drew closer to Port Royale, ships were becoming more frequent, and they had made two more raids in the last week. With every raid Brant felt more alive, his blood pumping through him and warming his extremities like a comforting caress.

Sword flashing, Brant attacked. He didn't even look men in the face as he ran them through. He went from battle to battle, reveling in how alive he felt. He'd forgotten the faces of the men he'd killed. He didn't care about their dying breaths or their looks of shock. All he cared about was the fight, the rush. This was what being alive really felt like; staring death in the face and spitting at his feet. How many times had the reaper come for him, only to be foiled by a piece of sharpened steel in Brant's hand?

Brant didn't even know if the ship they were attacking was French, British, Dutch or Spanish. He'd stopped paying attention to their colors. If the ship sat low in the water from a full belly, he attacked.

This particular ship fought bravely, refusing to surrender until only a few men were left standing. A couple surviving crew members supported the captain, badly injured and pale from exertion. He wouldn't survive long.

Brant walked back and forth in front of them, then turned to his men. "Give no quarter."

He'd never uttered those words before, but the moment they left his lips he knew it would change everything. In this moment he had crossed from play-acting, to the real thing. He *was* what people feared when they set sail for destinations across the great blue expanse. He *was* what boys dreamed about in the stories they read of gold and adventure, of ruthless attacks and terror on the high seas. He was a pirate.

Walking back to his ship, he was headed off by Matt.

"What are you doing?" he asked, anger written all over his face.

"Going to inspect the damage."

"No! Why ain't you givin' them quarter?"

"I'm putting them out of their misery. They wouldn't survive a day adrift."

"You've never taken the life of one who surrendered."

"I told you things were going to change around here."

Matt nodded, his lips pressed firmly together as if holding back words that threatened to spill out. His face was pale, whether from anger or fear Brant couldn't tell.

"I can't in good conscience allow this."

"It's too late. It's done."

"Then I'm leaving."

Brant's heart beat faster and heat rose into his face. He looked at his quartermaster, shocked. "Excuse me?"

"I told you that if things went further than I was comfortable with, that I'd leave. I ain't felt comfortable in a while, but I kept on 'cause I hoped you'd stop with this madness. But this killing men that surrendered; that I can't live with. We make port, I'm leaving."

Brant nodded. "If that's what you want. We'll be docking in Port Royale in a week. Does that suit you?"

"Well enough. And Nathan?"

"What about him?" asked Brant, annoyance leaking into his voice. He had managed to successfully forget about their prisoner, leaving his care to Matt.

"What will you do with him?"

"I haven't decided yet."

"Let him free in Port Royale. He ain't gonna report you."

Brant smiled wryly. "I'm sure he won't, but a dead man can't tell tales," he said with a chuckle, walking away from his seething quartermaster. "Oh, and you are expected to continue working for your keep until we dock. I'm not in the business of carrying passengers."

"Yes sir," Matt muttered to Brant's retreating back.

Brant walked his ship, checking the status of the damage, but he did so in a daze. He hadn't really expected Matt to leave. He had served on the *BlackFox* for years. Always a faithful sailor and someone Brant had come to consider a friend, if a captain could have a friend among the members of his crew. To hear him say that he was leaving was shocking, to say the least, and hit him like a punch to the stomach.

The *BlackFox* would miss him. Brant would have to find both a new sailing master and quartermaster. With Matt's intentions known, there wasn't any point in him acting in a position of authority for the last week at sea. He would work, but as a common sailor.

He mentally went over his list of crewmembers that might be good for the job. The problem was that although his ship was filled with good men, they all had a job and purpose. Those that were nothing more than sailors were not ready to take on quartermaster. He played with the idea of bringing someone new onto the crew, but he didn't like the idea of passing over one of his own men for the position.

Brant sighed, took off his hat, and ran his hand through his hair, then replaced it. He'd walked the entire ship without taking note of the damage.

Shaking his head to clear his thoughts, he pushed Matt out of his mind and returned to the job at hand. He'd deal with the issue of replacing him later. Right now he had to make sure his ship was sea worthy, and set Harold repairing what he could.

The rush and euphoria from the fight had vanished into thin air, replaced by the rising anxiety over losing his quartermaster. He couldn't even have this one moment of release without something going wrong.

CHAPTER SIX

Brant sat at his desk looking over his charts. His calculations showed that they were about two days out from Port Royale. Two days away from losing Matt. It was hard to imagine the ship without him; he'd been with the crew for close to ten years, and had become an integral part of the crew. Brant could still clearly remember the day they had taken Matt aboard. It was the same day he'd met Catherine—the day they had come across a raided ship; Matt and Catherine were the only survivors.

Matt had been badly injured, and it was hit and miss at first if he would survive. A few times they had thought he would succumb to his injuries, but he'd pulled through and had served aboard the *BlackFox* ever since then.

Brant hadn't been able to decide who to promote in his place. He'd spent many hours contemplating and dismissing various names, and so far the best contender was Christopher. He'd been around since Brant had first joined the crew of the *BlackFox* and had served faithfully. But, he'd also been a part of the mutiny against Captain LaFleur, and Brant was hesitant to promote any of the men involved in that to his second in command. After you turn on a captain once, you always have it in you to do it again.

But there was no one else. No one came remotely close to being able to handle the position.

Maybe Brant needed someone stronger, more ruthless and willing to take a chance. Obviously Matt was too soft for the new direction the *BlackFox* was taking. Christopher could be exactly who he needed.

Sighing, Brant resigned himself to sleeping on it another night. At least he'd narrowed it down to one capable crewmember. If he couldn't bring himself to promote Christopher, he would recruit someone new.

Putting away the charts that he had been staring blindly at while lost in thought, Brant got up from his desk and left his cabin. The fresh air on the deck immediately helped calm him and melt away the stress that had been building up ever since Matt announced his intention to leave.

It wasn't supposed to be like this. This was supposed to be a time of healing; of getting back to the man he wanted to be. He'd made too many compromises in the last few years; for James, Senona, and then Catherine. Somewhere along the lines he'd lost sight of who he was and what he wanted in life.

"Sail ho!"

Brant's gaze shot over to the shouting sailor, his eyes flashing and blood rushing in anticipation—an instinctual reaction for Brant. The sailor was pointing off the port side.

Pulling his eyeglass from his belt, he extended it, looking in the direction the sailor indicated. He brought his sight on the ship and then swept the glass upwards in search of the tell-tale flag that proudly displayed their allegiance.

"There she is," he muttered, catching sight of the union jack fluttering proudly in the wind. A British ship so close to Port Royale was no surprise, he had expected as much.

Panning down, he searched the deck for a clue as to the purpose of the ship. He didn't have to search long. It was more than apparent by the cabana set up for the ladies' afternoon tea.

The *Lady Luck* was a passenger ship. And, by the looks of her, not a poor one.

Brant continued to stare through his eyeglass at the ship and the happy passengers going about their day, completely unaware of the danger the *BlackFox* presented to them.

A touch met his shoulder, and Brant lowered his eyeglass to see who was disturbing him.

"Don't do it," Matt said, his eyes pleading.

"Why not? Think of the haul that ship will give us."

"A passenger ship, Brant? That ain't you. Ten years ago you were disgusted by Old Richard attacking one, and leaving Miss Catherine and me for dead."

Brant gritted his teeth at the mention of Catherine, but remained silent, allowing Matt to finish speaking.

"You gonna bring yourself down to that level? Become a common criminal? You'll end up hating yourself for it."

Brant shrugged. "Maybe I should never have set foot on that ship. Maybe I should have sailed on by and left well enough be. That ship was the beginning of all my trouble. If I hadn't stopped I never would have met her."

Matt's face remained firm, but his eyes flashed for a split second, betraying the hurt that Brant's words had inflicted. He immediately wished he could take back his words. If he hadn't stopped for that ship, Matt would have died.

"Those people are innocent. Pass by."

Brant shook his head. Those people weren't innocent.

They ruled the world from their cushy parlors, sipping expensive liquor and smoking while deciding the fate of lesser men. Nations rose and fell, wars were won and lost, due to the whims of these *innocent* people, and they just lined their ever deepening pockets with bloody money.

"Bring her about!" shouted Brant.

Matt shook his head, without uttering a single word he let Brant know he'd have no part in this, and disappeared below deck.

"Run up the colors!"

For the first time Brant could recall, his order was not met with cheers or enthusiasm of any kind. Instead, the men looked at one another, questioning and unsure. After what seemed like an eternity of shuffling feet and silent questions, the men slowly moved to action. They hoisted the flag and rolled out the guns, but even the thunder of the heavy guns didn't seem to instill in the men the anticipation and excitement that was so familiar to Brant.

"Look lively! You lot are about as intimidating as a load of mice!"

Those few words seemed to wake up the crew, and almost immediately they sprang into action. They went about their jobs with newfound energy, preparing for the fight at hand.

Brant lifted his glass and watched the activity aboard their prey. It was strange to watch the people who knew what was going on, but not hear the panic in their voices.

Passengers were being ushered away into their cabins, while sailors rushed about, opening sails and preparing to flee.

"You can run, but not for long," muttered Brant. The *Lady Luck* was a beast of a ship, a luxury liner made for leisurely cruises, not speed. With multiple decks and short jaunts between ports, she couldn't hope to be a match for the much smaller *BlackFox*.

The *BlackFox* gave pursuit, steadily gaining on her prey. They couldn't hope to flee to the shallows—they sat lower in the water than the *BlackFox*—nor were they near enough to a port to find refuge there. The only hope the *Lady Luck* had was if another ship was nearby. Since they hadn't turned around, Brant knew there was no one behind them, and he'd come across no one in front. It was just the *BlackFox* and the *Lady Luck* out here, in the middle of the ocean, and their luck had just run out.

Blood thundered through Brant's ears like waves crashing on rocks, as his adrenaline took over. Stowing away his eyeglass, he watched in anticipation as they closed the gap between them and the fleeing ship.

Brant could almost feel the pressure in the air building between the two ships that would explode in thunder of guns and lightning of clashing steel.

The loud popping of cannons shooting from the stern of the *Lady Luck* met Brant's ears. Warning shots. It was almost laughable as the shots fell short. Warning of what? She had no hope against Brant and his crew—they were grasping at straws, a last ditch attempt to tell their pursuers that they weren't going to go down without a fight.

"Fine then, it is a fight they'll have," muttered Brant.

The *Lady Luck* continued to fire shots from the two stern cannons, likely in hope that they would land a crippling blow that would allow them to outrun the *BlackFox*. But there was no lucky hit. Most of the cannon balls splashed harmlessly into the water, where they were only a danger to the fish below. The one or two that made contact didn't do enough damage to slow her down. It was like mosquitos biting Brant; a minor annoyance but no real threat.

The *BlackFox* closed in on the *Lady Luck*, and boarding hooks flew through the air, tethering the two ships together. Brant no longer had to imagine the frenzied shouts. He could hear them clearly now. There were no passengers on deck any longer, but the sailors present looked unsure and fearful.

"Hold steady, men!" shouted the captain as planks slammed into place, spanning the gap between the two ships.

In seconds Brant's men streamed onto the *Lady Luck*, menacing cutlasses flashing in the sunlight. Brant was thankful he wasn't the one facing his men. He could just imagine how they looked to the sailors; a horde of bloodthirsty pirates.

The clanging of metal on metal filled the air, followed shortly by the first screams of dying men, all joining together and escalating into a chorus. This fight wouldn't last long.

But, just as it looked like it would be the end, that surrender was only seconds away, the male passengers emerged onto the deck. A man in military garb led them, shouting war cries of bravado and anger. Brant swore softly. Of course the men wouldn't hide below deck with the women. They may sit in the lap of luxury, but they were raised to protect what was theirs, and it was quickly apparent that many of them were skilled with the blade as well as in marksmanship.

The sailors of the *Lady Luck* were no slouches themselves, and the added aid from the passengers gave them enough of an edge that the battle had turned from certain defeat to evenly matched, both sides fighting to gain ground that wouldn't give.

Unsheathing his blade, Brant ran across a plank onto the ship and joined in the foray. His blade bit into flesh and bone, shredding through guts and limbs, painting the deck in the slick crimson war paint that was the life blood of fallen men.

Men fell all around him, from both sides of the raging battle, but soon Brant could tell the tides were turning in his favor. Slowly men were losing their gumption, their drive, their bravery, and weapons fell to the deck as one by one they surrendered; all but the passenger in military garb.

He placed himself between Brant's men and the door to the hold and passengers' cabins.

"You've lost. Drop your weapon," stated Brant, breathing heavily from exertion and pain—having suffered some minor flesh wounds.

"And surrender our women and children to you? Never."

"You have my word that no harm will come to them. We're after your gold, not your women."

"The word of a pirate." The man spat at Brant's feet.

"Yes, the word of a pirate. And you'll accept it or I'll remove you."

The man stood firm, his cutlass raised and ready to counter any attack.

Brant sighed, drew his pistol, and fired. He didn't have time to engage in a duel with this self-righteous man. He hit the man square in the chest with an explosion of gunpowder, smoke, and lead. He crumpled to the ground, his eyes holding no shock, just a sad realization. Stubborn till the very end, he refused to give Brant the satisfaction of seeing him surrender.

Brant watched him as blood pooled beneath the man, staining his uniform and covering his medals in a macabre crimson sheen. Just another man painting the already red deck with his blood, but Brant couldn't look away. He could hear his men shuffling behind him as they wondered what to do, but it was as if he was glued in place, his eyes held mesmerized by the sight of the dying body of a proud man, a man that—he realized quite suddenly—reminded him a lot of his father.

He waved his men forward. "Do not so much as harm one hair on a passenger," he commanded, eyes never leaving the body of the dying man struggling for breath as he choked on the very liquid that had once offered him life.

Even after the man drew his last strangled breath, Brant stood rooted in place. All he could see was his father; all he could picture was him struggling for breath. Had it been his fault that he had died, as surely as if he'd shot him, like he had this man? Had his leaving been the cause of his father's declining health and ultimately his death?

He didn't notice his men as they moved around him, relieving the *Lady Luck* of her passengers' riches. Nor did he notice the passing time, until a hand rested on his shoulder, bringing him back to reality.

"We're ready to move out, Cap'n," said Christopher.

Shaking himself to try and regain his composure, Brant nodded. "Very good."

He walked away and surveyed the damage all around him. How had he been deaf to the groans of pain? Bodies of injured and dying men littered the deck.

"Why weren't our men taken care of?" asked Brant, his stomach clenching as a wave of nausea took over.

"Sir?" asked Christopher, pausing in his journey and turning back to his captain.

"Our injured. Why haven't they been taken care of? Why are they lying here suffering?"

"Sir, you said to collect the goods—"

"Men, Christopher. The men always come first. I shouldn't have to order that."

Christopher nodded. "Yer right, Cap'n. Matt usually looks after these things—I wasn't thinking."

But it wasn't Christopher's responsibility. He didn't even know Brant had been considering him for quarter master. If it was anyone's fault, it was Brant's. He sighed, letting his anger go with the dispelled breath. "I'm sorry. This is my fault, not yours. We all have to get used to Matthew not being around."

But even though his anger towards Christopher had dissipated, and blame lay where it should, on his own shoulders, Brant's decision as to whether or not Christopher would be promoted had been made. He wasn't quarter master material. If he was, he would have seen the men suffering and thought to look after them.

"Let's get these men moved over and the doc looking after them."

"And the dead?"

Brant looked around. How many of his own men lay dead amongst the carnage? Too many. More than he was used to seeing. "Take them too. They will have a proper sea burial. And get the *Lady Luck*'s doc. No sense in their men suffering."

"Very good, Cap'n."

Good? It certainly didn't feel like it. If it was so good, then why did he have a sick feeling in the pit of his stomach that threatened to have him hurling over the side of the ship? He was transported back to his first raid; when the coppery stench of blood had left him weak and immobile. Was it the innocent men he had slaughtered today that reduced him to his sixteen-year-old self? Was Matt right? Would he hate himself for taking a passenger ship? Or was it just one passenger, the haunting look of disappointment on his dying face that reminded him so much of his own father?

Brant shook the thoughts away, refusing to allow himself to walk down that path. Instead, he walked back onto his own ship, away from the carnage that he had caused. He went straight down to the hold where he found Matt conversing with Nathan, the captain from the last innocent ship that he had taken.

"We dock by the end of the week and I want you, and this *prisoner* gone," Brant ground out through clenched teeth. He'd had enough. Enough of Matthew's self-righteous behavior. Enough of Nathan's holier-than-thou attitude and preaching at him, like he needed to be saved.

"Then you'll let Nathan go?"

"I have your word you won't go to the authorities?" Brant directed the question to Nathan, who sat calmly on the other side of a set of bars.

"It is not my place to judge—"

"Is that yes?"

"Yes."

"Then I will let you go once we dock. Only because I should have left you with your ship, and I didn't. I won't have unnecessary blood on my hands."

"You mean like the blood of the men on the ship you just attacked?" asked Matt.

Brant turned sharply towards him, his eyes flashing in anger, and his hand reaching for his cutlass. "You hold your tongue. You may be leaving my ship, but while you are still aboard you will give me respect as captain. If you don't, you'll find yourself in the brig with Nathan."

Matt looked shocked, but he nodded slowly, offering no other words of argument or blame. Satisfied, Brant's hand left the hilt of his sword and he spun around, leaving the two men alone in the dark, musty brig. Once they were gone, then he'd be free. Then his troubles could begin to right themselves. It wasn't just Senona, or Catherine, or James. It was Johnny and Matthew. All these lost souls he'd taken under his wing, he'd somehow decided were his responsibility. But they weren't. They were their own people, and they had to look after themselves.

When had the *BlackFox* become a halfway house for the lost and alone? Was it when Karl had taken him aboard all those years ago? When had his life changed directions from being a captain, sailing a ship, and being free, to being weighed down with helping those less fortunate? Wherever that change had occurred, wherever that course had been altered, Brant now found himself miles away from the destination he had planned.

* * *

The groaning and moaning of men had quieted down some, as the ship's doctor went about treating those he could, and making comfortable those he couldn't. The bodies that lay in a row near the starboard rail, covered in an old sail, would not be the last to find their burial in the murky depths of the ocean because of today's raid. More men would join them before the week was through, some falling from loss of blood, others to infection. It was the cold reality of being a sailor and a pirate.

Brant made his rounds among the injured, who were made comfortable in their bunks. He stopped by each one, offering words of encouragement or bravado, whichever would be more welcome. Death was never mentioned, pain was scoffed at, and those dying smiled and spoke as if they would see many more sunrises. It was a room that stank of blood, sweat, rot, and denial.

No one asked for their last rites. There was no priest aboard, and although as captain Brant could play the role, it was never called upon. The men here all knew that no amount of confession or Hail Mary's would save their souls from condemnation. They were lost as sure as a man adrift at sea.

CHAPTER SEVEN

Catherine looked out from under the cabana she sat in, drinking tea with some of the female passengers, and watched Johnny conversing with the sailors. He had barely uttered a dozen words to her since leaving Spain.

He was angry. Angry with her for leaving Brant, for making him leave his life and future. Why couldn't he understand that she had been left with no choice? She had to honor their parents' wishes in sending Johnny home. The fact that the summons had come right when she had reached the point in her own personal life that she could no longer ignore how broken hers and Brant's relationship was, just made the decision easier.

She should have seen it long ago. She had been right the first time she'd turned him down, but had allowed her feelings to get the better of her the second time. She had known she wasn't good for Brant, that they were too different and that she'd destroy him, but she'd been selfish and had wanted him for herself. She couldn't let him go— until now.

It had been a hard decision to come to. For so long she'd ignored Brant's changes, his melancholy and unhappiness. She continued to plan their wedding while it got delayed again and again, first because the house fell behind schedule, again because of a shipping deadline... there was always something getting in the way. She kept telling herself that it was just life, these things happened.

But shouldn't they have fought harder for it? Senona and Caton had suffered similar delays with their wedding, but eventually they had decided to take matters into their own hands. Not Catherine and Brant, though; they just lived life and kept saying next spring, next fall, next month. After a while she couldn't ignore it. Brant wasn't ready to settle down, maybe he never would be. At least not in the way she needed him to.

Then the letter came from her parents; the situation with Spain was becoming increasingly unstable and they wanted Johnny out of there before it was too late. All she had to do was put Johnny on a ship and send him home, but she saw an out and she took it— packing her bags and severing the heart strings in one instantaneous blow.

So why did it hurt so much?

She knew, without a doubt, that she'd made the right decision, and yet her heart ached for the man that made her feel so alive. And seeing Johnny's unhappiness only succeeded in making her feel worse.

His dreams had been in his grasp, and in her taking the easy way out of the mess she'd made of her life, and not fighting for him to stay and follow his future, she had dashed those dreams on the proverbial rocks. It was as disappointing, and as destructive, as a siren's call. She wasn't sure he would ever forgive her for it.

Catherine continued to watch Johnny. He had removed himself from the other passengers, choosing to spend his time with the sailors learning and working. While Catherine sat beneath a cabana, drinking tea and eating cakes with the other women, Johnny would be climbing rigging or even swabbing the deck. At first she had been mortified as the women around her whispered in indignation, but she quickly learned to ignore it and enjoy the fact that Johnny was finding a little happiness in a less than ideal situation.

Now, as she sat having afternoon tea she listened silently to the women's gossip. Old news, Catherine was sure, but new to her as she'd been out of British circles for the last year. Back in Barcelona, she had a finger on the pulse of every scandal around. Lady

Carlotta Montez, Senona's mother, always knew what was going on, and she loved to share the latest news with Catherine during their weekly visits.

It had once been something Catherine had lived for and enjoyed, snickering and whispering behind poor unfortunate women's backs after they'd lacked the good sense to make the right decision. But now, all Catherine could think of was that within a month's time, give or take, these same women—and more—would be whispering and snickering about *her.*

A year ago she had left England and a prominent family to follow her betrothed to a new life. Now she was returning, scorned and rejected, with no ring on her finger and no husband by her side. There was just bitter failure and mistakes following her in the wake of the ship.

Johnny looked over and their eyes met for a minute before he waved and turned away. If only he would talk to her. He, of all people on this ship would understand what she was going through, what she was afraid of. But he was hurting too, so he didn't see her pain. All he saw were his dreams disappearing faster than the setting sun.

"Don't you agree, Miss Marshall?"

Catherine was ripped from her wallowing self-pity by the pretentious Mrs. Fairfield. She always insisted on talking to Catherine, never leaving her alone. Catherine was fairly certain she was keeping her close to try and get the first dish on the juicy gossip that her life was becoming.

"I'm sorry, agree with what?"

"That this trip has been much too dull."

"Oh, yes, much too dull," she agreed, not really caring. "We should be making more ports."

"And all you would do is drink tea and biscuits under a cabana just like this one. The only difference will be you can tell your friends in London that you visited Morocco or someplace equally as exotic," shot out Lady Henley. She was a widow, and a feisty woman at that. She didn't have much patience for the ups and downs of society, and she was old money—well connected. She didn't need to bow and scrape to be accepted, and she knew it.

Mrs. Fairfield forced a tight lipped smile and sipped her tea. "I'm sure you've been many places, Lady Henley."

"More than you ever will. And I saw a lot more than the inside of a cabana."

Catherine watched Mrs. Fairfield squirm in discomfort under Lady Henley's scrutiny, and she smiled in amusement.

"And you, Miss Marshall? Have you seen more than the inside of a cabana?"

"I've seen a few places, but only a small fraction of the world."

"Good. Then you understand that the world doesn't revolve around you, unlike Mrs. Fairfield here."

Catherine was sure her eyes widened into the size of tea saucers, but she nodded mutely before risking a glance over at the scorned woman.

Mrs. Fairfield's face turned red, and her mouth gaped open and closed like a fish out of water. Finally, she sipped her tea in an attempt to regain her composure.

"Have you given thought to going to the New World?" asked Lady Henley, directing her question to Catherine and completely ignoring Mrs. Fairfield's obvious embarrassment.

"I have not. My life has taken a recent change, and besides getting home, I've thought no further."

"You will go home to the gossiping jackals, like Mrs. Fairfield, here?" Lady Henley offered her a secretive smile.

Catherine raised her chin ever so slightly and nodded. "I have nothing to be ashamed of."

"Besides a failed marriage, of course."

"There was no marriage."

Mrs. Fairfield's eyes seemed to light up—she could sense the gossip that was about to be dropped.

"No, there was not. But you left London with a man, and are now returning a year later without him and without a ring on your finger. You think the jackals won't pounce on that?"

Catherine choked back the tears that threatened to overwhelm her. It wasn't so entertaining when the tables were turned on her, and Lady Henley was voicing the very insecurities that had just been running through her mind.

"It will pass. I have nothing to be ashamed of," she said, trying to sound strong and sure.

Lady Henley nodded slowly, knowingly. "You're a brave woman, Miss Marshall, I'll give you that. You come talk to me if you change your mind about the New World. I have an idea to head over there myself, see what all the fuss is about before I'm too old and frail to make the trip."

Catherine sipped her tea, looking for a moment to collect her thoughts. In this den of whispers and lies, it was hard to know who your friends were. Was Lady Henley a friend, or just looking to humiliate her before docking in London?

"Thank you, Lady Henley," she replied, choosing not to pursue the subject. It was a long voyage ahead, and there would be time to figure out Lady Henley. For now, she wanted to keep the spotlight off of herself. This voyage was supposed to be a reprieve, the calm before the storm that would hit when she walked through the doors of high society London.

Why, Brant? Why did you make me love you when you knew it couldn't work? I shouldn't be here sailing back in shame. I never should have left London. Why did you let me love you? She wondered to herself, her mind and heart spinning in turmoil while she calmly sipped at her quickly cooling tea and nibbled at biscuits.

Slowly, as if on stiff joints, Lady Henley got up from her chair, signaling that tea was over. "I'll see you ladies at supper."

Catherine nodded her good-bye, and watched Lady Henley as she made her way into the state room on top deck.

Catherine was stuck below deck. She could have taken money from Brant for better accommodations, but it didn't feel right. Instead, she took the money her parents had sent for Johnny, and covered both fares. Now they were traveling in bunks, not cabins—a fact that would likely be spun into the vicious rumors that would spring up about her.

Getting up, Catherine left the cabana and started walking around the deck, where at least she was away from the fake smiles and judging eyes of the other passengers. If this was a taste of what London was going to be like, maybe the New World wasn't such a bad place for her. She'd heard of people making lives for themselves, out there in the wilds of America. But she wasn't made for that kind of life. No, she'd stay in Britain and endure the scorn. Her mistake had been in leaving Britain in the first place.

Walking up to Johnny, Catherine placed her hands on the rail beside him. "I'm sorry," she said. "I didn't want to drag you away from there, from home."

Johnny nodded. "You're right, that was home. More of a home than any of the schools or manors ever was. You could have talked to father."

"You're right, I could have. But he's afraid for our safety. The political unrest—"

"We would have been fine. You know it, I know it. What are you running from, Catherine? And why are you dragging me with you?"

"Brant…" she trailed off and choked back a sob. "I couldn't marry him. I couldn't keep holding him back."

Johnny nodded. "Everyone else saw it."

"I didn't want to believe it. I wanted to think that I could make him happy. That he wouldn't need that life if he had me."

Tears flowed freely now and she swiped angrily at them. "I'm sorry, Johnny."

"You should have known that you can't change a man like Brant. We all knew it; we all saw that you weren't good for him and, quite frankly, I don't feel sorry for you when you were living under a rock."

"Johnny—"

"And think about what you put Brant through. He loved you and he was willing to change his life for you, even knowing he'd be miserable. You walked away from him, and left him with what?"

"Freedom."

"You left him with heartbreak. Don't fool yourself into thinking he's handling it well."

"And you, Johnny? What did I do to you?"

"Nothing I won't get over. I'm young and I've gotten out once, I'll do it again. This time without your help."

Catherine stifled a laugh. "You're so much like him."

"Brant?"

"Yeah." He was right, he would be fine. If Catherine knew anything, it was that men like Brant and Johnny were never held back for long.

She walked away, glad that she'd at least talked with her brother. In time, he'd forgive her. For now, she just had to make it through the rest of this voyage. Then London and the real battle, to hold onto her good reputation, would begin. She wasn't even afraid to explain to her parents what had happened, she was just afraid of the jackals, as Lady Henley called them, always looking for fresh meat. It was bad enough that she'd left with a privateer, but now she was returning with nothing.

CHAPTER EIGHT

The *BlackFox* docked in Port Royale right on schedule, but Brant found no relief in the familiar berth. Instead, he felt more anxious than ever.

Matt walked up on deck. Nathan, the captured captain who had taken up residence in the *BlackFox*'s hold, followed close behind. He was now a free man, as promised.

"Thank you for everything," said Matt, his small bag of possessions slung over his shoulder.

Brant just nodded. He had no words to offer his former quarter master and friend.

"I hope you find what yer looking for. Maybe we'll meet again, under better circumstances."

"It's a big ocean, Matthew."

"But a small world."

"You just make sure your friend there doesn't go blabbing about me to anyone." Brant indicated Nathan, who was standing a short ways away, waiting for Matt to disembark.

Matt nodded, slung his bag over his shoulder, and walked away. Brant didn't say goodbye; he was done with saying that. If people chose to walk away, that was their choice. It was the end, not goodbye.

Turning away from the retreating figures, Brant felt a pang of sadness—or was it regret?—but he quickly shook it off and went about his work. No crewmember left until everything was in order, not even Brant, so they worked tirelessly to stow away sails and rigging, tether the ship securely to the dock, and move crates around. Empty crates were offloaded to make room for resupplying. Goods that they had relieved ships of were sorted, some to keep, some to fence for gold.

The entire time Brant kept track of everything that moved through the ship. Without a quarter master, it was up to him to determine everyone's shares—and they had to be paid out by the time they left the ship that night.

At the end of the day, when the ship was in order and watches were assigned, Brant sat at a table next to the gangway and handed out bags of coin to each crewmember as they disembarked. Some of the men whistled in appreciation.

"Heavy bag, Cap'n."

"It's amazing how much more you get to put in your coffers when you aren't paying out to the king," said Brant with a wink, sending the sailor on his way.

It was true; the shares were the equivalent of what they would normally get, and this was only a portion of what they would pocket this time. There would still be more gold to be divided once goods were fenced and liquidated.

With the last man gone, Brant pocketed his own share, and walked off the ship in search of a tavern. It had been a long time since he'd sat and played cards in the taverns of Port Royale, too long. Since becoming captain, life had been too serious, and tonight he was going to let loose a little. He had no brother to look after, no estate to worry about. Just himself, and he was going to take full advantage and celebrate the good fortune their ship had come into this last voyage.

Sitting down in a dimly lit bar full of sailors, Brant ordered rum, and began wandering the room in search of a card game. It wasn't hard to find one, it was more finding the right one; one that wasn't closed to outsiders, or wasn't stacked too high against him.

Finding a table, Brant pulled up a chair and sat down.

"Deal me in."

"Buy in is five quid."

Brant placed the coins on the table, and cards were handed to him.

Brant won some hands and lost more. But it didn't matter; it was for the fun of the game to him, not for the gold—he had enough of that anyway. It brought him back to his school days, when he'd played with Leo—his roommate and friend. Last he'd heard, Leo had settled down on his father's plantation here in Port Royale, but he'd never bothered looking him up.

At some point early on in his days as a sailor, he had given up cards and gambling—disgusted by the way people would throw away the earnings that were meant to support their family, just on the hope that they would have a few more coins for bread or ale that month. Maybe he'd become jaded over the years, but he just didn't care about that anymore. If the men put their money in the pot, that was their choice. As long as he wasn't cheating, then all was fair in this game of luck and chance.

"Hey, Foxton, did'na think you were one to mix with us regular sea dogs," uttered a new voice, as a man took a seat across the table from him.

Brant looked up, and his eyes met those of Old Richard's. It had been a long time since they'd crossed paths, but every time they did, it was unpleasant.

"Richard, are you going to put your coin up against mine?"

"Aye, I think I might. Wouldn't mind a bit of that squeaky clean royal gold you got rollin' around in your coffers."

Brant smirked. "You haven't heard? I've gone independent."

Richard chuckled and threw down the allotted coins, while reaching for cards with his other hand. "So, yer joining us in more ways than just down-time, eh? Decided that you weren't so high and mighty after all?"

"High and mighty? No. Every man is the same out there on the water. But compared to you, Richard, I'm a whole different caliber. Your name will never be whispered in fear. I'd bet my ship that mine will be by the end of the season."

"I heard a passenger ship was taken not long ago. That you?" asked another sailor they were playing with.

Brant shrugged. "A gentleman never tells."

Guffaws circled around the table. "You ain't no gentleman no more, Foxton," offered one man, laying down a card. "Jus' a regular ol' criminal like the rest of us."

"And I'm sure I'll meet you at the gallows someday," said Brant, waiting his turn.

"Sooner rather than later, you keep making enemies," growled Richard.

"Enemies? I don't see any enemies, only friends."

"Friends in cards, 'cause we all want a piece of your gold. You turn yer back, yer liable to find a knife in it. That's what happens when you strut around these docks like yer better than the rest of us, taking *our* gold in the name of the *King,*" Richard spat on the floor. "Then decide to cash in on what we got. These men, they all smile at you now, but you wait. You can't just switch sides, switch allegiances, and turn enemies into friends. That ain't how the sea works."

Brant cringed at Richard's words, but he sipped his drink to hide his emotions and continued to play.

"Are you going to turn me in, Richard?"

The man chuckled, but it sounded more like a dying cough. "Turn you in? Nah, I don't deal with the authorities. I'm more likely to stab you while you sleep. Best keep one eye open, Foxton."

"Always do."

Brant lay his cards on the table face down, and scraped his chair backwards against the worn wood floor. "I fold."

He nodded to several of the men that he'd been playing with most of the evening, ignoring Richard, then walked over to the bar and ordered another drink.

"String o' bad luck?"

A doxy draped herself over Brant's shoulder, making it impossible to ignore her.

"Quitting while I'm ahead. You're wasting your time with me—I'm not looking for company."

"Everyone is looking for company," she purred, trying again.

Brant gently brushed her off so that she was no longer touching him. "I'm serious. I'm not looking for company."

His hand strayed to his pistol, and although he had no intention of using it, the action didn't go unnoticed by the promiscuous woman, and she flounced off with a huff to find someone else to prey upon.

Two drinks in, Brant glanced over as Old Richard sat down beside him and ordered a drink.

"It's on him," he said, indicating Brant. "He owes me."

Brant raised an eyebrow and shook his head at the serving girl. "I don't owe you anything."

Richard shrugged, and placed a coin on the counter to pay for his drink.

"Yer not one of us, Foxton. Never will be."

"Thank you, Richard."

"You can drink in our bars and play at our card tables. Even prey on our prey. But you ain't never gonna be one of us. There won't be no protection for you, when your time comes."

"No honor among thieves then?"

"Nah, there's honor for the brothers. But like I said, you ain't one of us."

Brant nodded and lifted his glass to Richard. "Good. I don't want to be like you."

Richard's brow furrowed. "You think yer better than me?"

"Yes, I do. Always have been, always will be."

Richard smirked and threw back his drink. "Prove it."

"Excuse me?"

Richard stood up and climbed up on his chair somewhat unsteadily, drawing his cutlass. "Prove yer better than me. I challenge you, Cap'n Brant Foxton, to a duel."

Brant snorted. Was he serious? Old Richard wanted to fight him? He was well-known for his skill with a cutlass, and here Richard was drunk, and challenging him—the odds couldn't be more against the man.

"Well, Foxton?"

Brant looked up. All eyes were on them. "You want to fight me, Richard? Fine, I'll fight you, but not like this. Sleep it off first."

"So you can turn tail and run? No way. Here and now. Clear the tables, gents."

Richard's original challenge had been met with silence falling over the entire bar, stillness, as the inhabitants waited for Brant's response. Now, it erupted in noise and cacophony as tables were moved, and men started placing bets on the outcome.

Brant shot back the last of his drink, shrugged at some questioning glances from a couple of his crewmembers that happened to be in the bar, and pulled out his cutlass.

"To first blood?"

"Let's make it interesting; death or mortal wound."

Brant nodded, pointing at his heart, stomach, liver, and kidneys.

Richard smirked. "Aye, those be the points that count. Any other crimson is just collateral."

Brant nodded his assent and he heard calls of "my money is on Foxton for first blood" and "Richard will take it, though."

Everything was a game in this life. Everything was a chance to make money, find entertainment, and create a story to tell over the next card table or roll of a pair of dice.

He could feel the adrenaline rolling through him, the rush of blood through his body, and hear his heart pounding in his ears. It was like before a raid, only better. It was personal, and it felt good. Then the clash of steel meeting steel resounded throughout the bar that had, in that split second, become deathly quiet. The dance began, and the voices grew in volume again, first a whisper, then a roar, as money was passed around and shouts of dismay or excitement were uttered.

But to Brant it was all just music, a symphony to the dance that he engaged in. He focused on the flashing blade, the clanging steel, and the shuffle of his opponent's feet, as he matched him step for step.

This would be it; to mortal wound or death. Richard would be out of his life forever. Him and everyone he had brought into it.

Memories flooded Brant, and he tried to shake them away, tried to concentrate on the fight. But he realized that in the split second he'd allowed himself to think towards the future, he'd left the fight, and now he was trapped down a road to the past. He thought about Catherine, hiding under a bed in the state room after her ship was attacked by none other than Old Richard; Matthew, as he lay dying in the infirmary of the *BlackFox* after being wounded by one of Richard's men; Senona, walking down the docks of Barcelona, having handed over most of her coins to Richard for passage to Port Royale—unknowingly handing her life over to a criminal—all the lives that had become entangled in his, all because of Old Richard steering him off course.

Richard's blade flashed into view, taking Brant by surprise, and nicking him in the leg as he jumped quickly to the left.

Shouts met Brant's ears as money was passed about for the drawing of first blood. Richard backed away, his small victory won, and smiled, taking a moment to breathe.

Brant briefly inspected the cut—it was nothing serious—and turned back to Richard, launching into a furious attack. If anything the injury had only succeeded in making him angrier. Richard was prepared, and it was quickly becoming apparent to Brant that he wasn't nearly as inebriated as he had thought, nor was this the easy fight he expected. Richard was skilled, maybe not in the technical aspects of sword play, but he certainly knew how to protect himself, and how to inflict injury on an opponent.

For a moment, Brant felt doubt—doubt that he could win this. Right now, with his mind far away and his anger taking over, Richard was gaining the upper hand.

Brant stumbled, tripping over a loose board in the floor, and caught himself in a crouch. Richard's sword flashed right on top of him, as Brant feverishly attempted to block the attacks and regain his footing at the same time.

But it wasn't just the physical attack from Richard. Inside there another war raged on, this one from the people that had taken over his life; Senona's smile, so radiant and alive, her laughter so full of joy and freedom. How could he say he didn't need her, when every part of him ached to have her around? Had he been lying to himself these last few weeks since leaving Spain?

And James… he had abandoned his brother.

A flash of steel met Brant's eye, and he threw up his cutlass to block the attack. The jarring clash traveled through his arm and into his shoulder—a brutal reminder of what was happening in the present.

He scrambled backwards on the ground, away from Richard and his attacks, stopping his retreat only to raise his blade in self-defense. Never had he been so close to defeat, never had he been in such a helpless situation.

The roar of the crowd was deafening. Men shouted at him to get up, others shouted encouragement to Richard. Brant saw, out of the corner of his eye, the doxy who had approached him earlier waving her fists in support of Richard. Even the men he had played cards with all night, seemed to be against him.

"You show him," was one shout.

"Privateer scum," another spat out as Brant's journey brought him near.

All it took was a moment's distraction by the crowd, and Brant could feel the icy bite of steel as it slid smoothly into his flesh.

Numbness filled him. Just one short moment of pain, and then nothing, as Richard stood over him, blade thrust forward.

Brant looked down, and saw the steel protruding from his belly. A dark crimson stain slowly spread over his shirt, and then the pain came back with a vengeance.

Searing pain like hot pokers from the blacksmith's fire filled his gut, traveling through his entire body like a desperate reminder that he was alive, that his body was fighting to hold onto the life that was trying to pull away.

And then he saw Catherine, her beautiful lithe body with flowing blonde hair, approaching him through the crowd like an angel come to take him home. Her smile, so gentle, so loving, radiated and took away some of the pain, and when she reached out to him her touch was a soft whisper.

"I'll never stop loving you, Brant," she whispered. And then, as if a wind had come through and blown away a wisp of smoke, she was gone.

She was never here, Brant realized as the pain returned for just a split second, and Richard's leering face filled his view—a stark contrast to the ethereal beauty that Catherine had inspired upon him only a moment before.

"You lose, Foxton. See you in hell."

Everything went black and silent.

CHAPTER NINE

Catherine sat across from Brant in the garden, a small table between them set with tea, coffee, and biscuits. The sun was warm on Brant's neck and inviting him into a blissful sleep, yet he felt restless and uneasy. He could see the ocean, and his ship bobbing up and down on the waves just on the horizon. A longboat was waiting for him on the beach, Johnny waving him over, away from Catherine who smiled at him and sipped her tea. It was like two different scenes were melded together, and he didn't know where one began and the other ended.

"I'm sorry, what did you say?" he asked Catherine, realizing that she had been talking.

"I said I'm so glad you're here to stay now. It was the right decision, letting Johnny take over the captaincy of the *BlackFox* so that you could be home to help raise the family."

Brant frowned. Family?

As if on cue, two children ran out and started frolicking in the grass—or was it sand?—in front of them.

Brant nodded at Catherine's words, but couldn't look away from the children playing in front of him. If they were his, why didn't he feel the love he should, or joy at watching them? Instead he felt... nothing.

He looked over at Catherine. He was numb. It was as if she didn't exist, for all the emotion she instilled in him. The only thing he felt was the longing, the draw towards the ocean, the waiting longboat, and his ship. They were so close, and yet so far away. They were out of his grasp, as Catherine shackled him to the solid earth and this building they called a home.

"No," he whispered.

"No?" Catherine questioned.

"No, it wasn't the right decision. I shouldn't be here," he said, more to himself than to Catherine.

Her face fell and tears welled up in her eyes, which had been shining in happiness only moments before. "Don't say that, Brant. You told me we were enough for you. You said that we would be enough—"

He shook his head and stood up, walking away. She wasn't enough. He knew that, she knew that, so why had they been holding on? Through all the hurt, and anger, and tears their relationship had endured, they had continued to hold on, lying and saying that their love was *enough*.

He could hear her calling his name, but he kept walking…walking towards his ship, towards his freedom, and away from the woman who trapped him.

As he walked, a pain filled his gut, slowly working its way through his body. He felt weak, each step becoming more and more of a struggle. He looked down and saw blood seeping from a stomach wound. Everything came pouring back; the duel, the fatal blow. This world, this conversation with Catherine had never happened, because she had been the one to leave weeks ago, and now he realized she was right. They never would have worked out, and he would have ended up resenting her for holding him back.

"He's coming to," said a voice that sounded distant, but was slowly drawing closer.

Brant blinked, and the scene before him disappeared for a second, replaced by a dismal looking room, but only for a moment. Blinking once, twice, every time he closed his eyes he saw the room, until finally he shut them, and he didn't return to the beach.

Instead, he was in a dark, damp room. A man was washing his hands in the corner, and he turned to Brant with a smile.

"You had a nasty wound."

"Will I be okay?" croaked out Brant through a parched throat.

The doctor handed Brant a glass of water and shrugged.

"Only time will tell, but you're heading to lockup, so I don't put much stock in it. If you survive the wound, you'll go to trial."

Brant grimaced as he choked on the water. His freedom was to be so short lived.

The doctor waved in a couple of guards who were standing just outside the doorway, and they marched in, positioning themselves on either side of Brant's cot.

"I've done what I can. The rest is up to nature," said the doctor, waving them away.

The guards moved, each to one end of the cot, and picked it up, marching themselves and their prisoner out the door, and down a long stone corridor. They didn't take him far. Obviously they had already been in the prison building, and he was now being transferred to the cell that would be his home until he either died from his wound, or he was hung.

Placing him in a cell by himself, they left the cot on the floor with a small pitcher of water beside him. No one was there to help him drink or sit up. He was all alone, except for the echoing calls from prisoners elsewhere in the building.

Time passing was measured by the shadow moving across the floor. Even then, Brant had lost track of the days and evenings he'd spent in the cell. Most of the time he drifted in and out of sleep, his waking hours filled with pain that had no relief.

Three times a day he was given food—if it could be called that—and a guard helped him eat, and checked his wound. Besides meals, he had no contact with another human for days. Rats ran across his prone body, and nibbled at his soiled, shredded clothing.

Brant found himself lost in his thoughts, realizing over the days that, for the first time since he'd sailed away from Spain, he was at peace with Catherine leaving. Maybe it had been the pain induced dream, but he no longer missed her, nor felt any anger towards her. She had done what he hadn't had the courage to do—and what they had both been denying for over a year.

He had traded his emotional pain for a physical one. The thing that really irked him was if he'd let himself come to terms with this during the weeks he'd spent at sea, he never would have lost to Old Richard, and he wouldn't be lying here rotting away in a jail cell awaiting his death.

A clang sounded on the cell bars, ripping Brant away from his thoughts.

"Foxton, you got a visitor," said the guard.

Brant looked over and saw Matt standing at the bars. "You look terrible, Cap'n."

Brant smiled. "I feel terrible. What's happened with my ship?"

"She's just off the coast, laying low. I told the men that those who didn't want to stick around and wait for me, could find a new billet."

"You staking claim, then?"
"Figured there was no one else."

"Good. If I don't make it out of here, I'll know the *BlackFox* is in good hands."

Matt shuffled awkwardly and looked at the floor. "Yer still Cap'n. I'll come back to visit in a couple days, just wanted to let you know what was happening on the outside."

"Thank you. And, Matthew…" Matt looked up.

"You were right; I was looking to fill a space in the wrong places. I realize that now."

Matt nodded, no words needed in the situation. Brant's apology was accepted before he even uttered it; that was apparent by Matt's efforts to look after his ship, as well as check in on him. Despite his best efforts, he hadn't managed to chase all his friends away. And for that, Brant was thankful. Because right now, as he lay here wallowing in pain and guilt and sorrow, he could really use a friend.

* * *

Days passed by, meal after meal being fed to Brant, and yet his pain didn't diminish. He was as helpless as a baby, lying on his cot with only the rats for company. No one came to visit; just the guard who helped him eat his food. There was no talk of a trial or hanging, there was no mention of his wounds, just an ever-increasing pain, and a growing weariness that seemed to be accompanied by dreams of the strangest sort.

How many times had Brant woken up from nightmares of the ocean swallowing him up? He'd lost count. All he knew was that every moment, both awake and asleep, were filled with horror. He found himself praying, for the first time in years, for someone to come, anyone, that he might get the help he needed.

He was no fool. He knew what infection was. He knew the smell radiating from him wasn't just filth and his surroundings; it was the distinct smell of rot. Yet no one called a doctor. He knew that the bouts of sweating and shivering had nothing to do with the atmosphere, but instead was because of the invisible force attacking his body at his weakest point.

"Please, God," he sobbed, one evening after a particularly terrifying nightmare. "Please, send Matt. Send help."

After that, he lost track of time. He drifted in and out of a feverish sleep. He would go from being unbearably hot, to shivering in cold. He couldn't eat anymore. He had no recollection of when, or if, a guard came to feed him.

At one point, when he was awake, he called out hoarsely for water, but no one came or, if they did, he had already fallen back into unconsciousness.

How many days had passed? How long must he suffer? It was getting to the point where Brant just wanted to die.

And then, one day, when he opened his eyes, he saw Matt. He stooped beside him and mopped his brow, bringing a glass of refreshing cool water to his lips.

"I'll bring help, Brant. Just hold on," he said before Brant passed out again.

The next time Brant opened his eyes, a girl knelt beside him. He had been stripped of his soiled clothes, and she gently washed him with a pail of warm soapy water and a sponge. It felt heavenly on his aching joints and filthy skin. Was this the last moment of compassion before he passed on?

"Priest," he whispered, too weak to get out any more than just that single word.

The girl stopped her work and looked at Brant, a stern look on her face. "I'm not calling a priest for you, Captain. You aren't dying yet."

"Priest, please… sins…"

She just shook her head and continued cleaning his body.

Brant didn't know how long she dutifully toiled over him, cleaning him and his wound. He passed in and out of consciousness numerous times. Sometimes he opened his eyes and she was gone, then the next time he woke up she'd be back.

"Here, eat this," she said, as she held a piece of bread to Brant's lips. He nibbled at it. It had been soaked in some kind of soup or broth, and the bread tasted fresh and warm. This wasn't prison fare.

"Who are you?" he asked.

"Faith Howard. I'm a friend of a friend," she replied with a smile, offering him another bite of bread.

They spent most of their time together in silence. Brant didn't have the strength to talk, though questions about this woman plagued him when he was coherent enough to wonder. Most of the time, he lay there silently as she administered to him, cleaning his wound, bathing him and feeding him. Yet she still refused to get him a priest, no matter how many times he asked.

"You aren't dying, not yet," she always replied. "Not if I can do anything about it."

Days, or maybe weeks went by while this woman held Brant on the precipice between life and death, never letting him fall over. His fever came and went, always threatening to make all her work for naught, always threatening to drag him down. Some days were better than others, but mostly everything was a blur.

And then one day Matt was there instead. He didn't bring food, but he helped Brant drink.

"Why did you get help? I'm going to die either way," asked Brant. It was a better day, and he was feeling strong enough to converse a little.

"Because, you did it for me once upon a time, and if you're going to die, it isn't going to be at the hand of infection. It's gonna be proudly, as a captain."

Brant smiled slightly. "Thank you."

Matt talked for some time, telling Brant about the weather outside, stories of what happened down at the docks, how Old Richard fled Port Royale after the guards arrested Brant. Most of it was trivial and washed right over him, but it was the simple comfort of hearing a human voice that gave him a sense of contentment and happiness—human connection was not to be scorned. The power it held was magnificent, because suddenly Brant found himself *wanting* to live. And when Matt left that day, he resolved to fight with every ounce of strength he had left. There would be no more asking for a priest. There would be no more despair. He would fight until the very last breath was ripped from his body. And if he had sins to confess, he'd do so at the judgment seat.

CHAPTER TEN

Catherine looked over the letter. She had docked in England only a day ago, and the letter had been waiting for her when she arrived at her family's townhouse. She read it over for what was the fifth or sixth time this evening.

Brant was injured and dying. If he survived his injuries he would go to trial, and likely be hung as a pirate.

The letter was from Matt. He said that he had written a similar letter to Senona and Caton, but he didn't have much hope they could do anything to help. Catherine, on the other hand, had connections. Her father was a powerful man, and if he appealed to the right people, Brant may be spared.

Catherine stared at the letter. It was dated weeks old already. For a letter from her father to get to the governor, or anyone else of importance before the trial, was unlikely. But could she just let him go? Brush it off as reaping the rewards of his chosen life? Could she just forget the love that she felt pounding through her body for this man, as he stood on the brink of death? Closing her eyes, she let a tear slip down her cheek and fall to the parchment that had been folded and unfolded repeatedly since her return.

"What's wrong?"

Johnny walked into the room and sat down, slouching in a chair across from her.

Catherine said nothing, handing the letter over to her brother who, at the very least, seemed to have forgiven her for her role in his return to England.

The room was silent as he read the letter over. Then, he looked up. "Have you spoken to father yet?"

Catherine shook her head.

"You'll let him die?"

Her tears began anew. "I don't know what to do. I walked away from that life, from him. I'm not responsible for him anymore—"

"You were in love with him and you'll let him die?"

"It is a consequence of the life he chose."

"If you won't talk to father, I will," said Johnny, getting up, still clutching the letter tightly in his hand. "I won't sit idly by if there is still time to save him. And if you ever loved him, neither should you."

He stalked out of the room, presumably to talk to their father who had holed himself up in his study after supper.

Catherine got up and followed Johnny. If he spoke to their father, she would be there for support. After all, he was speaking for the man that had once been her fiancé. He was right, she shouldn't even consider sitting idly by while he sat in a jail cell waiting to be hung.

Johnny didn't even bother knocking, just burst into their father's study and strode right over to the large desk, where their father was situated, writing a letter.

"I would appreciate a knock," said their father without looking up.

Johnny planted his hands on the desk and waited for their father to look up, while Catherine stood behind him, watching things play out in silence.

"How can I help you?"

"Read this." Johnny shoved the letter from Matt in their father's face and waited as he took it gently from his son and perused it. Finally, he placed the letter flat on his desk and looked up.

"So you want me to intervene?"

"You have connections. You're a powerful man."

"Connections that will take time to talk to and convince. Time that I'm afraid Brant Foxton does not have."

"You'll do nothing?"

Their father sighed and ran his hand through his hair, then looked past his son at Catherine. "I'll talk to some people and see what I can do, but I doubt it will get back to Port Royale in time to save Brant; for all we know he's already dead."

Catherine nodded. "Thank you."

Johnny shook his head. "Let me sail to Port Royale."

Attention back on Johnny, the room got tense. "And what do you hope to accomplish there?"

"I could speak on his behalf. As your son—"

"You will hurt our name more than you will help his."

Johnny looked back, catching Catherine's eye. Their father had forbidden him from leaving, but she could see just by the look in his eye that he would be gone by sunrise on the first and fastest ship bound for Port Royale.

She smiled, but it wasn't out of happiness. Her brother would run off in the middle of the night and take to sea. He was so like Brant, and she could only pray that his life wouldn't end up the same way in a few years. But she wouldn't stop him, because she couldn't, and because she didn't really want to. She knew that Brant's best hope was with Johnny, and he wasn't going to just go to Port Royale to speak on his behalf. He was going to rescue Brant, if it came down to it. That was the kind of person Johnny was; just like Brant, reckless, stupid, and brave.

"Thank you, Father. I know you'll do everything you can."

She gave Johnny a pointed look, and they left the study. Once in the hall she closed the door behind her and leaned against it. "Should I say goodbye now?"

"I can't just let him die, and you know that father's efforts will be too little, too late."

She nodded. "I won't stop you."

"I'm not coming back."

Their conversation was short and clipped. Facts were stated and emotions kept out of the situation.

Catherine swallowed the moment of sorrow that threatened to overtake her, and nodded slowly, tears welling in her eyes. "I feared as much."

"I don't belong here. I'll save Brant, and from there… who knows?"

Catherine nodded again and took a deep breath. "Come see me before you leave, please," she said, walking away to find privacy. Not only would she lose Brant, but she was losing her brother now too.

* * *

Johnny didn't say goodbye. Catherine woke the next morning to him gone, and the house in an uproar. Her father immediately knew what had happened and was attempting to assuage her distraught mother, but Catherine could see the anger smoldering beneath his eyes.

But no move to chase their prodigal son was made. Instead, after a week of tears and angry outbursts, Johnny was slowly forgotten. *Well, maybe not forgotten,* thought Catherine as she paused her work on a needlepoint. No, forgotten wasn't the right word. Ignored perhaps. Or better yet, considered dead.

As if in mourning, his name was carefully avoided for fear of some kind of emotional response. Catherine walked on eggshells around her parents. But she was almost relieved that the disappearance of Johnny took the attention off of her and her failed engagement—if only for a while.

It didn't take long for word of her return to make its rounds in the circles of society. And soon enough invitations for tea, and other social events, came in. At first, Catherine turned them down. But soon she was looking for an excuse to get out of the house and away from the building tension and suppressed emotions.

"Catherine, tell us, are you just back for a visit, or for good?" asked an older woman.

Catherine plastered on a fake smile. They all knew very well that she was back for good, and without the fiancé she had left with. "I'm here to stay."

"Your sailor wasn't good enough for you?"

"Captain, actually."

"Frankly, I'm surprised you gave him any attention, much less considered marriage. He is beneath you."

Catherine gritted her teeth beneath her false smile. "Captain Foxton comes from a good family. One that would have placed him as your superior in social standing had he chosen to stay, rather than serve his King."

Soft sounds of disapproval filled the room. "If he walked away, he is beneath you. I'm glad you came to your senses."

But Catherine didn't sense gladness coming from the women, or even good will. All she felt was the growing joy over a scandal that was sure to sweep the social circles at her expense. Sitting through the rest of tea was torture, as she deflected various questions, and hoped she wasn't giving the women anything concrete to base their rumors on.

When the time came that she could excuse herself, she did so in a hurry, hailing a carriage and hiding in shame the whole way back to her parents' townhouse. And to think that this was just the beginning. Wait until news of Brant's imprisonment and charges of piracy came to light. Then tongues would really start to wag.

After that, Catherine hid in her home. She refused all invitations to come out, but she still heard the vicious rumors as she walked down the halls of her own house and maids whispered amongst themselves, having heard stories from the neighboring houses.

Finally, her mother pulled her aside.

"Dear, you can't keep hiding. You will only give them more fuel by doing so."

"How so, Mother? If I go out into society, I will be bombarded with questions that will fuel the fires more than my silence will."

"If you continue to hide as if you have something to be ashamed of, they will treat it as such. You must get back into society and hold your head high. Only then will they lose interest. Surely you knew this was coming, that they wouldn't leave you alone."

"I had hoped…," Catherine trailed off. No, she hadn't even dared hope. She did know that this was coming, and when the storm hit she cowered down and let it tear her apart, rather than weather it bravely.

"Whatever you had hoped doesn't matter now. You made your choice to leave with a man of questionable nature, and now you're reaping your rewards."

Catherine bit her tongue as an angry retort sprung forward. She wanted to blame her mother for allowing her to go, for not talking some sense into her, but she knew the fault lay squarely on her own shoulders. She had proposed marriage, she had asked for a big society ball to celebrate her impending marriage, she had sailed off into the sunset with a privateer, and had deluded herself into thinking she could make a life out of only half the ingredients required for two people to make a life together.

"You're right, Mother; I'm reaping my rewards. And I would appreciate your silence as I gather my strength about me to face this. The sad thing is if it wasn't your daughter, if it was someone else's daughter that had made the same mistake, I know you would be wagging your tongue right alongside the worst of them."

Her mother's shocked and hurt face gave Catherine a small sense of victory. If only for a moment, she had stood in front of society and held fast. It was the first step in a long climb to victory, but she knew that if she could gather her wits about her and respond to every woman like she had her mother, she could come out victorious. She could return to her place on top of society's ladder.

"Catherine…" her mother's mouth opened and closed like that of a fish out of water until she found her words. "I'm glad you found your tongue. Now maybe you should find the right target to attack," she replied angrily, leaving the room in a rustle of skirts.

Catherine smiled. She would persevere.

CHAPTER ELEVEN

Brant lay on his cot, watching a stream of light move across the floor as the sun rose outside. He was doing much better. He could feel himself getting stronger each day, with the help of Faith—the woman who had been nursing him back to health.

He was still too weak to sit up on his own, and was mostly confined to his cot. But he could sit up with help, and Faith had promised that soon he'd be looking out the window and watching the sunrise, instead of just watching the beam of light across the floor.

Bars clanged and the door squealed as it opened, admitting the young woman into the cell.

She was young and beautiful, in her own right. Red hair and a pink tinge to her cheeks gave her a girlish look, one that would keep her looking younger than her age for years to come. Her brown eyes were soft and spoke of kindness and gentleness, while flecks of green near the pupil seemed to tell a tale of a dangerous storm brewing. She was, perhaps not one to make heads turn; she was plain in her appearance and dress, but her smile could light up a room.

"Good morning," she said, kneeling beside him and helping him sit up.

Brant grunted from exertion and smiled. "It is now."

A blush spread across her face and she lowered her head so that her hair blocked her embarrassment.

"You look like you're doing well today. A bit more color in your cheeks," she said, the slight blush receding from her face.

"I could say the same for you."

"I see you've found your tongue as well."

Brant grinned at the girl. She was quick; he liked that. It made teasing her all the more entertaining.

She worked in silence as she removed the bandage around Brant's midsection and gently swabbed the now healing wound with clean water. It looked good, on the outside. The skin was starting to pucker together in the formation of a scar, but the internal muscles were taking much longer to heal.

As she wrapped him back up, to both protect the still tender wound from dirt, and to add support to his healing insides, she looked up at him. "I think you can start sitting up on your own. As long as it doesn't hurt too much, I think it will be good to work the muscles just a little bit."

"And walking?"

She shook her head. "Not yet."

Brant sighed but didn't protest.

Faith pulled up a stool and took a seat, opening the book she had been reading to Brant for the past week. She read until breakfast came, and then she brought that to him. She offered help when it was needed, but allowing him the dignity of independence as much as she could.

Now that he was sitting up he could mostly eat by himself. He just needed things handed to him.

Once breakfast was over, Brant knew his time with Faith was nearly over for the day.

"What are you doing the rest of the day?"

"Helping my ma with the children."

"Are there many of you?"

Faith nodded. "Six. I'm the oldest."

"How did Matt find you? Are you…"

Faith blushed and shook her head. "No, there is nothing between myself and Matthew. He met my father not long ago, and when news of your injury came to him he asked for my father's help. He sent me."

"I'll see you're handsomely reimbursed for this."

Faith smiled gently and placed her hand on Brant's arm. "It is my pleasure to help you in your time of need. I don't require anything in return."

"You know I'm well past the critical point. You don't have to keep coming here."

"I enjoy our visits. Besides, this is more enjoyable than running after children."

Brant chuckled. "Tell me about your days, Faith. I'd like to hear more about life outside these dank stone walls."

"I'm sure my stories are boring, compared to some you could tell about your life on the high seas. My father always came back with the most fascinating stories—makes me want to take to the ocean myself, and see a bit of the world."

"I'm craving a bit of normality. Adventure is what got me into this situation in the first place."

"You regret your life choices?"

Brant was silent for a moment, deep in thought. Did he regret them? Over the weeks since Catherine had left him, and the weeks he'd spent in jail, he'd had a lot of time to think about his life and the choices he'd made, the path he'd chosen to walk. He could pinpoint a lot of mistakes; turning points in his life that had changed the course he had set for himself. But did he regret them? He had treated people horribly over the years, people that cared for him. But their loyalty still shone through it all—every mistake he had ever made. Each choice, each step he'd taken, and subtle nuance in conversation, had brought people into his life that cared for him, people that were there for him when he needed them most.

He shook his head slowly. "Regret? No. But I've made mistakes, and now I have to live or die by the consequences."

"You won't die," Faith said matter-of-factly. To her it wasn't a question of if. She was completely confident.

Brant smiled and patted her hand. "Don't be so confident. You're only setting yourself up for disappointment and tears."

"You think I'll cry over you?"

She was feisty, he'd give her that. "I think you'd cry over your hours of nursing me back to health going to waste."

"If you die, I'll chase Matt down for some gold."

Brant burst out laughing, clutching his sides in pain. It felt good to laugh, to feel a little joy in life. It had been too long since he'd enjoyed himself without the adrenaline rush of a battle. When was the last time he'd sat, conversed, and had a good laugh? Too long. Just more evidence of how broken his relationship with Catherine had been.

He hadn't even noticed when things had changed. It had probably been gradual; a growing discontent.

When he looked back now, he could see it more clearly.

More and more nights spent in Caton's townhouse. Less supper parties and more drinking in taverns. It had been subtle, but the shifts were there; an avoidance of the legitimate lifestyle he had attempted to adopt for the sake of the woman he had tried to love.

His laughter died out as more sobering thoughts took over, and for a moment he forgot that Faith was there. Instead, he was immersed in memories of the last year, and how his life had changed. No wonder he'd gone off the deep end. He'd been silently calling for help for months before Catherine had left, and the sudden change had been too much to deal with, too much to come to terms with when his life was in such a confused state.

"Are you okay?" Faith's voice cut through his thoughts. "Yeah, just thinking."

"About what?"

"Life and how I got myself in this predicament."

Faith smiled sadly and stood up, picking up her stool to take out of the cell. "You'll get out, I promise. Matt is working on something."

"With your father?"

She shook her head. "No. But I've already told him I'll do what I can to help."

Brant didn't need her to elaborate to know that their plan involved breaking laws, and was a last shot in the dark scenario if his trial ended up going south. "You sure you're willing to risk your neck for me?"

"I told you I wanted a little adventure. Maybe this is my way of finding it."

"Just be careful what you wish for. Your neck is much too pretty to have a rope adorning it."

She smirked and called for the guard to let her out of the cell. While waiting, she turned to Brant and winked. "Now, where would be the fun without risk?"

The guard came stomping down the hall then, and let Faith out. He attempted to make conversation with her, asking her about her day and how her family was. Evidently he knew her from around town, but she didn't give him the time of day. She cast her eyes to the ground and lowered her head so that her hair hid her face—a defense tactic Brant had come to realize she utilized quite often—and answered in quiet, one word responses. It was like he was seeing two different women; a shy proper young maid to some, but in his presence a woman full of energy and life, willing to put herself in danger for a man she barely knew. She was the kind of woman you wanted at your side when the winds turned against you.

* * *

James stood on deck with Caton, as they oversaw the loading of supplies. They were scrambling to get the ship ready to go on short notice.

After receiving word a couple of days ago of Brant's injury and imprisonment, they had quickly shuffled around cargo from one of their ships preparing to head out, to a few other ships, and rushed the preparation to sail. They'd be going bare bones. No cargo besides the stores needed to get from Barcelona to Port Royale.

James' heart pounded beneath his rib cage as he waited impatiently for them to set sail. It had already been two days too long, and they should be well on their way to help his brother. For all he knew he was already dead. A letter would have taken weeks to reach them. If Brant had died of his wounds, James was headed for a funeral, not a trial.

"You're making me nervous. Take a walk," said Caton.

James hadn't even noticed the impatient twitching, but now that his attention had been drawn to it, he realized he was stepping from foot to foot and crossing and uncrossing his arms in an attempt to hold in his nerves.

"What if he's dead?"

"You can't think that way. Take a walk around the deck, keep yourself busy. Soon enough we'll be on our way, and then it's just a matter of time."

"You don't have to come with. You have a new baby."

Caton shook his head. "The only way I could keep Senona and the baby at home was by promising *I'd* go."

James chuckled. He could imagine Senona raging about the house, her baby clasped tightly against her chest, telling Caton that she was going to rescue Brant and there was nothing he could do to stop it.

"I'm surprised you managed to convince her at all."

"Bringing up the well-being of our child does a lot to convince a mother. But don't think she won't be wearing a path in our floors with the pacing she'll be doing for the next few months."

"Weigh anchor!" came a call from the captain.

James looked at Caton and smiled, but it was half-hearted. "Here we go."

"Off on a swashbuckling adventure."

"This won't be an adventure. This is us bailing Brant out of trouble, once again, because he just couldn't follow the rules."

James knew he sounded bitter, but he felt like he was sailing to his only living relative's funeral. A funeral that could have been avoided, if Brant had only stopped for a moment and thought about the people who cared about him, the people he was responsible for. They shouldn't be sailing across the Caribbean to try and bail him out.

"He's your brother—"

"Don't act like you don't think he brought this down on his own head," spat out James. "He always does this; acts without thinking about the consequences."

"Maybe this time he'll learn."

James scoffed and walked off with a wave of his hand, mumbling under his breath as he went.

"Brant Foxton will never learn. He's just like our father: stubborn and unchanging, right 'til the very end."

CHAPTER TWELVE

Brant grunted as he forced himself upwards, and off of his cot. Pain ripped through his mid-section, but he refused to give up. He was done lying on a cot, unable to see the sky just outside his window. Weeks of lying here, helpless and confined, were enough to drive any man to beg for death, but Brant refused to stoop that low.

So, before Faith came for the morning, when the first hint of sunlight touched his cell floor, Brant slowly shimmied up into a sitting position. He swung his legs off the cot and slowly, with the help of his hands pushing him up, he stood.

Pain coursed through him, taking his breath away and threatening to make his knees buckle. He was surprised how weak he had become since being injured. His body was shaky from lack of use and muscle atrophy. How quick a strong man was brought down to nothing. Standing for a moment, Brant waited for the pain to subside and his legs to gain balance and steadiness. Once confident he could stand, he took one hesitant step forward, then another. He inched along the cell wall, not caring about the dirt and the grime that his hands rubbed against as he supported himself.

His progress was maddeningly slow, but Brant didn't push himself. He rested when pain hit, and he moved forward when his body felt ready. Slowly but surely, he made his way around the perimeter of his cell to the window. When he finally made it to his destination, he grasped the window grate with his hands and pressed his forehead against it to get as close to the outside as he possibly could. He watched the sun rise fully into the sky, and then closed his eyes as the warm light washed over his weary body. Brant was sure that this was the most beautiful sunrise he had ever seen.

He stood there long after the sun had made its way clearly into the sky, watching the hustle and bustle below. People walked around the streets as shops opened and homes came to life. The whole town slowly woke up below him, and Brant felt more alive just watching it.

He looked out to the ocean and saw the ships docked, some leaving port and others just coming in. Brant could taste the salt in the air, and imagined the feel of the rolling deck beneath his feet. He longed for the ocean, longed to return to the place he felt the most alive. Would staring out a window at the glistening water be the closest he'd get to returning to sea?

A throat cleared behind him and Brant turned slowly, his healing body not allowing him to move any faster, and met Faith's angry face. Her hands were firmly planted on her hips in a decidedly mother hen pose.

"What do you think you're doing?" she asked, incorporating a very motherly tone. Apparently being the oldest of six children gave her a lot of practice with the "I am very disappointed in you" tone.

"I wanted to watch the sunrise."

The excuse sounded lame, even in Brant's ears, so he added what he thought was a charming smile to the end of his words, hoping that Faith would forget her anger and help him back to his cot—he wasn't sure he could get back alone.

"I told you that you weren't ready to get up."
"You said I could sit."

"Standing and walking is not sitting."
"I took it slow."

"If you ripped anything open, so help me..." she trailed off, her face turning red in anger.

Brant had to bite back laughter that threatened to boil over. "Why don't you come and check?"

A blush spread across her cheeks, but she was too angry to hide it. Instead she stalked over and held out her arm to help Brant back to his cot.

They slowly hobbled arm in arm back to the cot where she, without a word, helped him lay back down. She didn't speak at all as she lifted his shirt and unwound the bandage, carefully inspecting the wound before cleaning it and re-dressing it.

"Looks fine, doesn't it?"

She nodded, still not speaking.

"This isn't the first time I've been hurt. I know what my body can take."

"So you're willing to put all my work at jeopardy just to watch a sunrise? Or was this a failed attempt at buying more time before your trial?"

"Your hard work? It's my body. And seeing as we haven't gotten a trial date yet, I have nothing to try and postpone."

Faith glowered at Brant, then turned on her heel, calling for the guard.

"What, you won't stay for breakfast? Read me our book?"

She turned to face him, anger still written all over her face. "No. I have a lot to do today, and obviously you don't value my time, so I'm leaving."

"It's boring without you," he said with a pout.

"Prison isn't supposed to be comfortable, Captain Foxton. I suggest you listen to me a little better from now on if you want *company.*"

The guard came and let Faith out. "Everything alright, Miss?"

She nodded. "Fine, I just can't stay today."

"The prisoner didn't hurt you at all, did he?"

She shook her head and offered a smile. "On the contrary, he seems to be doing quite well, and may not be in need of my services anymore."

Brant watched Faith and frowned. What was she playing at, not needing her services? Didn't she know that her short visits every morning kept him hoping?

She glanced over her shoulder, the anger all gone and replaced with sadness. "Actually, I think he's fine without me. Have someone check his wound from time to time, but he's healing well."

Fine, if she wanted to play that game and remove herself from his life, just because he hadn't listened to an instruction, he'd just have to play along. She needed to learn that he wasn't a child to be bossed around. And at least he wouldn't have anyone yelling at him for wanting to watch a sunrise for the next few days. It's not like he needed her. Soon enough he'd be out, or so she kept saying—Matt had a plan.

But she'd be back. She was just teaching him a lesson, that's all.

* * *

Johnny climbed the rigging to unfurl a sail with practiced ease. He felt at home, once again at sea and doing what he loved. Callouses that had begun to soften during his voyage to London had reformed. His muscles had ached the first few days, but they quickly became accustomed to the hard work.

It was amazing how fast a body went soft. Johnny had helped the crew out with small jobs on the voyage from Spain to England, but the trip had been, for the most part, leisurely. In only a couple of months he had gone from calloused, energetic, and strong to soft, tired, and weak.

"Marshall, pick up the pace!" shouted the sailor working opposite him.

Johnny nodded and moved his out-of-practice fingers faster, in an attempt to keep up with the seasoned sailor.

He knew he frustrated some of the men, working slower than he should for the experience he had. But it had only been a week and he'd already improved a lot. All it took was time. They teased him, some good-naturedly, some not-so-much, about being a land lover. Johnny laughed and promised them he'd be giving them all a run for their money by the end of the month.

"You know, there are bets on you leaving this crew at next port," his partner said as they climbed back down to the deck.

Johnny smirked. "Next port being Port Royale? I'll let you in on a secret: I am."

The sailor laughed. "Not so cut out for this life after all, eh?"

"This billet was just a means to get me there. I planned on leaving from the start."

"And what's in Port Royale for you? A sweetheart?"

"A friend that needs help."

"And after that?"

Johnny shrugged as his feet met the deck floor. "Whatever life brings my way."

The sailor chuckled, and they walked off together to their next task.

"Life don't always bring about the right path. You gotta go looking for it."

"Well, I want to sail. And someday I'm going to be a captain."

"Lofty goals for a deck hand."

"Just you wait and see. You'll be hearing the name Captain Marshall before long."

The sailor shook his head and laughed. "Yeah, and I'll be the King o' England. Stop dreaming, Marshall. That's your problem, you know. You dream too much and don't work hard enough."

Johnny grinned. The sailor's words didn't bother him. He didn't know that Johnny had connections or money. He only saw him as a half-useless deck hand that could barely tell the starboard side from port. And that's all he needed to see. The last thing Johnny needed right now was them thinking he was some rich dandy trying out how the other side lived.

They were making good time. The winds were favorable and the ship was fast, despite being weighed down by cargo. But Johnny couldn't complain about the progress they were making. If Brant survived his wounds he should make it there in time for the trial, if he hadn't—well, it was too late anyway but at least he could go and claim his body, and make sure he had a proper burial.

Had James gotten word of his brother's injury? Was he sailing from Spain to Port Royale at this very moment? Johnny had read and re-read Matt's letter, and from what he could tell, he wasn't about to allow Brant to die. That meant that if the trial didn't go according to plan, there would be a rescue attempt. That was why Johnny was sailing as fast as the winds would carry him.

He knew he didn't have the influence his father had, and no amount of speaking at the trial of someone who had been accused of piracy would save Brant. The only hope that the trial was going to go in Brant's favor was if Johnny's father managed to pull some strings and favors in time to influence the decision. Johnny was going there with the intention of breaking laws and saving a friend and mentor. He knew he wouldn't be able to return home for quite some time after that. He'd have to wait for his father's anger to simmer down, and maybe he could get his name cleared in a few years. But the minute he'd stepped foot on the ship and sailed out of the London harbor, Johnny knew he'd signed away the life he knew for one completely foreign to him.

He wouldn't be living comfortably while learning to sail, like he had been the last year with Brant. The *BlackFox* would be a pirate ship. The men involved in Brant's rescue would have a price on their heads. Even Brant wouldn't be able to return to the life he had once known—he would be back to having nothing but his ship and the ocean around him.

A part of Johnny was scared, terrified even, of this leap off a proverbial cliff he'd taken. Sure, he wanted a life at sea, but at what expense and with how much sacrifice?

* * *

Catherine stood stoically near the center of the room, conversing with a friend while hearing the whispers all around her. It was the first supper party she'd been to since arriving back in England, and apparently long overdue. The rumor mill had been hard at work with her story, and people seemed gleeful with her appearance into accepted society, despite her supposed shame.

"I heard he ran off with another woman," whispered one woman, only a few feet behind Catherine. Close enough that she could hear.

"No! How horrible for her. She won't be able to catch a man like she once could, now," responded another.

Catherine grimaced and turned around, joining the small circle.

"I'll have you know that Captain Foxton did not leave me, but we parted ways on amicable terms. I have the greatest respect for him, but we come from different worlds. You should probably get your facts right before spreading rumors, ladies," she said, a smile plastered on her face the entire time as she soaked in the looks of shock and contempt from the small circle of women.

When no one responded, Catherine lifted her glass in mock toast. "I'm off to refill my refreshment. Have a nice evening, ladies. I'll see you at supper."

Walking away, she could feel her body shaking. Whether from adrenaline or raw nerves, she didn't know. What she did know, was that the smile plastered on her face was very real, and very triumphant. She felt elated, despite the weakness of her limbs, as she made her way to the refreshment table to refill her wineglass and await the call that supper was served.

"For you, m'lady," sounded a voice behind her.

Catherine turned to see an offered glass of wine and the very handsome Charles Henley, son of Lady Henley, smiling at her.

"Thank you," she said, accepting the glass.

"You look awfully happy for a scorned woman."

Catherine didn't reply instantly, instead she studied Charles' face in an attempt to gauge his disposition. Was he being friendly? Or did he too wish to attack her for the mistakes she made? He looked innocent enough, his face kind and welcoming. There didn't seem to be any hint of mocking directed at her. Rather, his face seemed to hold something akin to respect.

"I am. I just got to give a few women a piece of my mind after I caught them talking behind my back, literally."

Charles chuckled and offered his arm, leading her on a stroll around the room. "I suppose their reactions would warrant the smile."

"But they won't stop. They're probably back to whispering about how I have some gall, showing up here tonight all high and mighty."

"You were invited, why wouldn't you come?"

"I'm told that if you're the subject of the rumor mill, you're supposed to lock yourself in your house and wait out the storm."

"But you aren't one to go with conventions, now are you? After all, you were betrothed to a privateer."

"Would you believe me if I said that I am normally a very proper and conventional lady?"

"No, I wouldn't. I'm afraid your reputation is forever tainted." Charles laughed.

Catherine smiled slightly, but a part of her felt sad for the loss of who she once was, a person she would likely never be able to recover after everything she'd seen and done. "It's probably for the best. I'm afraid I'll never be the proper lady my mother raised me as, not anymore."

Charles led her around the room in silence, and Catherine studied his face, looking for some indication of his thoughts.

"You know, I think it makes you more appealing as a woman. My mother was never a very conventional woman, and look where she is. No one dares speak against her."

"She has the money and standing to make her untouchable."

"She has the attitude to make her untouchable. You know as well as I, that money and title don't make a difference in the tea room. You keep doing what you're doing, standing up for yourself and making it uncomfortable for the women to talk, and you'll be just fine."

"And if I'm not?"

"There is always the option of hiding behind a closed door and waiting out the storm."

Catherine chuckled, and as they turned a corner around the room they were called into the dining room.

"I do believe I am your dining partner tonight," said Charles Henley.

"Did your mother feel sorry for me?"

Charles shook his head as he led her into the dining room and, much to Catherine's surprise, seated her to the right hand side near the head of the table. "On the contrary, my mother seems to admire you. I believe she is hoping we get along."

Catherine took her seat and waited for Charles to take his next to her before responding. "And do we?"

"I can see where my mother's admiration comes from, and I

believe we'd make good friends, but beyond that…" he trailed off.

Catherine could feel the heat of a blush rising up her neck and face. "Oh, I didn't mean it like that! I'm not," she paused for a minute before whispering, "I'm not husband hunting."

Charles burst out laughing, much to Catherine's chagrin, and didn't stop for quite some time. She sat there, awkwardly waiting for his outburst to silence, and wishing she could take back the last few sentences she'd said.

Finally, he settled down, his face red from laughter, and he grasped Catherine's hand in his. "You, Catherine Marshall, are one of a kind."

"I am sorry; I shouldn't have been so blunt."

"On the contrary, I enjoyed that. And don't worry, I think if anyone is on the hunt, it is my mother. She has been begging me to marry for years."

"And why haven't you? Any one of the single women here would be glad to be seen on your arm."

"They would be glad to be seen on the arm of my money and title. As for the man attached to that arm, I think they could care less. Besides, I have hopes to sail for Jamaica in a few months' time. Not many women are willing to follow me there."

"No, I don't suppose there are." She thought back to her time in Jamaica with Brant. She had to swallow hard to hold back the tears that threatened to rise up. The wounds were still so fresh; memories of Brant still so dear.

Supper was served and their conversation was cut off. Lady Henley, who was seated at the head of the table, talked with Catherine, asking her about how she was enjoying being back in England.

Few others approached her in conversation, though they were limited to those seated in the direct vicinity. But Charles Henley continued to be charming throughout the evening, and when supper came to a close and his duties as her dining companion were over, he continued to entertain her. He brought her about the room, pulling her into conversations with his friends and acquaintances. All of them were gracious, though it was apparent from the looks that she received, that many were disapproving of her and her presence here—especially that she was on Charles' arm.

Catherine refused to be the first to leave, but once a few carriages left, she turned to Charles and led him out of the group he was conversing with at the first opportunity.

"I'm going to take my leave, Charles."

"So soon?"

"I've had my fill of stares and whispers for the night, I'm afraid. But you have been a wonderful and gracious host. Thank you very much for an enjoyable evening."

Charles led her to the entrance and waited with her as her carriage was brought around. "It was my pleasure, Miss Marshall. If you ever require a supper companion, I am at your disposal."

He opened the carriage door for her, and offered his hand as a support as she climbed in.

"Aren't you worried about how keeping company with me will affect your reputation?"

"You said yourself that my title and money make my family untouchable. I am unconcerned about my reputation, and more concerned about keeping enjoyable company."

"Then I'm sure we will cross paths again."

Charles closed the carriage door behind her, and it pulled away, rattling down the cobblestone streets towards Catherine's home.

CHAPTER THIRTEEN

Brant looked up to see Matt standing at the bars of his prison cell, watching silently.

"How long have you been there?"

"Long enough to see yer going a little crazy cooped up in here."

Brant chuckled from where he sat near the window, and slowly got up. It had been over a week since Faith had left, and she hadn't returned. He'd lain in his cot diligently for the first two days, awaiting her return so that he could show her that he could listen, but after that he had grown restless and had taken to slowly moving about his cell. Mostly, he moved between his cot and the window, watching the harbor for hours and hoping that he could once again taste the salty sea air as he sailed through her waters, instead of just imagining it from this stale dank prison cell.

"It gets lonely from time to time."

"You upset Faith." It wasn't a question.

Brant grimaced. "Apparently enough to make her go to you. What am I supposed to say, Matthew? I'd been stuck lying on that cot, on the brink of death for how many weeks? I needed to see the outside world. She can't hate me for that."

"Hate you? No. Far from it. She's worried about you and she's worried you'll end up hurting yourself. The longer you stayed immobile, the longer we could hold off your trial."

"Does it matter? Let's get it done and over with. What's the point in holding off the inevitable?"

"I contacted Catherine."

Matt's words were blunt and flat, hitting Brant like a cannonball in the gut. "You shouldn't have done that."

"Her father is a very influential man—"

"And I failed his daughter. I doubt there is any love lost there. You shouldn't have done that, Matt," he repeated.

"One letter from him and we could put this all behind us."

"The letter won't come."

"I also contacted Senona… James will come."

Brant sighed and ran his hand through his dirty, knotted hair; his fingers getting caught in snags instead of moving smoothly through as they normally did. He felt disgusted at the state he was in.

"You shouldn't have done that." He knew he was repeating himself, but what else was there to say? Good job, thanks for involving every person I've hurt? "Senona has a baby, James doesn't need to know about the mistakes I've made."

"It's done. There are people who care about you in this world, Brant, and you need to stop pushing them away."

"Is that what you're saying I did to Faith?"

"No. Faith will come around, and when she does, please apologize. I don't care if you think you didn't do anything wrong. She's important to our plans so you need to make things right."

Brant nodded. "Okay. Just make sure she comes back."

"She will. We got word of your trial date."

The air seemed to thicken around them as Brant waited for the words to be spoken. Matt didn't speak though, not at first.

"Well?"

"Two days, then you'll go before the governor."

Brant nodded. "You have your plan in place then?"

"I will."

"Then we wait."

* * *

Brant looked up when the rattling of keys met his ears. He sat next to the window, as he did most days, but upon seeing Faith standing outside the bars, he slowly got up and walked over.

"I see you're feeling better," she said, her voice flat as she entered the cell and the door was locked behind her.

Brant sat on his cot and smiled up at her. "I'm sorry. I didn't realize you were trying to hold back the trial."

She nodded and without a word started pulling Brant's shirt off to take a look at his bandages. She was all business today, not making any indication that she was interested in conversation, but Brant kept pushing.

"I have a hard time thinking of others. It's something I have to work on."

"Mmmhmmm," she agreed, sponging off the wound that was now completely closed, and had the beginnings of what would be a scar.

"But everything will work out. Matt has a plan—"

"No thanks to you. The wound is looking good. I don't think you did any harm."

"Will you stay today? Read to me or talk, I don't care which."

She sighed and then slowly nodded, as if unsure of her decision. Pulling out the book from her bag, she began reading where they had left off a couple weeks ago. At some point breakfast was brought, and Faith put down the book, pulling out a loaf of freshly baked bread.

Brant's mouth began watering as she broke off a piece for him and another for herself.

"I take it you've forgiven me."

"Tomorrow is your trial. I just thought that you could use a few luxuries before you were sentenced to die."

Brant grimaced, but bit into the still warm bread. It must have come out of the oven just before she'd come here.

"This is probably the best tasting bread I've ever had."

"I was walking by the bakers on my way here and he had just taken the loaves out of the oven… I couldn't resist," she said with a smile. "But don't tell my father. He'd be upset that I wasted money on fresh bread."

"Even as a kind act for a man on death row?"

"That, he might forgive."

"You say Matthew met you through your father?"

Faith nodded. "Yes. They met on your last voyage, so I suppose you met him as well."

Brant frowned. "Is your father Captain Nathan Howard?"

"Yes. Is that a problem?"

"I don't suppose he told you how we met then, did he?"

Faith shook her head.

"How..." Brant trailed off, at a loss for words. "I don't understand why he would send you to help. Not after how I treated him."

Faith looked confused. "What do you mean, how you treated him? You brought him home safely."

Brant shook his head. "No, I didn't. I attacked his ship, and the men that I didn't kill I left for dead. The only reason your father is alive is because of his bravery and Matt's intervention. I would have set him adrift..." he trailed off, waiting for Faith's angry outburst.

Instead, she sat in silence for a minute or two, as if digesting what had just been confessed to her, and then she nodded. "But in the end you made the right choice. You let him go."

"But I would have killed him."

"Are you trying to make me hate you?"

Brant shrugged. "I don't know. Maybe you should. I certainly don't deserve your friendship."

Faith smiled sadly and took his hand in her own, squeezing it gently. "I never fooled myself into thinking you were a good man, Brant. I know you've done some terrible things; otherwise you wouldn't be in this situation. But I chose to look past that, because Matt told me that despite your many failings you are a good man and you're just a little lost."

"I've been lost for a long time."

"I think you're beginning to find your way."

Brant nodded and removed his hand from hers, uncomfortable with the familiar touch of one so kind and innocent. He felt as if his very presence was sullying her; ruining her innocence. "Can you keep reading?"

Faith nodded and opened the book back up, continuing where she had left off earlier.

She stayed longer than she normally did, and when she finally closed the book and placed it back in her bag, she leaned over and brushed Brant's hair away from his face.

Her fingers touched his skin ever so lightly, but the warmth sent a shiver through Brant and it took everything in him to refrain from grabbing her hand and holding it against his face.

"I'll be by early tomorrow. We have to get you looking presentable for the governor."

He nodded and smiled at her. "Can you ask Matthew to come see me before the trial?"

"Of course."

"Thank you, Faith."

She called for the guard and was let out of the cell.

"Don't worry, Captain Foxton. I'm sure things will go favorably for you tomorrow," she said, her tone becoming distant and formal now that the guard was present.

Brant could hear the guard trying to talk to her as he escorted her out of the prison building, and he wished she would respond. That one simple gesture of her brushing his hair was enough to make him realize where this was going, and he wasn't comfortable with it. He'd learned his lesson; young women like Faith, like Senona, or Catherine; they thought they wanted adventure. But after his experience with Senona, and then Catherine, he knew that he was bad for them, and he'd be even worse for Faith. A prison guard would be a much better choice for her. He would be able to take care of her, and she'd never have to worry about if he'd be coming home at night.

The prison guard would always be safely here in Port Royale, never at sea for months at a time with her wondering if he'd make it home by summer and with money to put food on their table.

But here she was, entertaining some kind of attraction to him, to a man who was bound for the gallows, and would have to live on the run if he managed to escape. He couldn't allow that. He couldn't allow her to throw away her life in the process.

Whatever Matt's plan was, however it involved Faith, it would have to be changed. Faith would have no further involvement with him, this trial, or the escape. She was a nice girl with a promising future. She would make a good wife to a nice man. As much as Brant loved her quick wit, temper, and strong personality, he couldn't have her for himself. For once in his life, he was going to put someone before himself. Faith deserved a good life, and he could never offer that. Not now. Not after everything had been stripped from him.

With a sigh, Brant slowly got up from his cot and made his way back to the window, where he sat and watched the ships. Moving around was easier now, and although it took a lot of energy, it no longer hurt to make the short trek across his cell. Was the *BlackFox* sitting out there now, ready to make a quick getaway if things went south? Or was she still docked off the coast?

Either way, as soon as he escaped, the *BlackFox* would be a hunted ship and fair game for any privateer or servant of the king. No matter where she was, she wouldn't be safe for long.

Tomorrow Brant would have to stand before the governor and plead his innocence; innocence that was a lie. He deserved to die. He deserved to be hung like a common criminal as a warning to other men who might walk his same path. He had sent countless souls to their eternal resting place, he had stolen more gold than he could count, instilled terror in the hearts of otherwise strong men and women. Yet, he would stand before the governor tomorrow and say he had done no wrong, that he only served the king and that a mistake had been made.

Could he do that? Could he stand and lie; accept life knowing that it had been given under false pretenses? Or did he admit his guilt, confess his sins, and accept what he had coming? One word from him and Matt would leave, abandon his rescue attempt and allow Brant his death in dignity. Did he give that command? Did he stop ruining other people's lives on his account, and accept his fate?

There wasn't enough time to decide that, nor was it a decision he could make. He wanted to live. He didn't have a death wish or a martyr's complex. But he also didn't want to ruin Matt's life. Not when he'd told him he didn't want to be involved. Not when he'd warned him that this would be the outcome. He didn't deserve this. And Faith, she was blindly following feelings. Feelings that she never should have allowed to foster towards a criminal like him. Feelings that he had turned a blind eye to for far too long.

Brant sighed. Matt would come, either tonight or tomorrow morning. His decision had to be made by then. Would he accept his fate, his punishment for the wicked he'd done? Or did he fight for life, lie about his sins, and hope to change his ways and make up for his wrong doings in life?

He couldn't keep thinking about himself.

Getting up, he slowly walked to the cell door and called out for the guard. It took a few calls, but eventually someone came.

"What?" the guard asked brusquely.

"Could I get a writing desk? I'd like to write some letters."

The guard nodded. "Ready to face your sentence tomorrow?"

"As ready as I'll ever be."

The guard left and returned a little while later with a small desk, equipped with a quill, ink pot, and a few parchments of paper. He set the things down near Brant's cot, and then left. "Call me when you're done," he said, locking the door.

Brant sat down and pulled out the first sheet of paper, addressing it to Senona. Her letter would be the easiest, a simple goodbye. She wouldn't need an explanation or an apology. She understood him better than anyone else.

With her letter done, he pulled out another paper and addressed James. This one was much harder. He had let his brother down countless times, and now he was leaving him alone in the world.

He knew no apology would be enough to fix the wrong he did to James, but he tried. He made no excuses for his behavior, only wrote of his regrets and how he knew he'd done wrong.

I thought I was giving you a better life, a life that our father never could give you…

Brant wrote, then paused, collecting his thoughts.

I guess the apple doesn't fall far from the tree. I didn't know any way to live except for myself. I learned that from our father—not that I blame him— and I could never get past that. It's what killed him, and it's what is killing me.

I hope you can learn from our mistakes and break the pattern.

Senona and Caton are good people, and they'll look after you, but you're a man now and have to make your own decisions. It won't be long before you get your inheritance and you can go where you want. But I hope you stay with those that care for you. I learned too late that you need people in your life. You can't live on your own—you'll never thrive.

I love you, James, and I'm sorry I couldn't be a better brother for you.

Brant

He sprinkled the parchment with sand to help the ink dry, and read over the letter one last time. He knew it would do nothing to assuage James' pain, but they were things that needed to be said. Perhaps it would at least help James come to terms with his death.

Lastly, he had to write to Catherine. This would be no short letter—there was a lot to apologize for, a lot to admit to and to say.

Dipping his quill in the ink pot, he began.

Dearest Catherine...

CHAPTER FOURTEEN

Catherine looked up from the book she was reading, when the maid walked into the drawing room.

"Excuse me, ma'am, Mr. Henley is here to see you."

Catherine set her book aside. "Send him in, and prepare some tea for us," she said, getting up from the sofa to greet her guest.

She hadn't been expecting any visitors, least of all Charles Henley. It had been a week since the supper party and she hadn't heard from or seen him since. She had written him off as a charming and polite companion for the night who had no intention of continuing to pursue friendship. Maybe she'd been too quick to judge.

Charles walked in, all smiles, and immediately greeted Catherine with a kiss on her hand and a sweeping bow.

"M'lady, I hope I'm not disturbing you."

Catherine smiled at his antics and removed her hand gently from his. "Not at all. Please, sit. Tea will be out in a moment."

Charles walked over to a large easy chair, but didn't seat himself until Catherine had situated herself back on the sofa.

"Already have tea brewing and I barely stepped in the door."

"It is about that time of day anyway. What brings you here? I was beginning to think you had forgotten all about me."

Charles shook his head. "You are a difficult woman to forget. No, I'm afraid I've been quite busy this past week. But I had the afternoon free and I couldn't think of any better way to spend it than with you."

Catherine could feel the heat of a blush rising up her neck and into her face, and she dropped her eyes in embarrassment.

"You flatter me, Charles."

His attention made her nervous. She didn't trust the kind and flowery words coming from his mouth, despite his kind exterior. She already knew his mother had ulterior motives in introducing them. What were his motives?

"I'm sorry, I'm afraid I've been too forward."

"Just a little," she replied through a tight lipped smile. "For future reference, I prefer a man who speaks plainly instead of hiding behind flowery words and compliments. They're not needed here."

"You don't seem to fear speaking your mind."

Conversation paused as tea was served with cake, and Catherine had a few minutes to consider how she would respond while they prepared their beverages.

"I've learned that it never hurts to be up front. If one doesn't appreciate that, then they likely aren't someone you can trust to have around anyway."

"But society is built on lies and flattery."

"And that is why people crumble. What good is it to put on an act when at the first sign of scandal or trouble they can no longer keep their head above water? They become scorned and unwelcome where they once walked freely."

"And yet you haven't been out since my mother's supper."

He was right, she was hiding. She had continually turned down invitations for tea and supper. Now the invitations had slowed to a trickle.

"I'm afraid I'm not as strong as I'd like to be."

They sipped at their tea in silence for a time. Catherine studied Charles, waiting for him to reopen conversation, preferably to a more comfortable subject, but he looked deep in thought.

"I think you have plenty of strength, Miss Marshall. If I thought you were a weak woman, I wouldn't be here."

"And why are you here, Mr. Henley?"

"To get to know you better. Since you have requested my frankness, I'll be exactly that. You've intrigued me, and although I don't know what that means or where it will lead, I do wish to see you—if you'll allow it."

Catherine looked down at her feet, unable to meet his kind eyes. She couldn't say she wasn't really expecting this, not when he showed up at her doorstep unannounced. But she was in turmoil. She had just left Brant, a man who she truly loved, and she wasn't certain she was ready to forget years of emotions and transfer her affections to another man.

"Charles," she started, and immediately his face fell. She sighed and started again, unwilling to allow his disappointment to stop what she was going to say.

"Charles, I appreciate your gesture of friendship—you know I need it now more than ever, and invite it with open arms. As for seeing me on a more… personal level, I can't allow that. It isn't that I don't think you are a wonderful man, and it isn't that I'm not interested. But I was betrothed to a wonderful man, who I was in love with for years, and it is going to take some time to heal from that. Until then, I can't in clear conscience allow you to pursue me. It wouldn't be fair to either one of us."

Charles nodded. "But we can be friends?"
"Of course."

"I appreciate your candor, though I must admit I am disappointed."

"Not used to disappointment?"
"I'm afraid not."

Charles spent a bit more time, drinking tea and conversing with Catherine. Conversation came easy to them, as they talked about the weather, politics, and social plans. He even convinced her to attend another supper party with him at the end of the week. When he took his leave a few hours later, Catherine got up to take a walk, not wanting to miss out on the warm spring sun—a rarity in their rainy climate.

Almost ready to walk out the door, her mother walked by, stopping when she spotted Catherine.

"Was that Charles Henley I saw here earlier?"

"Yes, Mother. He stopped by for some tea."

"Oh?"

Catherine could see the expectation in her mother's eyes and smiled slightly. "And he is a friend, nothing more. Don't get your hopes up."

"There is no interest? None at all? He could save your reputation."

"He could do more than that, Mother. I think Charles Henley would be a fantastic suitor even with my reputation intact. There is interest on his part, but I'm not ready."

"Not ready! You have a man like Charles Henley calling on you and you make sure you're ready. You had better get over your feelings for that pirate, and fast, if you don't want to miss out on this opportunity."

"Privateer, Mother."

"What?"

"Brant is a privateer, not a pirate."

Her mother waved her hand to dismiss what was obviously a trivial fact to her, and sighed. "Please don't send Charles Henley away. You couldn't ask for a better marriage prospect and after this debacle with Brant Foxton, I'm afraid you won't have an easy time finding those—not ones that aren't just looking for your money or status."

Catherine smiled slightly and embraced her mother. "Thank you for caring. I promise I won't send him away. But you need to allow me to do things on my terms. If that means turning down Charles Henley in the future, then you need to trust that is the right thing for me to do."

"The right thing," her mother scoffed. "The right thing would be to marry well and sort out the rest later. You aren't getting any younger."

Ignoring her mother's comment, Catherine finished doing up her shawl. "I'm going to take a walk."

Escaping out the door before her mother could get another word in, Catherine walked more swiftly from the house than was needed, but once she turned the corner of the block, she slowed her pace to a leisurely one and enjoyed the scenery and the warm afternoon sun.

But she was plagued by thoughts. Between Charles' visit and her mother's chiding, Catherine felt lost. She knew she'd done the right thing by turning Charles down, but had it been the right thing for her? Her mother was right; her reputation was in shambles and it would take years—or the next big scandal—to bring it back to what it once was. She had no hopes of marrying well in the next year or two, not after she'd belonged to a "pirate".

Catherine had never put a lot of stock in marriage. She had always pushed it away as something that would come later in life, when the right person came around. She'd never been in a hurry because men had always been there, lining up for dances or to be her companion at supper parties. They would stop by for afternoon tea often. To have men calling on her had been a normal occurrence, and one that she had never thought twice about. When she was ready to marry, there would be men to choose from.

But the words that had stuck with her the most were that she wasn't getting any younger. It was true. She was getting to the upper ages of what would be considered peak of eligibility. She'd likely never get a suitor of Charles' caliber again—young, rich, and handsome didn't go for older women with a broken engagement.

She had no desire whatsoever to end up an old maid. That would hurt her pride more than a loveless marriage ever would. Catherine wasn't like Brant or Senona. She did put stock in society and the expectations it had of her because, unlike them, she had to live in it.

And Charles Henley would make living in society more than just bearable, he could resurrect her reputation. She didn't have to love him… how many people married for love? Very few. People married for status, money, connections, and reputation. Love was not a luxury the rich had, and Catherine knew that. She'd known it all her life.

Rounding another bend in the road, she willed her mind to slow down, to take a minute to breathe before jumping to the decision she knew her heart had already made.

Brant was likely dead. She knew she wouldn't, and couldn't, run back to him. Charles Henley was here, alive, and interested in her.

She would let things sit for a few days, but when she accompanied him to the supper party later that week, she'd tell him she'd changed her mind, that she would very much like to see more of him. Sure, she wasn't in the husband hunting business, but when one presented himself, she'd be a fool to pass him by.

* * *

Matt stood at the bars of Brant's cell. "You asked to see me?"

Brant nodded. It was late, the sun had gone down a few hours ago and he hadn't been expecting Matt to come anymore that night, so he'd fallen asleep.

Rubbing away the heaviness from his eyes, Brant got up and walked to the door. "I want to talk about the trial tomorrow."

Matt nodded. "Whatever the outcome, we're going to get you out. You don't have to worry."

Brant shook his head. "That's what I want to talk to you about. I don't want a rescue attempt."

Matt stared at Brant, a look of shock on his face. Not that he blamed him. "What do you mean? You just want to give up and die?"

"No, but I'm done putting myself before others—or trying to at least. Rescuing me; you'll be on the run for the rest of your life, you and whoever else is involved. I can't ask that of you or Faith, especially Faith."

"Yer not asking, we decided we can't let you die, and that's just the way it is."

Brant shook his head again, this time more adamantly. "Matthew, I need you to promise me that you won't try and rescue me. Take my ship, give her a legitimate life and… help Johnny find his way back to the sea if you can."

Matt nodded slowly, offering no argument.

"I have letters…" Brant pulled out the sheets of paper he had written on earlier. "I need you to send them out to Catherine, Senona and James. Can you do that?"

"Of course."

"And keep Faith away."

"What?"

"I don't want her here tomorrow; I don't want her to come to the trial. She needs to distance herself from me."

"Why?"

"Just… tell her I don't want to see her anymore."

"Brant, that's ridiculous. She's done so much for you, what happened?"

"It's for her own good," he said, refusing to elaborate.

Matt sighed and didn't speak for a minute, but Brant could see the annoyance building behind his eyes. What must be going through his head, when he was called here to be told that his efforts needed to be abandoned, that his friend and captain was resigning himself to die, and not only that, but he was cutting ties with the people that had been there for him through all of this.

"I need some kind of explanation, Brant. I can't just tell her you don't want to see her anymore. She'll march right on over here and give you a piece of her mind. And quite frankly, everything you're telling me tonight is insane. I think this cell is getting to you, making you wish for death."

"I don't want to die, Matthew. I just don't want to ruin your life, or anyone else's. Faith is getting too close, too involved. I don't know how that trial is going to turn out tomorrow, but if I'm sentenced to hang, then I will hang, and I don't want her to have to deal with that. The more distance the better."

"So you want me to go tell her not to come here tomorrow morning, not to dress your wound like she has every day since you landed in here, not to care for you and feed you, because you're going to die? I'm not doing that. You want her to stay away, you tell her that yourself. See how well it goes."

"That's the problem, Matthew! It won't go well. She's too involved. Don't you get that? She… cares for me… and she can't do that. I'm a bad person and I'll destroy her."

"You can't decide how she feels, Brant. Like I said, you have something to say to her you better be saying it to her face. She's a strong woman, she can handle it."

"I know she can," said Brant with a grimace. "I'm a little afraid of what she'll do to me."

Matt chuckled. "Now that makes sense. I'll see you tomorrow, Brant. Don't you go entertaining thoughts about death now. You're going to live, that's final." Matt held up the letters. "And these, I'm not sending them until you take your last breath, cause I don't plan on that being for a good many years."

"Matt—"

He shook his head and turned, walking away, leaving Brant alone once again.

Turning, he walked back to his cot and lay down. He could move around with only a little tenderness now, a testament to Faith's dedicated care of him.

That conversation didn't go at all like he had hoped, but he should have expected as much. Basically, he was still where he was before Matt came. Matt wouldn't hear of him giving up, and he wouldn't keep Faith away. All Brant could hope for was a favorable trial tomorrow.

Stretching his arms behind his head, he stared at the ceiling, watching bugs skitter across it. Faith would be here tomorrow morning to make him presentable. She would bathe him and clean him like she had countless times before, yet now that Brant had realized their relationship had turned to more than just nurse and patient, it made him uncomfortable. He would send her away.

After the trial he would either sail out of her life, or he would be dead. Either way, the problem would be over and she would move on.

He would have to put his foot down with Matt and this rescue idea, but he could do so after the trial, once they knew where he was headed.

With his mind made up, Brant closed his eyes and attempted to sleep, but even though he had come to terms with the Matt and Faith problems, there was still the trial tomorrow that he wasn't ready for. He ran scenario after scenario over in his head, wondering how it would turn out, if the governor would be kind to him, if his family name still held any clout around here.

He tossed and turned for hours, every time he almost fell asleep a new thought sprung to life, a new idea for what he could say. As the sun began to peek over the horizon, and touch his dark cell with the slightest hint of light, Brant's thoughts turned more morbid. Would he be hearing a death sentence today? Or a promise of life? Would he walk that well-worn path to the gallows in only a few days' time, feel that rough rope around his neck, be covered by the dark hood that would hide his dying face from the watching crowd? Would he feel it, the snap of his neck? Or would it be quick and painless, over in a second? Either way, Brant wished he'd insisted on a priest back when he was in his feverish daze. The only thing that scared him more than death was what came after.

CHAPTER FIFTEEN

Docking in Port Royale should have felt like a relief to Johnny, but instead it was accompanied with dread. He wasn't sure what would be waiting, but he was sure it would be unpleasant.

He went through his duties on board grudgingly, both eager to be off and hesitant to leave the safe confines of the ship. His sailing mates could tell his mind wasn't on the task at hand, and he'd lost track of how many times they'd yelled at him this morning—not that he cared all that much. It wasn't like he'd ingratiated himself with the crew very much during the voyage. In fact, he wouldn't be overly surprised if the crew forgot all about him the moment he walked off the ship and onto solid ground.

They disliked him because he was soft and spoke fancy. No one had offered to be even remotely friendly with him. But he'd made the weeks more bearable by telling himself that someday he would be commanding men like this, and he wouldn't be looking for friends.

Finally, when the docking procedures were done, Johnny was free to go. Knocking on the door of the captain's cabin, he was welcomed in.

"Hello, Sir," greeted Johnny, walking up to the desk the captain was seated at.

He looked up for a minute and frowned, as if trying to

recollect the name of the sailor standing in front of him.

"Hello…" he started and trailed off, obviously at a loss for who he was.

"Johnny, Sir. I joined up in England."

"Right, Johnny," he said with a snap of his fingers. "What can I do for you, my boy?"

"I was wondering if I could get my pay."

The captain nodded and got up, walking over to a safe.

He spun the dial and then opened it. There wasn't much to reveal; a few sacks of gold and some papers. The captain took out a single bag and counted out fewer coins than Johnny would have liked, then brought them over, dropping them onto the desk.

Johnny bit his tongue from asking if that was it. He was used to seeing much larger shares being given out by Brant, but he accepted the coins quietly. Still, he didn't move to leave.

"Was there anything else?"

Johnny nodded. "I'm taking my leave now."

The captain smiled. "I had a feeling you were just signing on to get to a destination. All the best, my boy," he said, standing up and offering his hand.

Johnny accepted it with the hand that wasn't full of coins, and shook. The captain was a kind man, and understanding. He could have chosen a worse ship to sign on to, and they'd made good time to Port Royale—which was really all that mattered.

Taking his leave, Johnny left the cabin and pocketed the coins as he walked. Leaving the ship with a small burlap sack filled with the few possessions he had, he walked down the docks of Port Royale. He was unsure of where to go, but he needed to find Matt. He started at the docks, wandering from tavern to tavern in hopes that he would recognize someone from Brant's crew. But after hours of searching and no success—the sun having gone down, Johnny headed for the prison where he hoped to find Brant was still alive. If he was, he might be able to see him, and find out where Matt was located.

"Johnny?"

Johnny looked at who had said his name, and grinned. There was Matt, walking out of the prison directly towards him. He'd searched all day only to stumble upon him here, the very place he should have started.

"Matt! I've been looking all over for you. Please tell me he's alright."

Matt nodded. "He survived his wounds, but his trial is tomorrow. Any luck with your father?" he asked, hope shining in his eyes.

Johnny shrugged. "He said he would try his best, but he didn't think any of his efforts would be in time. If the trial is tomorrow, I fear he is right. I left the day after we received your letter, and my father did not have the chance to even speak to any of his connections in England that may have been able to help."

"Come, let's go somewhere we can talk in private, and perhaps get a hot cup of coffee."

They walked together down the streets until they made it to a small, warmly lit house. Matt didn't bother to knock, just walked in as if he owned the place. Inside was the family whom the house belonged to.

The family seemed accustomed to Matt's presence as they went about their various tasks. The mother was standing in the kitchen preparing bread dough for breakfast in the morning, while a daughter sat near the fire mending some clothing. The father sat nearby, reading from a well-worn book that looked like it could be the Bible.

"Nathan, I brought a friend," said Matt, taking a seat at the scuffed and scratched kitchen table.

The father, whom Matt had addressed as Nathan, stood up and greeted his guest. "Pleased to meet you. You be a friend of Brant's as well?"

"Johnny Marshall."

"This is my daughter Faith. She's been helping heal your friend. And my wife Mary. Our other children are in bed, but I'm sure you'll meet them in the morning. You'll be staying here, with us?"

"I don't want to impose."

Johnny looked around at the small, humble house. He knew he shouldn't turn up his nose at it. He was used to living in a ship's hold, yet when he was on land he was used to a certain level of luxury, a level that this house came nowhere near with its single room making up the main floor, and a crude staircase leading upstairs, presumably to bedrooms.

"Nonsense. We won't have you put up in a tavern room. I'm afraid the house is getting a bit cramped, but I think the food and company should make up for it."

"Thank you, I'd be happy to stay," replied Johnny, putting aside his pride and taking a seat beside Matt. "Now, fill me in on the situation."

Faith, the daughter, seemed to perk up at this. "You just came back from visiting Brant, right? How is he?"

Matt sighed, running his hands through his hair and shaking his head. "I think he's losing it in there."

* * *

Johnny woke up the next morning to the smell of baking bread and the sound of children squabbling and playing downstairs. What time was it? It felt too early for so much noise in one house. Slowly rolling out of the bed, which was more of a cubby, that Johnny was sure one of Nathan's children had given up for him, he stretched and pulled on his boots, walking down the creaky stairs into the loud and bustling kitchen.

There were people everywhere. Mary was trying to wrangle four, no five, children who seemed to want to run in all different directions. Nathan and Matt were nowhere to be seen, and Faith also seemed to be missing.

"Good morning."

"Morning," said Mary, not looking up from arranging the children in their chairs around the table. "Bread is just fresh out of the oven, and I got some porridge here on the table. Just help yourself."

Johnny took a seat next to one of the younger children, and ladled the thick goop into a bowl. The child stared up at him with wide eyes.

"Are you a sailor like my pa?" he asked.

Johnny laughed. "I am. What does your father do on his ship?"

"He's a cap'n. But his ship sunk so he ain't a sailor no more."

"Anymore," corrected Mary from across the room.

The boy nodded in agreement.

"Nonsense. Once a sailor, always a sailor. Your father will find a new ship. My name is Johnny, what's yours?"

"Phillip."

"That's a good strong name, Phillip. Will you be a captain someday too?"

The boy nodded excitedly. "Yes sir, I will."

Johnny laughed and shoveled the porridge into his mouth. The steaming breakfast tasted a lot better than it looked, flavored with sweet sugar and what Johnny guessed was cinnamon. He ate it with enthusiasm.

"Where are Matt and Nathan?"

"They went out to attend to some last minute business before the trial, and Faith went to the prison."

"What time is the trial?"

"Ten, I think. Matt and Nathan will return for you, don't worry."

Just then Faith burst through the door, her braid swinging back and forth and she breathed heavily, her eyes flashing in anger.

"What's wrong, Faith?" asked Mary.

"That pirate! I hope he hangs!" she burst out.

Johnny looked at the angry girl in confusion. "What did he do?"

The girl turned on him and he immediately shrunk into his seat, wishing he could be a bit smaller and less noticeable under her furious gaze.

"He had the gall to say I was falling in love with him. Falling in love! And then he sent me away, saying he didn't want me around anymore and not to come to his trial."

Johnny swallowed back a chuckle that he was sure wouldn't be appreciated by the angry and hurt woman. From Faith's reaction, he'd guess that Brant wasn't far off on the love thing. Maybe it hadn't progressed that far, but with the eagerness she'd swallowed up the news about him last night, and the anger she carried now, there were definitely feelings at play—her anger was the sign of a scorned woman, if Johnny had ever seen one. What was Brant thinking, estranging an ally right when he needed them most? Of course, Matt had said he was asking for them to accept his sentence, no matter the outcome, so maybe he wasn't looking for allies anymore. Maybe he was looking for an end.

"I'm sure it's just the pressure of his life being on the line. I wouldn't take it too personally," offered Johnny.

Mary stood in the background, silent. Johnny wished she would jump in and assuage her daughter. But she seemed to be content to leave it up to him, a stranger.

Faith started pacing the length of the small house.

"Pressure? I've been going to that prison each and every day to nurse him back to health. I bathed him and read to him, and this is the thanks I get?"

Johnny shrugged, not sure what to say. She had a temper and he wasn't enjoying being on the receiving end of it.

Matt and Nathan walked in, the door banging open and admitting them and a flurry of sounds from outside. Matt took one look at Faith storming around the house, and chuckled.

"I take it Brant talked to you."

"You knew?" she asked, turning her anger on Matt.

Johnny leaned back in his chair, relaxed now that the attention was off of him, and watched the woman say basically the same thing she had said to him just seconds earlier, but this time to Matt. He chuckled slightly. Despite the gravity of the day, this small bit of drama seemed to take the heaviness out of the morning, and gave Johnny a reason to smile; something he hadn't done enough of since leaving Spain.

But the amusement was short lived. Nathan held up his hand to his daughter and she obediently stopped her tirade.

"It's time to go. Faith, you'll stay here?"

She scowled, hands on her hips, and shook her head.

"No, I'm coming. I don't take orders from a man with prison fever."

Matt smiled slightly, but the gloom seemed to have returned and the four of them—Johnny, Matt, Nathan, and Faith—left the house. They walked towards the town square in silence. Johnny didn't want to discuss the reason for their journey, and he didn't feel right talking about other, more trivial things.

The town square was full of people, tightly packed together and craning to get a better look. The trial of an accused pirate was considered entertainment around here. And with Brant's family name, Johnny doubted it was a trial that anyone wanted to miss. Their small group pushed their way through the throng of people. They didn't apologize for bumping or pushing as they fought against the crowd. These vultures were here to see their friend hang, and there was no room for apology with that.

Brant stood on a platform, shackled at his hands and feet. He looked surprisingly presentable for a man who had spent the last few months in a prison cell.

The governor paraded out with other council members of the town, and sat in a stand set near the gallows. It was meant to intimidate. They wouldn't hang Brant today, but they would make him stand and stare at the noose while he awaited judgment.

Johnny could feel his heart rate pick up as proceedings began, and a deathly silence fell over the crowd. He could hear the crickets chirping gleefully as everyone waited for the governor to speak. He looked over at Matt and Nathan who appeared calm and stalwart, but Faith clutched her skirts so tightly her knuckles were white.

Then it began.

The charges were brought forward of piracy, crimes against the king, treason, and unprovoked attack on civilians.

Johnny paled as he heard and his eyes shot over to Matt. "What?" he mouthed silently. These charges didn't sound like Brant. Not the man he knew.

Matt nodded, confirming that it was true, making the situation all the more shocking and leaving Johnny confused. What had come over this man who he had carried so much admiration for? Had Catherine leaving him sent him over the deep end? Or had these criminal acts always been sitting right under the surface, just waiting for release from society to be set free?

Johnny was certain the proceedings would be quick and straight forward. He didn't even think his father's influence could have helped this situation. To attack a British civilian ship... it made Johnny sick to his stomach to think about it. The innocent lives lost for what? Gold? The rush that accompanied a fight?

"Do you have anything to say, now that these accusations have been brought forward?" asked the magistrate.

Brant held his chin high, staring directly at the panel of men who would decide his fate, and smiled slightly, almost sadly. "I have nothing to say."

Johnny nearly choked. Did he have a death wish? Out on the high seas it was one man's word against another's. He could at least attempt to plead out, but instead he stood there proudly and accepted his fate.

"Then you admit your guilt before all these witnesses?"

Brant closed his eyes, just for a moment, as if collecting his thoughts, then nodded. "I admit that I have made mistakes and have broken the agreements to which I was granted the letter of Marque by Governor Modyford. I cannot deny that. I have seen the error of my ways, though I doubt that will make any difference to you, and will accept judgment as the king and his majesty's representatives see fit for my treason."

Johnny shook his head and turned away. "I can't stay for this. He just threw away his life," he ground out through gritted teeth to Matt, before pushing his way back through the crowd as quickly as he could, eager to get away from the macabre proceedings.

After Brant's statement, they would only be minutes away from announcing his sentence. Once free of the pressing crowd, Johnny took off running towards the docks. He needed to distance himself. Maybe he was a coward—even Faith was still standing by, supporting a man she barely knew, a man that she had said just this morning *should* hang—but he couldn't hear that a man he had come to think of as family was to be hung by the neck until death.

He just couldn't.

But he didn't have to hear the words to know they were spoken. Even a few blocks away, he could hear the eruption of the crowd, which could only mean that a hanging would occur in the near future.

As the wave of noise washed over Johnny he collapsed on all fours and rejected his breakfast all over the cobblestone streets.

He'd be the first to admit he was soft. It was one thing to observe or hear a raid from a distance, and to witness the death of strangers. It was completely different to be faced with the death of someone he had come to think of as family. He should have stayed. He should have stepped forward and tried to speak on his behalf. But it wouldn't have done any good. Brant would hang—and from what Matt had said last night, he seemed determined to do so. He didn't want rescue—though how they'd accomplish that, Johnny had no idea—and he'd thrown away any chance of clearing his name this morning. Had he come all this way just for a funeral?

Slowly getting up, Johnny brushed off the spittle and vomit from around his mouth, and walked the remainder of the way towards the docks. He walked in a daze, unaware if people were even around him. For all he knew the streets were abandoned, everyone in the town square.

He didn't notice anything until a hand touched his shoulder, and he spun around quickly to face Caton, concern etched through his questioning eyes and stolid lips.

"Johnny, we called you three times. Are you okay?"

Johnny nodded slowly and looked over at James, who stood next to Caton, looking equally scared.

"Brant. Is he...?"

Johnny nodded again. "He's alive."

A sigh passed through the two men in unison, but Johnny shook his head, not to encourage their relief. "For now. He didn't succumb to his wounds, but he just stood in front of the governor and admitted to treason."

Caton nodded. The words didn't need to be said; they hung unspoken between the three of them, heavy and ominous.

After a moment or two of silence, James' eyes flashed in anger. "Let him hang. He deserves it," he spat out.

CHAPTER SIXTEEN

The minute the magistrate read his sentence, reality crashed in on Brant like a twenty foot swell dropping on a ship being tossed to and fro. He was going to die and he wasn't ready.

Any thoughts of selflessness evaporated with the simple words of "hung by the neck till death". His knees went weak and he felt a chill fall over him despite the warm temperatures. He looked over to where his friends were standing. Johnny wasn't there anymore. When had he left?

Catching Matt's eyes, he offered a weak smile before being led away by his guards, back to his jail cell.

It took everything in him to place one foot in front of the other, and hold his head high and proud. Despite the shock that kept rolling through him, he refused to show weakness. He couldn't hear the cheers and jeers of those around him through the pounding of his heart in his ears, as he walked through the crowd, his shackles making each step smaller than he'd like, and making the journey take longer than he could stand.

What day had they said would be his last? He couldn't even remember the rest of his sentence. He hadn't heard anything after they'd said he'd hang. Did he have 24 hours? Three days? A week to dwell on the mistakes he'd made?

He never should have admitted guilt. He should have lied,

should have fought harder for his life. He wasn't ready to die. He wasn't ready to meet the judgment that awaited him beyond. He couldn't die with all these sins weighing down on him. He'd done so much wrong, he wasn't sure even a lifetime of doing good could save him—and he didn't have a lifetime. He had a matter of days.

Once back in his cell, alone and out of the public eye, Brant collapsed against the wall near the single window, too weak to stand. He contemplated praying, but it didn't feel right. He'd given up asking for forgiveness for all the lives he'd taken many years ago. Who was he to turn to religion now, in the last hour? He would be a hypocrite, and a just God wouldn't listen to the likes of him.

Instead, Brant sat and looked back on the years of his life that he'd lived so wrongly. He thought about the faces that belonged to the lives he'd taken, and mourned over the fact that most of them had no faces to remember, just instances in time that passed quickly and without notice. What he remembered, more than individuals, was the feeling of taking a life. The slice of his blade or the recoil of his pistol; those stood out so much more than the people he had killed.

How long had he sat there before the echoing footsteps from down the hall brought him back to the present? Long enough to make all his joints sore and stiff as he stood up and stretched.

When he looked over at the door, he saw the angry face of his younger brother, James.

His heart plummeted. He'd come too? Brant had hoped he wouldn't be here to see him in such a low place, to see his death. Mostly, he hadn't wanted to deal with the disappointment. Anger hadn't been something he'd expected though.

"You shouldn't have come," he said.

James continued to glower at his brother, and Brant found himself wondering when he had grown up so much. Looking at his brother now he didn't see the boy he remembered, but instead a man. At seventeen years of age he stood tall and muscled, and looked even more like Brant than he cared to admit.

"You're right, I shouldn't have. I stupidly thought that even after all the mistakes you'd made you would have at least *tried* to clear your name. If not for yourself, then for the people that care about you."

Brant knew he could try to explain himself. Tell him that he thought he was doing what was best for the people in his life. But seeing James' face now, he knew he'd been mistaken, and any excuses would fall on deaf ears. Instead, he nodded. He had no words right now. What was he supposed to say? "You're right, but it's too late now"?

"What is wrong with you, Brant? Catherine leaves and you decide to throw your life away? You decide that it doesn't matter anymore? That's not the Brant Foxton I know."

"It's not about Catherine... not anymore. I was trying to feel alive..." he trailed off, his words sounding foolish even to him.

"And now you're going to end up dead. I hope you're happy. We all knew you were walking this path anyway. Guess it shouldn't come as such a surprise."

Brant opened his mouth to argue, but closed it as James turned around and walked away. What was the point? James was right. It was ironic that the very things he'd been doing to try and feel life pumping through him, were what landed him at the end of a noose. It was almost comedic, if the situation hadn't been so sad.

He'd managed to chase away Catherine, Faith, and now James. How long would Matt stick around? And Johnny? He hadn't seen him at the end of the trial. Had he abandoned him as well? He wouldn't blame him if he did. Nathan... he didn't owe him anything, and was likely only there because Matt was. He wasn't a friend, and he wouldn't put his family at risk for Brant. If anything, he should have been up there testifying against him.

No, Brant was utterly alone in the world because he'd either run from, or chased everyone away. He would go into his last hours alone, he would hang alone—to the cheering of a blood thirsty crowd—and he would face judgment alone.

Brant Foxton didn't have a soul in the world standing beside him. He had thought the ocean was enough for him, but when it came down to it she couldn't stand beside him.

All she ever did was take; unable to give back. For the first time in his life he was truly terrified.

* * *

Catherine laughed as Charles twirled her around the dance floor, her dress swishing around her legs as her feet deftly made the memorized moves to the lively waltz being played. Music from a string quartet filled the ornate hall, as partners moved around in rustles of silk and taffeta in a beautiful moving rainbow of color.

"I'm so glad you changed your mind," whispered Charles in her ear as he drew her close.

Catherine smiled in response. Charles had been courting her for a little over a week now, and already it had made a difference in her social status. Women were suddenly interested in being her friend again, if only because they saw her as the future Mrs. Henley, and they knew they had to stay on her good side. The Henley name held power, and no one wanted to get on the wrong end of that.

It was a relief to be nearly back to the old Catherine; accepted and flourishing in society. It didn't hurt any to have Charles' doting and obvious admiration poured upon her on a daily basis either. He was the ever attentive suitor. He came for supper daily. He took Catherine out, showing her off proudly on his arm. And now he had taken her to one of the most anticipated balls of the season, one that she likely would not have garnered an invitation to. Her reputation had been in shambles before Charles stepped in and resurrected it from certain death.

When the song ended, Charles led her off the dance floor towards a mixed group of men and women.

"Would you like a drink?" he asked before they made it to their destination.

"Yes, please. White wine."

"Your wish is my command," he said with an adoring smile that made Catherine's heart ache. Why couldn't Brant ever have smiled at her like that?

Arriving among the group of people, Charles introduced her. "You all know Catherine Marshall?" He didn't wait for their response. "Catherine, this is Lord and Lady Fairfax, Duke and Duchess Nightingale, and Lord and Lady Hunt."

"Pleased to meet you. I believe you know my father, Lord

Marshall."

"Yes, I've had the pleasure of dining with your parents on many an occasion," replied Duke Nightingale.

Conversation flowed easily, and Catherine felt completely at ease—almost like the woman she had once been. At first she had expected sneers and judging looks, but instead kind smiles greeted her.

Charles stood by her a few minutes, then took his leave, offering to fetch drinks for anyone else in the intimate group that needed refreshment.

Left alone, Catherine felt a moment of hesitation and fear pass through her. Would these people be different around her without Charles? She realized quickly that she had nothing to worry about, as the men and women continued on in their conversation as if nothing had changed.

"Tell me, Catherine, how was your recent trip to Spain?" asked Lady Fairfax.

Catherine's heart skipped a beat. There it was; the segue to the mistakes she'd made. But she offered a smile and held her head high. "It was wonderful. So nice to experience the country for a longer period of time."

"I hear there is some unrest between our countries now," said Duke Nightingale.

"Yes, it is why I returned. My parents didn't feel it was a safe environment for me and my brother any longer."

"And your brother, he isn't home anymore? I heard he left almost as soon as he arrived."

"Yes, he left for Port Royale."

Catherine didn't offer any more information, and no more was asked. Her audience seemed content with her answer. To her relief there was no mention of Brant. It was as if they had forgotten the reason she had left Britain in the first place—or perhaps they chose not to mention it out of respect for Charles.

With their questions assuaged, conversation turned to more trivial matters and Catherine was content to stand and listen quietly. Charles returned with her drink, and placed his hand protectively on her lower back. Leaning in, he whispered,

"Everything okay while I was gone?"

She nodded with a smile in response. He was taken with her, and she needed him—it was the perfect arrangement to benefit both parties. But she didn't realize how much she needed him until she had him. He erased everything; all her mistakes, her scandal, Brant. Charles silenced the whispers just by being there —whispers that had been more harmful to her than she had ever realized.

She was a shell of the woman she once had been. Catherine Marshall from a year ago never would have found herself on the arm of a man just to improve her status. Catherine Marshall from a year ago never would have feared to attend an afternoon of tea or a supper party. She used to thrive in those environments, and had never needed someone to protect her. But here she was, on the arm of a man she was lying to, because she wasn't certain he would appreciate the situation the way she did.

After a polite amount of conversation had passed, the small group dispersed, and Charles led Catherine back onto the dance floor where they spent the majority of the evening. Charles was a fantastic dancer, leading her around the floor in perfect grace and litheness. She felt weightless in his arms, but when the evening came to a close the ache in her feet reminded her all too well of the amount of movement they had made that night.

Charles called for their carriage to take her home, and helped her climb in, sitting across from her on the plush seats. They rode in silence, Catherine exhausted from the night's events. When they arrived at her home he helped her disembark and led her to the door.

"Did you enjoy your evening, Miss Marshall?"

"Very much so, thank you," she replied.

"Every moment with you is a pleasure, Catherine."

Hearing those words stung more than they should. Everything he did that was kind and courteous, that showed his devotion and admiration, had her feeling guilty. What if she married him? Would she feel this guilt for the rest of her life—knowing that she'd used him?

Instead, she put on a smile and allowed him to plant a kiss on her cheek before she escaped into the safe confines of her house.

She let out a sigh and leaned against the door, trying to hold out the guilt associated with the man she had left on the other side.

"Is that you, Catherine?" called her father from the den.

"It is."

"Join me for a night cap."

Catherine walked the short distance to the dimly lit den, and found a seat on a large wing back chair beside her father, who was staring into an unlit fireplace.

"How was your evening with Charles?"

"Beautiful. We danced all night."

Her father got up and walked over to the decanter and glasses set on a stand near the wall, and poured Catherine a few ounces of port. He returned to his seat, handing her the glass.

"I'm glad to see you smile again," he said, taking a sip from his glass. "I hate to see you so sad."

"I wasn't sad, Father. Just..." she trailed off. What had she been? Sad wasn't the right word. More like defeated.

"Regardless, you weren't the woman I know you to be. Charles has been good for you, I can see that."

Catherine nodded. Yes, Charles had been good for her, and would continue to be good for her. He could only bring her up, improve her, her social standing, money, authority. But was she good for him? She couldn't help but feel like he was just another man she would ruin. With Brant they'd had the love, but they had been from different worlds, and they couldn't live between them without being torn to pieces. With Charles, they were from the same world, but there was no love—at least not on her part. And it terrified her that having a one-sided relationship was almost as toxic as being from different worlds.

"Have you heard any news of Brant?" asked her father after they sat in silence for some time.

She shook her head, knowing that what her father really wondered if she'd heard from Johnny. "Nothing. It's too soon to expect any news back. Give it time."

But she knew that time wouldn't bring news of Johnny. He was gone and he wouldn't return; not now that he was free. Her words were an empty and meaningless attempt at comforting her father. How many doubts were going through his head right now?

She could almost see his thoughts passing over his face. Was he a bad father? Had he pushed Johnny away? She wanted to tell him that he was realizing these things all too late. That all the signs had been there for years, and all Johnny wanted was love and support for his choices. He would still be around then, and she wouldn't have lost her brother. But she couldn't, because the pain crossing her father's face told her he was enduring punishment enough for his short comings. And who was she to judge?

"How is mother handling things?"

This time it was obvious they were talking about Johnny.

"You know your mother. She refuses to acknowledge anything is wrong and is distracting herself with her excitement over Charles Henley courting you."

And there was the guilt again. Not only was she using Charles for her own gain, but now her mother's happiness seemed to be riding on her contrived relationship.

"That's probably for the best," muttered Catherine. "He's a good man, Catherine."

She smiled. Her father saw right through her, saw her doubts.

"I know you really cared about Brant, and those wounds are still fresh, but Charles is a good man and you'd be a fool to doubt that."

"I know."

Setting down her empty glass, she got up from the chair and walked over to her father in a rustle of skirts, and planted a kiss on his forehead. "I'm going to turn in. Try and get some sleep."

He smiled up at his daughter tenderly. "You know me too well."

"I mean it. Sleep tonight. It won't do you any good to dwell on things," she said, before taking her leave.

Catherine had always been close with her father, and she knew exactly what he was like when he was troubled about something—he wouldn't sleep. He would sit there in that chair in front of the fireplace all night, refilling his glass of port, and running things over and over in his mind until it made sense.

He had always said that night was the best time for thinking, for sorting things out. There were no distractions; just him and his thoughts.

Climbing into bed after her maid helped her undress; Catherine stared up at the ceiling going over her own thoughts. The dark offered a calm and undistracted environment for her to contemplate the things that had bothered her all evening. She had learned a thing or two from her father.

But the last thing on her mind before sleep claimed her, was dancing the night away in Charles' arms, and how much fun she'd had. Pushing any guilt she'd been feeling away, she smiled and embraced the memories she had made that evening, and accepted that what her father said was right; Charles was good for her, and she'd be a fool to let him go.

CHAPTER SEVENTEEN

Brant woke up as the clanking and jingle of the cell door opening met his ears. He opened his eyes, but didn't move. He didn't have much interest or energy in sitting up, and the sight of Nathan, standing there looking as self-righteous as ever, did nothing to change that.

"You've come to tell me how I'm reaping the rewards of my sins?" he asked, closing his eyes again and wishing silently that the man would just go away before he even got started.

"No."

Footsteps echoed across the stone floor and Brant opened his eyes again to see Nathan approaching.

"Then why don't you leave me be?"

The guard returned and placed a chair next to Brant's cot.

"Thank you," said Nathan, taking a seat. Then he turned to Brant. "Please sit up and pay attention. I have something to say and you *will* listen."

Brant looked at Nathan in surprise. He wasn't used to being commanded by anyone, especially not the mild-mannered Nathan. He sat up and sighed. "Say your piece and then leave me alone. In case you didn't hear; I'm going to die soon."

"That's why I'm here."

Brant raised an eyebrow and waited for Nathan to speak again.

"Faith told me you asked for a priest when you thought you were going to die from infection."

"I was delirious."

"I'm not here to listen to a confession," continued Nathan, ignoring Brant completely.

Brant could feel his irritation growing towards the man. Something about him rubbed him the wrong way, and brought out a hostility that Brant wasn't used to feeling.

"I'm here to tell you a story."

"Stories aren't going to help me, old man," he ground out through gritted teeth. "Why don't you just stop wasting your time and go home?"

"A lost soul is never a waste of time."

"Get out," said Brant. He closed his eyes and took a deep breath, trying to contain his annoyance. He was not some project to be saved. There was no hope for him anyway; he was a sinner through and through. Still, Nathan sat there. But he didn't speak. He just smiled and sat. And that smile made Brant angrier than any words ever could.

"Get out," he repeated, this time with more anger leaching into his voice.

"If it's all the same to you, I'll just sit here until you're ready to listen."

"Get out and leave me alone. Can't you let me die in peace?"

Nathan nodded and stood up. "Very well. But I'll be back. You're more lost than you'd like to think, and there's only one way I know that will help you find your way."

Brant's heartbeat raced as he attempted to control his anger. Nathan didn't know him, and couldn't help him.

"Guard!" he called, then rolled over and turned his back to the man. He was done listening.

* * *

James paced the length of Nathan's house as he listened to Matt lay out the rescue plan. He resisted the urge to walk right out the door. This whole thing was foolishness. They were throwing away their lives and their freedom for a man who was too selfish to even care. But if they were willing to do it, James wouldn't be the one to walk away.

"Faith will get the key," outlined Matt, "and hand it off to me. After which she'll go about her day as normal."

Faith nodded, her face serious and eyes wide. James could almost see the spiraling thoughts of fear going through her mind as she attempted to remain brave and unfazed.

"I mean it," said Matt. "You ain't sticking around."

"Don't worry, I'm not daft."

James heard Johnny trying to stifle a chuckle. Even though he said nothing, James could tell what he was thinking, and he was right. He wouldn't put it past Faith to do something foolish. She seemed to thrive on being needed—he barely knew her, and even he could see that.

"Good. Now, Johnny, you are going to be on the *BlackFox* arranging for a quick getaway."

"Wouldn't that be the first place they'd look for him?" asked Johnny, frowning, his amusement gone.

James scoffed. "This plan is going to go nowhere. They'll go after the *BlackFox* the instant they discover he's gone. Then what?"

"He won't be there," answered Caton.

James stopped and all attention turned to Caton once again.

"Matt, you want to continue?" asked Caton.

"Johnny will be ready to sail away the instant we spring Brant. Caton is going to create a distraction nearby, drawing the guards away from the prison."

"Why Caton?" asked James.

"I have no affiliation with Brant that anyone here knows of. They won't connect the disturbance with his escape."

"Once the majority of the guards have vacated, I will go in and spring Brant and we'll make our way to Caton's ship. That's where you'll be, James.

"Brant will go aboard Caton's ship, and from there Caton will join them and they'll sail towards Spain, where he should be safe from the British—which is our biggest concern right now. I will make my way to the *BlackFox* and join Johnny there. We'll sail to

Tortuga to keep attention away from you, and after we'll join you in Spain."

Johnny sighed. "This all sounds good and well, but what about Brant not wanting to be rescued?"

James frowned. "What do you mean he doesn't want to be rescued?"

"It's just the closed spaces getting to his head. Brant Foxton has never had a death wish, and that hasn't changed," said Matt, his voice leaving no room for argument.

But James smirked and tried anyway. "Really? From what I heard, he basically gave up at his trial. Maybe he does have a death wish. You ever stop to think about that?"

"Did the Brant Foxton you know ever do anything but love life?"

"The Brant Foxton I knew wouldn't have attacked innocent people and landed himself with a piracy charge on his head. He's changed, Matt. This whole thing with Catherine broke him."

"Wait a minute—" inserted Johnny, but Matt held up his hand to stop him.

"Let's not get into this, boys."

"No, let's," cut in James. "You don't think this is all Catherine's fault? If she had just stayed in England where she belonged we wouldn't be in this situation."

"Brant chose to love her. How is that Catherine's fault?" bit back Johnny.

James knew he shouldn't be attacking his friend's sister, but his words were directed by emotion, not logic right now. All he felt was anger coursing through him and he was unleashing it on whoever was willing to take it—Johnny and Catherine were prime targets.

"She knew better. She knew she'd ruin him. It's why she left. What I don't understand, is why she didn't let him go when it was first apparent it wasn't going to work—when he was chasing after Senona."

"Is that what this is all about? You think if Brant had ended up with Senona he'd be happier with his life?" asked Caton, who had been listening silently up until this moment. "I have news for you,

James; it wouldn't have made a difference. If Senona hadn't put an end to things, they would have walked a similar path. They weren't meant to be. They fed off of each other and continually pushed each other to get closer to the edge. Eventually they would have fallen off.

"Brant and Catherine made the mistake of thinking they could work together. But that doesn't mean he was supposed to end up with *my* wife."

James felt heat creep up his face as the husband of the very woman he had wanted Brant to marry rebuked him. Caton was right; Senona and Brant were like tinder and fire, while Brant and Catherine like oil and water. Both would have ended disastrously. And in bringing up issues that had long since been buried, he had hurt the people he considered family.

"I'm sorry, Caton," James mumbled.

Caton nodded his acceptance. "We're in a tense situation. Brant's life is on the line, and I don't think this is the time to argue about what brought him to this point. If you have an issue with Brant's behavior, or Catherine's, or anyone else's, take it up *after* we are all safe and sound."

James' head bobbed up and down in agreement and he glanced over to Johnny to see him mimicking his actions. He felt like a child being rebuked, and had a hard time meeting Caton's eyes. Instead, he looked over at Faith. She stared at Caton, studying him. What was going through her mind, and what was her role in all of this? James had assumed she had some kind of connection with Matt, but as he watched her he realized she seemed to have very little interest in Matt, aside from his role as the self-proclaimed leader.

He'd have to ask Johnny about her later, when they were alone. Pushing Faith from his mind, he directed his attention back to the conversation at hand. Matt and Caton were winding down with explaining things and answering a few questions that had arisen. James' role was fairly straight forward: have the ship ready to go and wait for Brant. There was nothing complicated about what he had to do.

"What happens if things fall apart?" asked James.

"It's game over," replied Caton, much too calm.

"But it won't. It's a good plan and it'll work," put in Faith, speaking for the first time since they'd begun their discussion.

James nodded. "Are we operating on 'no man left behind'?"

Matt nodded but Caton shook his head, contradicting him. "We can't risk it," said Caton. "If things go south we won't get another chance at breaking anyone out, and it's only a matter of time before the authorities drag the rest of us in. It's not like we haven't been seen together. If anything goes wrong, the rest of us leave."

James raised his eyebrows in surprise as Caton spoke. He hadn't ever pegged Caton for someone so willing to do what needed to be done. *Senona must have rubbed off on him*, he thought, bringing a smirk to his face. But it quickly disappeared. With the idea that things might not go as planned hanging in the air, the room suddenly felt dark and depressed. Nervousness and fear rippled from person to person like a fast moving virus, and James saw that the danger of the situation hadn't dawned on Johnny or Faith. It hadn't even dawned on him until he'd asked the question.

"I'm going for a walk," said Johnny, getting up and leaving the house.

"Me too," said James. He halted his pacing that hadn't stopped during the entire conversation, and followed his friend out into the fresh air, needing to get away from the stifling disease-like fear. "Hey, wait up!" he called, trotting after Johnny.

Johnny paused and waited, giving James a questioning look. "Didn't think you'd want to talk."

"I'm not angry with Catherine, I'm angry with Brant. I never should have attacked her."

Johnny shrugged. "The whole situation is unfortunate."

James fell in step with him. Just like that, things were forgiven and forgotten. "So, what's Faith's role in all of this? Is Matt courting her?"

Johnny chuckled and shook his head. "She has no interest in Matt. Brant on the other hand—"

"That's bad news," cut in James.

Johnny nodded, looking just as serious as James felt. "You should have seen her yesterday morning. She was so upset and insulted that Brant had insinuated she might be interested in him. In my mind, she only made her interest more apparent to everyone."

"Is Brant handling this?"

"I assume he is discouraging it. That would be part of the reason for her tirade."

"How did she get involved in all of this? I can't see Nathan being enthusiastic over the danger his daughter could be in."

James looked around, recognizing the street they were on as one that led to the center of town and away from the docks.

"Something happened with Matt and Nathan on the voyage here. When Brant got injured, Matt recruited Faith to help nurse him back to health and she's been around ever since. Like I said; I think she's quite taken with him."

James shook his head and sighed. "If Brant survives this he needs to take his ship and leave us all alone."

Johnny raised an eyebrow. "Bitter?"

"Maybe. But you know as well as I, that he's dangerous to those around him. If you and I have any hope of living a normal life he needs to stay out of it."

"Will you return to Spain?"

"I haven't really thought about it. Senona and Caton are there... but it's not home. I don't really have a home. Half my life I've been sailing around with Brant, a vagabond in this world. I guess the *BlackFox* could be considered home, but I don't feel any connection to it anymore and I don't want that life; Brant's life."

The words hung between the two boys, and James realized that Johnny's lack of response wasn't because he didn't have anything to say; it was because he didn't agree with what he was saying. He'd been trying to get away from a normal life for years. The realization made James feel completely alone. He and Johnny had become friends because of what they had in common, but over the last year something had changed. James had changed, grown up, and realized that he didn't want this life, while Johnny was fighting tooth and nail for it.

As they walked in silence, James looked over at Johnny. They'd stay friends, he was sure, but he saw a rift between them that would never grow smaller.

* * *

Brant looked up as his cell door clanged open and admitted Faith. He'd slept leaning against the cold, dirty stone wall—unable to find the will in himself to get up and move to his cot.

Faith looked at him and rushed over, kneeling beside him. "Are you alright? You look like death. No fever? Soreness?" she shot off questions in rapid succession, not waiting for Brant's response.

"Didn't think I'd see you again," he muttered, ignoring her concern. He didn't deserve her pity.

"Why not? I've been here nearly every single day. You think I'd stop just because you're living on borrowed time?"

Brant shrugged. "That, and the way you stormed out of here last time."

"You insulted me."

He smirked, but didn't say anything. She was volatile when it came to bringing up what her feelings might be—he liked that about her. In some ways she reminded him a lot of Senona, but she lacked the disregard for social rules, and surprisingly, he found himself admiring her for that.

"And I don't abandon friends just because of an insult," she added.

"Friends?" teased Brant.

"After the hours we've spent together, I think it's safe to say that I consider you a friend."

"But not more than a friend?"

He had to stifle back laughter at the bright red that flared up Faith's neck and across her cheeks, but her eyes flashed in anger, countering her embarrassment. "Don't flatter yourself," she bit back.

"Just making sure you're not falling in love with a man doomed to die."

"All men are doomed to die; it's just a matter of when."

"So you don't deny that you're falling for me and my pirate charm?"

"Pirates don't have charm, Brant. There is nothing charming about a noose around one's neck. I feel sorry for you."

"And I'm your friend."

"Because I feel sorry for you."

Brant frowned. "Don't. I brought it upon myself. Can we forget about all this for just a while? All I can think about while I'm alone is the mistakes I've made. I'd like to use the short time I have with you as a distraction."

"Maybe you *should* be thinking about your mistakes. Then you'll know what changes to make when we get you out."

Brant glanced around quickly, ensuring that they were completely alone. "Keep it down. You can't talk like that here."

"No one is around."

"Sound travels here." He glanced around again. "I guess that means Matt hasn't given up on me?"

Faith chuckled and shook her head. "You have so little faith in your friends? They care about you, Brant. They won't see you die."

"So they're willing to sacrifice their freedom for me?"

"When people care about you they're willing to put their lives on the line. Johnny, James, Caton… they're all here to help."

Brant let a smile curl at the edges of his lips. How had he not realized how loved he was? Why had he run from a good life? James, Johnny, and Caton had dropped everything and left their lives behind for him. Caton had even left behind his wife and child. And Matt—Matt had seen a way out of this life, and instead of taking it, he had sacrificed his escape in order to help Brant.

"They shouldn't be here. I don't deserve them."

"It's not about deserving."

"I'd do anything for them. I hope they know that."

"I think they do. Otherwise they wouldn't be the friends that they are."

Faith got up from where she sat on the floor next to him, and placed her hand on his shoulder. "Keep positive and be ready. We're going to get you out soon."

Brant nodded, and then looked up at her. "Promise me you won't involve yourself, Faith. Your life is here, in Port Royale."

"I'm part of the plan." Her voice was firm. "Change

the plan. I don't want you involved."

"They'll never know. Matt has it arranged so I'm not at risk. I'm touched by your concern, though."

"If you're involved there is a risk. I can guarantee that after these daily visits they'll go straight to your house and question you. The only way you'll be safe is if you aren't involved."

Faith smiled. "It's too late for that. I guess I'll just have to be elsewhere when they come looking."

Brant shook his head. She was so stubborn and no one could tell her what to do if she set her mind on something. He'd known the minute she'd said she was involved that she wouldn't back out now. But he had to try—he'd never forgive himself if he ruined her life. He had to talk to Matt, but if he asked Faith to tell him he wanted to see him, she would know that it would be to convince him to cut her out of the plan. She wouldn't allow it. He'd have to wait and hope he'd come. If not him, someone else, anyone other than Faith. He would even be glad to see Nathan again if it meant he could talk to Matt.

"Faith, please, think about how it'll affect your life. That's all I ask."

She walked towards the cell door and called for the guard before turning back to him, her face serious. "I can think about it, but it won't change my mind. My life in Port Royale is not important. I help my mother raise her children and I pray my father makes it home safely from a voyage."

"That's a lot to lose. That's your family."

She nodded. "You're right. But eventually I have to find my own way in the world."

Brant clenched his jaw tightly. He wished he could make her understand that family was the most important thing in the world.

CHAPTER EIGHTEEN

Johnny looked over at Faith, positioned between him and James as they walked through the market to collect food for their supper. She had been quiet and preoccupied when she'd returned from the prison earlier this morning, but when Johnny had tried to ask her how the visit went, she brushed him off saying everything was fine and Brant was ready for when they made their move.

He could tell there was something more, something bothering her, that she tried to keep hidden beneath the surface. But now, walking with her and James, she seemed to have forgotten whatever was bothering her and was showing a fun and playful side that he hadn't seen before.

Their situation had been a bit dark and dismal as of late, with Brant's future still unsecured. But this afternoon the sun shone, and for just a little while the three of them could forget the circumstances that had brought them together and just enjoy the beautiful port city. They laughed and joked. Faith was an easy mark as she had a bit of a temper and got flustered easily, and Johnny enjoyed seeing her reaction, but James eventually put a stop to it. She had a quick wit too, and could have James blushing with a couple well-chosen words.

After supper everyone went to sleep for the night, leaving Johnny and Faith the last ones awake, sitting next to a smoldering fire. They didn't speak at first. Johnny knew what he wanted to say to her, but he wasn't sure if he had the right to pry—they barely knew each other.

"What's on your mind?" Faith asked, breaking the silence.

Apparently we know each other well enough, he thought, smirking slightly. Then answered, "You."

"Me?" A blush crept up her cheeks, barely noticeable in the dim light of the lantern. The pink tint offered her an innocence that Johnny hadn't associated with her before.

Whether or not she was falling for Brant was debatable, but Brant would have to be blind not to be attracted to this woman, Johnny realized.

"Well, not you as much as how you were acting after your trip to the prison today. Did something happen with Brant again?"

She smiled slightly as if in an attempt to assuage his worry and shook her head. "He doesn't want me involved."

"He's probably right; you shouldn't be. If things go wrong it could ruin your life, and your reputation. At the very least it would destroy your chance at a good marriage and at most—" he trailed off. It wasn't often a woman was hung, but helping a convicted criminal escape might be enough to warrant that kind of punishment.

"I'm not backing out."

"I figured. So why were you troubled?"

"Because I think he might be right about something else."

Johnny didn't say anything, just waited patiently for her to get up the courage to voice what had obviously been eating at her all day, from the way she had fallen into silence or offered distracted answers during conversations.

"I think I might care about him… more than I'd like to admit."

* * *

Catherine's hand rested on the crook of Charles' arm as they walked through the grounds of the Henley's country estate.

"It's beautiful here."

"Anytime you need to get away from the busyness of London,

my home is yours."

"Perhaps I should hideaway out here and never return to society. I could be happy in relative solitude."

"And deny the world of your beauty and grace? That would be a shame. I don't think you could stay here for long, though."

Catherine blushed. Charles was right; she wouldn't be happy hiding out here. Ever since she started seeing him, and her scandal slowly disappeared into the background, she found herself enjoying her old life again. Afternoon tea was now a daily occurrence, and no one dared to whisper Brant's name. Not when she had the potential of being the future Lady Henley.

Of course, her mother was ecstatic with how things were going, and never passed up an opportunity to invite Charles for supper—but with the number of supper parties they had been attending, that didn't happen often.

After a few weeks of social obligations nearly every day, Charles had decided it was time for a break, and invited her up to his family's country home. They had spent all day yesterday travelling, and arrived late at night to a lavish supper the servants had prepared for the two of them. This morning she had awoken to breakfast on the terrace overlooking an immaculate garden.

It was the perfect escape—for a short time. But this place reminded her too much of Foxton Estate, and she knew she wouldn't be able to stay here for any length of time. Then again, everything reminded her of Brant, and sooner or later she'd have to get past that.

"What's on your mind, my dear?" asked Charles, pulling her from her thoughts.

"Just admiring the scenery."

"I'm told Port Royale has some beautiful surrounding country."

Catherine nodded. "Yes, it does." Why was he bringing up Jamaica? She knew he wanted to go there and see the Henley sugar plantations, but he hadn't brought it up since they had first met.

"My father is sending me there," he said, after what seemed like an eternity of silence.

She turned sharply towards him to study his face. Surprisingly, he looked sad. She expected excitement.

"Don't you have anything to say?" he asked, and she realized she had been staring, shocked.

"What should I say? Congratulations? I'm happy you're getting what you want, Charles. You deserve to go and do what you can in life, and if that means going to Port Royale, then I'm happy for you, I truly am."

Charles face fell and she knew instantly that she'd said the wrong thing.

"I don't want to go anymore. Not without you."

"Don't say that," she whispered, turning away. She didn't deserve him. She had let it go on too long. She'd known all along that he was more invested in their relationship than she was, but she had selfishly refused to let him go. She liked the shield he was, and the status he gave her. For her, he was nothing more than a salve to help heal her wounds, and for him she was quite obviously so much more.

It terrified her, to know that he was willing to give up his dreams for her—not because she asked it of him like she had of Brant, but because those dreams paled in comparison and became meaningless without her. It made her sick to realize that she would destroy him with what she had to say next.

She turned back to face him, determined to give him the respect he deserved. What she had to say needed to be said to his face, not with her back turned like a coward.

"You know I can't come with you, Charles. My home is here, in England."

Charles' face fell, and the hurt in his eyes made guilt rise up in Catherine in the form of a sick feeling in the pit of her stomach. *I'm a horrible person*, she thought, averting her eyes from his expression of pleading and hurt.

"Do I mean nothing to you?" His face contorted in anger that Catherine knew she more than deserved. It didn't make it hurt any less though, and threatening tears choked her.

"Was I only a tool to fix your reputation?"

Catherine couldn't reply. She couldn't say it aloud; admit to the wrong she committed against a man who had been willing to give her anything she asked for, and more. *I should have lied*, she thought. *I will never do better than this man. It wouldn't have hurt me any to make a life with him.*

"You mean so much to me, Charles. I just…" she trailed off, searching for the words to finish her finely woven truth. "I can't go to Port Royale."

"I thought you were different, Catherine. That's what I liked about you. But now I see you're just as manipulative and self-driven as every other self-absorbed society lady. You made one mistake, though; you grew a conscience. If you had held on just a little longer, you could have had the world at your fingertips."

Charles' words stung and brought tears to Catherine's eyes more effectively than a slap in the face could have.

"I'm sorry."

"Don't be. You were just looking out for your future. And really, I should have known when you changed your mind about seeing me. I think you should leave now, though. I'll have the carriage pulled around for you."

Catherine nodded mutely, standing frozen in place as he walked away. Sobs wracked her body. Was this what she had become; selfish and self-absorbed? Slowly she forced her feet to move, carrying her step by step inside the manor and to her room to collect her things and leave.

* * *

Brant sighed, standing up and walking over to the bars of his cell where Nathan stood waiting. No guard let him in today. Instead, he pulled up a rickety looking wooden chair and sat outside.

"You're back," said Brant, staring down at him, his hands grasping the cold steel bars.

"I am."

His eyes were drawn down to Nathan's lap, where his hands rested on a worn leather book.

"Are you going to read me a story?" asked Brant, smirking.

Nathan nodded slowly and offered him a smile. He wished he

wouldn't. He didn't want this man's kindness. He hated the guilt that Nathan's visits instilled in him—yet another reminder of the wrong he'd done in his short life.

"I don't suppose asking you to leave will work?"

Nathan chuckled and shook his head. "I'm afraid not."

He opened up the book on his lap, leafing through the thin pages filled with words, and stopped somewhere about two-thirds of the way through.

He started reading, and Brant immediately recognized the passage as one from the Bible. He really wasn't that surprised. Nathan had always preached at him, but this was the first time he'd pulled out the actual book and read from it.

There were parables, stories of Jesus' life. He flipped back and forth between the old and new testaments, picking and choosing stories to dictate to Brant.

Brant didn't listen... at first. He'd heard all these stories before, preached to him during his youth from tall foreboding pulpits in great cathedrals and ornate churches. But after a half an hour he began to listen.

There was David, the giant slayer; Peter, the doubter; Samson, the man with a weakness for women. Every story showed Brant a deeply flawed man, or woman, full of sin, and yet repentant and accepted by what Nathan claimed to be a forgiving and loving God.

Nathan stopped and looked at Brant, who was still standing, leaning against the bars.

"You're listening," he stated, looking surprised.

"The stories are interesting. If you didn't think I'd listen, why did you even bother coming?"

"It's my duty to try. I could only hope God would work in your heart."

"After everything I did to you, you still won't give up?"

"We are called to love."

"I am a wicked man, Nathan. All these stories you read were of godly men who sinned. They don't apply to me."

Nathan pressed his lips together in a thin, tight smile. Brant saw a hint of what he thought to be sadness behind his eyes, and waited for the man to speak again.

"I have one more story for you today," he said, leafing through the Bible.

Brant waited for him to find his spot, and then listened intently as Nathan read the story of Jesus' crucifixion, and the thief on the cross. Nathan finished with the simple words of "today you will be with me in paradise", then closed the worn book and stood up. "The thief was a sinner. He was not David, or Moses, or Samson. He was like you, Brant, and God forgave him. Think about that," he said, then walked away.

Brant sighed, letting go of the bars and running his hand through his dirty, greasy hair. He slowly sunk to the floor, leaning against the bars and sighed again, closing his eyes. A tear slipped through his eyelids, then another. Maybe there was hope for him after all.

"Please Lord," he whispered. "If you forgive wicked men, forgive me."

CHAPTER NINETEEN

James walked with Johnny through town, always keeping the prison in view as they watched the guards—making note of their shifts and movements throughout the day. They had walked these same streets already four times today, and it was getting old. But they couldn't afford mistakes.

"I spoke with Faith last night about Brant," said Johnny, drawing James' attention away from the prison.

"And?"

"She loves him. She might not know to what extent yet, but…" he trailed off.

James sighed. "Matt should never have involved her. Brant is only going to destroy her life, like he has everyone else's."

"You think Brant doesn't know that? He's not the villain you make him out to be. Sure, he's made mistakes—more lately. But life hasn't been kind to him, and he's trying to find his course."

He grimaced at Johnny's words of defense. Had Brant not hurt his sister time and again in his selfishness? He had just as much reason to be angry with Brant as James did, and yet he was risking everything for him. Guilt plagued James, always there whenever he took a minute to think about the situation he and his friends were in. He knew he had a right to be angry and bitter, but if anyone should have been defending Brant it was him. They were brothers, for goodness sake. Brant had practically raised him—and if Brant had ever been selfless in an area of his life, it was where James was concerned. Even in leaving him behind in Spain, as much as it had hurt, he knew Brant thought he was doing what was best. And yet he couldn't bring himself to say even a single kind or redeeming word in Brant's defense. No, he left that to the man who had more reason than anyone to be bitter.

It was an embarrassing realization, but it was also not something he could just change. His feelings remained the same, even if he knew they weren't right. Brant had done too many wrong and selfish things in the past; that didn't just change because Johnny said it should. If anything, it made him a little angry with Johnny.

"You defend him because he's your hero, always has been. But you need to realize that his life has been empty and lonely. Don't follow the same path and end up unhappy and alone. Don't you see that Brant does nothing but chase people away?"

Johnny offered a half-smile and stopped his walk to face James, "Brant hasn't chased anyone away. We're all here, putting so much at risk because we care about him. He's hurt some of us, but he's done so much more *for* us. You especially. What is your problem, James? You're angry that he's in this situation but then you say he deserves to die? You're upset that Faith is falling in love with him—quite frankly I think she would be good for him. Why?"

James shrugged. "You barely know him. Just be careful... and don't make the same mistakes he did."

"I think I know him quite well, and I value my neck enough to be smart about the choices I make."

"You ran from home to get what you want. I'd say you're off to a good start."

James could see the sarcasm stung Johnny, but he didn't care. He was sick and tired of these irresponsible choices that affected everyone. Johnny had a promising life ahead of him, and he was throwing it away to live the same life as Brant. And Faith—she was a nice girl. She had skills that could open so many opportunities. She could marry a respectable man and have a happy and comfortable life, but she was giving her heart to a man that could give her nothing but heartache in return—just like he had Catherine and Senona. Yet no one warned her that she was being foolish and throwing her life away. Why?

"If that's how you feel then you should probably go hole up on your ship. We don't want you involved if it's such a burden. And quite frankly, I don't want you around if you're going to judge me. Last I checked, you and I weren't so different, so where do you get off sitting on your high and mighty horse? Wake up, James. You aren't perfect either."

"I never claimed to be."

"Talk about chasing your friends away, James. You're doing a really good job of it right now."

Johnny turned around and walked back in the direction of Nathan's house, leaving James standing alone in the street.

He hadn't intended to argue with his friend. Johnny had always been the person he vented to, but the different direction their lives were taking erased the understanding they once had.

It hurt to have his friend walk away, and he couldn't help but think that maybe it was a sign of the future—a consequence of their drifting apart and taking different paths in life. But what Johnny didn't understand, was that he wasn't chasing him away. He wasn't like Brant, he was just changing and so was Johnny. Their friendship just wasn't surviving it.

No, Johnny just didn't understand. He wasn't like Brant. He couldn't be.

* * *

Johnny walked into Nathan's house and immediately felt a calm pass over him—the sound of happily playing kids and the smell of bread baking in the masonry oven instantly erased all the problems he faced.

"I thought you were watching the guards," said Faith when he walked in. And just like that, he was reminded of everything he was dealing with right now.

"I was, but figured James could handle it on his own," he shot back, more harshly than he had intended. It wasn't as if he was angry at Faith, but the argument he'd had with James had him on edge.

"Something wrong?"

"Let's just say that James picked up a self-righteous attitude, and he needs to lose it."

Nathan picked that moment to walk in the house, a concerned look on his face. "Everything alright?" he asked, looking from Johnny to Faith.

Johnny nodded. "Just a disagreement with James."

"If you boys want to rescue Brant, you best not be fighting amongst yourselves," he advised.

Johnny grimaced. "I know, but he is making it hard."

"He is hurting right now, and could use a friend and some understanding. Remember, his brother is in prison and has been condemned to hang. That's enough to make anyone act out of character."

Johnny sighed and nodded. "I hope you're right, because I'm afraid I'm losing him as a friend."

Nathan placed his hand on Johnny's shoulder and smiled. "Just be a friend to him, and he'll come around. But I best be heading back to the docks. I've been talking to some people about getting a new ship."

"Best of luck with that."

"Don't need any luck. Either I'm blessed with a ship, or maybe my life is meant to take a different direction," he said as he walked back out the door after grabbing a banana from a bowl on the table.

Johnny turned to look at Faith, who had been silent during the exchange with her father. "How can he be so at peace with everything?"

"He trusts in God. Strongest man I know, my father. He never doubts we'll be provided for."

"But to be willing to give up his livelihood…"

"Everything happens for a reason. Just think; if Brant hadn't taken my father as a prisoner, if Matt hadn't become friends with him, Brant wouldn't have had the help he needed. He probably would have died from his wounds long ago."

Johnny nodded, thoughtful. He had never thought to leave

things to fate. He always liked the idea that he was the master of his own destiny, not some uncontrollable, invisible force.

He'd gone to church with his family and at boarding school nearly every week, but he couldn't say he believed it. He saw the people who attended, and saw that they lived very different lives outside of Sunday. But Nathan and his family showed a calm and peace in life that he had seen in few people, and it made him wonder if maybe there was something to religion. Maybe humans needed something to believe in, whether it was God, or the ocean, or an invisible force.

"And you, do you believe?" he asked Faith.

"I see the peace my mother and father have, and I know that God has to be real to give them that. But it's a struggle to remember that I'm not in control of my life, and at the same time it is comforting to know that I have a path to walk. This whole situation with Brant has only solidified in my mind that belief."

Johnny nodded. "Seeing your family has made me want to find something more. I just don't know how religion could possibly fit me."

"Then maybe you should be changing your course. Whether you choose to believe or not doesn't make your sins go away. You're just choosing to ignore their existence."

"Want to go make this speech to Brant next?" asked a new voice, interjecting into their conversation.

Johnny and Faith looked up to see James standing in the doorway. Neither had noticed his arrival, but it was obvious from what he'd said that he'd been listening for a while.

Faith chuckled, but Johnny saw it was just a cover for the tears she wanted to shed. "I don't think he'd appreciate it much. He isn't the type of man to hand over control of his life."

"If you care about him then you'll try to fix him."

Johnny raised his eyebrows in surprise and looked over at Faith, whose reaction seemed similar to his own. He offered her a half smile as if to say "see what I'm frustrated about?" He couldn't quite believe that this was his carefree friend from boarding school. Then again, even back then he had been Machiavellian.

"It's my experience that if you care about someone you don't try to *fix* them. You care about them, faults and all, because that's what makes them who they are," she replied calmly, though Johnny could see the annoyance smoldering in her eyes. "My father has been visiting him—I honestly think he is the best person to be talking to him about a change in his life. He doesn't need all of his friends preaching at him too."

James shrugged and walked back out the door.

"He's just hurting and we need to be understanding, right?" asked Johnny, smirking in an attempt to hold his annoyance in check.

Faith scoffed. "He needs a smack over the head."

Johnny chuckled. Yeah, that'd probably do the trick.

CHAPTER TWENTY

Catherine realized news of her and Charles' falling out traveled quickly when she received no invitations for tea or supper parties all week. She was back to being a social pariah in the span of a day or two following their parting of ways. But unlike last time, she felt like she deserved to be shunned, and accepted her punishment with grace.

Her father was particularly understanding, though he seemed to think her sadness was over losing Charles. She didn't bother to correct him. She didn't want anyone knowing about how she'd used him.

Staying at home allowed her to avoid the gossip that was sure to be worse than before. Yes, her life was gossip gold at this point, between running off with a pirate and then using the most eligible bachelor to rescue her reputation. Maybe her parents didn't see the truth of the matter, but the ladies of society certainly did.

Catherine filled her days at home reading and helping her mother run the household. Her evenings were often spent in discussion with her father, when he wasn't out or having guests over. She always appreciated the way her father conversed with her as an equal, never once making her feel less intelligent because of her gender. In a way, she was happy for her extra time spent at home, allowing her to spend time with him. She hadn't realized how desperately she had missed him over the year she'd been gone.

"Your mother says people have been talking," her father said as they sat in his study that evening with a nightcap.

"About me and Charles?"

He nodded but didn't speak. Catherine knew he was waiting for her to explain. He was never one to pry in her life; he always trusted that she would make the right choices, and if there was ever a situation she couldn't handle she would come to him. She smiled to herself; he treated her so differently from Johnny. She didn't understand why he was so much harder on Johnny. If her father treated him with an ounce of the respect and love she received he may not have run off. Her smile faded. She realized it was time to tell her father the truth of the situation.

"I made a mistake."

Her father nodded. "You were only with him to shield you from the whispers."

She nodded mutely. He had known, all along. She should have realized that, but a part of her wanted to believe that he wasn't privy to her shameful behavior.

"So many women do it. The difference is you felt guilt about it, and you couldn't let it continue. Most women would have married him."

"He wanted me to go to Port Royale with him. His father is sending him to run their plantation, and he asked me to go with him. I couldn't do it. Not after Brant."

Her father nodded and sipped his drink. "It's too soon. You made a hard decision, and you need time to heal. Charles will forgive you."

"I do care about him, though. I just don't love him."

"Your mother will never forgive me for saying this," he said, a smile tugging at the corner of his lips. "You don't need a man. You're intelligent and strong, and if you don't marry you'll still do great things with your life. No matter what society says, or demands, great women have refrained from marriage in the past."

Catherine smiled. He was right; she had never needed a man in her life before, and it was time she found the strength she had once possessed.

* * *

Brant paced his cell back and forth all night; still unable to sleep, but too restless to lie down or sit. As morning dawned he continued to walk—his toes dragging from exhaustion, and he was beginning to shake. The only thing that made the dawning of a new day any better than the night before was that Faith would be here soon and he wouldn't be completely alone.

The sun rose higher in the sky, breakfast came, and was taken away, and still Faith did not come. Eventually he had to give in to his exhaustion, his legs refusing to hold him up any longer, and sat down by the window. Still, sleep did not find him.

He had asked Faith not to come anymore, but he hadn't really expected her to listen. He realized now how much he missed her when she wasn't around. It was selfish, really, because he knew she was better off staying away, and even though he was disappointed, he was also glad. Maybe he had been wrong about her having feelings for him. Or maybe he'd just insulted her one too many times.

Eventually sleep found him. But it wasn't restful. He kept waking up from cramping muscles and sore limbs, and the nightmares didn't help either.

That was the main reason he wasn't sleeping—he was afraid the nightmares would come. He'd been having them ever since Nathan had visited and he had prayed, searching for some kind of peace. Instead he got terror—it felt as if it was God saying he had been weighed and found lacking, undeserving of salvation. The dreams were always the same: he stood at the gallows, a noose around his neck and an ominous storm rolling in. The clouds weren't normal; they had the shape of an armada of ships rolling towards him, and the flashing lightning appeared like the flashing of cannon fire with the accompanying thunder.

The nearby ocean rose up, and the whitecaps grew larger and more ferocious.

He stood alone on that platform. Not even the hangman with his dark hood to hide his face was around. A wave rose up and crashed over him with an overwhelming force, knocking him off his feet. For a moment he floated, but as the water drew back into the ocean, his feet were swept from under him and the rope tightened around his neck, blocking the flow of air to his lungs.

Brant kicked his legs back and forth in an attempt to catch his footing, but they floated over nothing but air.

It seemed to take an eternity. What should have been a quick death as his neck snapped from the force of falling into the noose, had been turned into a slow strangulation by the ocean rising up against him—his executioner.

Finally, as the light faded and the rolling storm and ocean grew silent, a new kind of horror met him. All around him were hundreds of faces, pale and rotting, barnacles and other sea creatures and debris made their homes on their corpses. And they all spoke in unison; "you killed us. You stole our lives. Burn, burn, burn!"

Brant screamed, clawing desperately at his assailants, but to no avail. He *knew* it was a dream. He'd lived through it enough times to recognize that. But this time was different. This time the dream went longer and as the corpses chanted 'burn', they moved in on him, reaching for him, pushing and pulling. Brant felt the terror course through his body as he realized the angry mob would rip him apart. It wasn't enough that he had to die once at the hand of his beloved ocean, but now he had to die again at the hands of those he'd murdered.

As hands pulled at him he began to sob out, "I'm sorry! I'm sorry!" But the men only continued to chant their calls for revenge.

Then a voice came through the gloom, calling his name and begging him to wake up. *I can't*, he thought. *I'm dead and there is no escaping hell.*

But slowly the grappling hands and faces drew back, the darkness faded into a soft orange glow, and he opened his eyes, finding himself back in his cell. The sun had set, and the orange glow he'd seen was the flickering of a lantern beside him on the floor.

Faith knelt on the floor, holding him firmly in her arms, binding his arms across his chest with her own.

"It's okay," she whispered. "It was just a dream."

Realization dawned on him, and he relaxed into Faith's arms, letting sobs of relief wrack his body as the terror he felt left him in the form of tears.

Brant had never cried in front of anyone before, but Faith's comforting whispers broke him and let his feelings open to her. As the tears subsided, she released her grasp and moved back just far enough so that they were no longer touching.

"Nightmares?" she asked, wrapping her arms around her body as if to shield it.

"For the last few nights. I tried not to sleep…"

Concern etched on Faith's face. "We're getting you out soon. You won't have to live like this much longer."

Relief coursed through him. He didn't let the guilt set in. He couldn't live like this anymore; it wouldn't take many more nightmares before he'd be begging for the noose just to make it all end.

"You didn't come this morning," he said, changing the subject.

"I'm sorry. I had to help my mother today. This was the soonest I could get away."

"I thought maybe you'd listened to me."

Faith smiled. "No matter how many times I tell you I'm around to stay, you won't believe me, will you?"

Brant shook his head. "I'd like to believe you'd wise up at some point and realize I'm a bad man."

Faith blushed and lowered her eyes. Brant loved how she could be witty and sharp, but how that rosy glow could find its way to her cheeks and give her a young naiveté that she had managed to hold onto, despite being exposed to the rougher side of life here at the prison and at the docks. Somehow it didn't surprise him that Nathan had raised a strong and independent woman, who hadn't been corrupted by the world. He saw the same hidden strength in her that he had seen in her father, and had fascinated him so much.

Since it was evening and Faith didn't have to leave to get chores done for the day, she stayed longer than usual. This time she didn't read to him though. Instead they talked for hours. Brant told her stories about his life on the high seas. Most of them were funny or of good times. He didn't go into the darker side of his life, not at first anyway. But as the moon rose higher in the sky he opened up to her even more.

"If I get out of this, I don't know what I'm going to do with my life."

"Keep sailing," she answered, as if it was a fact that could not be changed.

"I don't know if I can. I feel like the ocean has become a stranger to me. I used to feel so connected to her, like she was a living, breathing being, but this past year I've felt alone out there.

"I know I don't have it in me to be a merchant—nor can I be after all this. I'll be a wanted man. I tried that, and I ended up more lost than ever. I need adventure, but I'm done with this illegitimate life. I don't have the stomach for it anymore, Faith."

Her hand touched his shoulder. "You'll figure it out. There is something out there for you, I promise. Even my father found his place in life."

Brant looked at Faith. Nathan, if anyone, had everything together. He had his beliefs, his family, and his ship—up until Brant sunk it. He had everything a man could ever need. How could she compare Nathan's life to his own?

She must have recognized his questioning look, because she chuckled. "You think my father has always been the man he is today? He used to sail on a slave trading boat."

Brant grimaced in disapproval—slave trading had always been where he drew the line. A human being was a human being, no matter the color of his skin.

"A lot has changed since then, but he had to make some changes, and find a way to live his life that would make him happy. He never had that call for adventure and freedom that you have, but he did feel the call of the ocean—like so many sailors do—and he couldn't leave her."

"But he was able to be a merchant, and be happy doing it."

Faith nodded. "Yes, he found what made him happy, and so will you."

She stood up and smoothed her skirt, looking down on Brant still sitting beside the window. "Try and get some sleep tonight, okay? I think the nightmares might leave you alone."

Brant snorted in disagreement, but slowly got to his feet, walking stiffly with Faith towards the cell door. He felt old. His joints were stiff from the damp cold of the cell and lack of exercise and pacing. His muscles were atrophied. He used to be strong and agile, now he was weak and slow.

The guard let Faith out of the cell and she turned to face him, reaching her hand back through the bars and grasping his.

"It'll all be over soon," she whispered, brushing her thumb against the back of his hand. "Soon you'll be free."

She pulled her hand away; a pink hue covered her face. Brant suspected it was from the moment of intimacy they had just shared, but he said nothing. For once he didn't want to tease her, because she had just said the very words he needed to hear more than anything else.

Soon he'd be free.

"Can you do something for me?" he asked.

She nodded, waiting for him to continue.

"Ask your father to come see me?" He needed to talk to Nathan, to find out why he was still haunted and unforgiven, and how he could find the peace Nathan had.

She smiled. "Of course."

He stood by the bars listening to Faith's retreating footsteps, and found himself wondering what she was heading home to. He wanted to see her outside of this prison environment. He wanted to see her laugh in the sunlight, to see her with her brothers and sisters, her parents. He wanted to see her dance to the music of a fiddle—he couldn't quite imagine her dancing a waltz. He wanted to see her alive and in her world, he wanted to know the *real* Faith.

Brant didn't know when those ideas, those feelings had arisen. But it was a realization that he had only just come to. He cared about her and those feelings had been growing since the first time he had laid eyes on her.

Brant shook his head and walked to his cot, lying down and staring up at the ceiling, wishing it was stars he was seeing. A tear slipped down his face. Even if he got out of this alive, he would have to leave Faith behind. He would never be able to know the woman she was outside of these dark stone walls.

CHAPTER TWENTY-ONE

"You asked for me?" asked Nathan from outside Brant's jail cell.

Brant got up, walking over. "The last time you came here you told me if I repented I'd be forgiven," he spat the words out, fear coursing through him, leaving him shaking and his knuckles white from clutching the bars. All he'd been able to think of was that Nathan would hear what he said and tell him that he was beyond saving.

"Have you repented?" asked Nathan, as calm as ever.

Brant could feel his heart rate pick up as annoyance towards the man grew. Of course he had repented. He did exactly as Nathan had told him, but something had gone wrong.

"I prayed, like you told me to, and I've had nothing but nightmares since. Not peace, just terror. God rejected me."

Nathan smiled as if he knew a secret Brant didn't, stepped forward and rested his hands on top of Brant's right hand. "My friend," he said, his voice soothing and calm. "Repentance is not just a onetime deal. You must change your heart, strive to do good, and always seek the Lord's will."

Brant sank against the bars. "You're sure there is still hope?"

He nodded, his face calm, impassive, confident. "The Lord rejects no one who comes to Him in true repentance. You keep praying, friend. You'll find the comfort and peace you seek. Just remember, faith does not make life easy, it just gives us the grace to accept what comes our way."

He lifted the worn, leather Bible he held in his hand and slipped it through the bars. "Here," he said, "you need this more than I do right now."

A tear slipped down Brant's face as he reached out and accepted the heavy book. "Thank you," he whispered. "I do not deserve your kindness."

* * *

James stood on the deck of Caton's ship. Everything was in order. The crew was busy getting ready to depart. Things would look normal to anyone passing by; just a ship getting ready to leave port. But to James, the energy, whispers, and nervous glances amongst the crew was anything but normal.

They were alive, a living, breathing organism, as sailors ran around shouting at each other. Supplies were moved into the hold and rigging was prepared. But amidst it all, James and the captain stood stalwart and silent.

James noticed everything, yet he couldn't seem to consider anything beyond their plan. Today, if all went according to plan, Brant would join him aboard this ship and they would sail off towards Spain. His brother would be alive and well, and for that he would be thankful. But he wasn't sure he *wanted* his brother back.

But it was too soon to count on anything. If things went right, he'd figure out what to do then. But everything could very easily go wrong, and if they did he had to stick to the plan. Sail away. Save his own neck.

James chuckled. *It seems there is no honor among thieves.*

* * *

Johnny paced the deck of the *BlackFox*. His heart pound a marching beat in his ears and he attempted to take large, deep breaths to assuage some of his nerves—not that it was doing much good.

166

He was relatively safe where he was. But breakfast that morning could very well have been the last time he'd see Caton, Matt, or James again.

He'd already said his goodbyes to Faith. He had grown fond of her over the week or so they'd spent together, planning Brant's rescue. He saw a lot of strength in her, and wisdom that he wished he could possess, but at the same time her temper made her seem unbridled and passionate.

Johnny looked around at the activity on the deck of the *BlackFox*. They were loading supplies, making every effort to look like they were going on a legitimate merchant run, rather than breaking a convicted criminal out of prison. If anything, they had one of the more dangerous roles. Brant wouldn't step foot on this ship while in British territory, but that wasn't to say they wouldn't all get arrested and hung if the governor was looking for a scapegoat. But Johnny had no intention of even a single member of the British navy or royal guard stepping foot on this ship, and Brant would be safe enough with James, aboard Caton's ship.

Maybe Brant would set James straight during the time at sea they would have. Apparently the few months away from his older brother had not done James any good—he had turned from happy and carefree, to bitter and angry.

He sighed. Time couldn't be moving any slower than it was now, waiting for Matt to return and to set sail. The sound of the thunder of boots on planks as soldiers ran past ripped him from his thoughts.

This is it, he thought. *The alarm has been raised. Where is Matt?*

* * *

Brant stood by the window in his cell. It was early morning, the sun just barely peeking over the horizon. He could hear footsteps approaching his cell—there were two distinct sets, the heavy, marching like steps of a guard, and the softer tap of Faith's slippers.

When she came to the door and the guard unlocked it, she placed her hands on his arm and smiled. "Thank you," she said, glancing down, a blush rising up her cheeks as if on command.

Brant had to stifle back a chuckle as he watched the young guard's reaction. She was playing him like a well-tuned harp.

"Will you be around when I leave?" She removed her hand from his arm and raised it to her hair, twirling a loose strand around as if to mesmerize him.

He nodded, grinning. "Of course."

Faith offered him a glowing smile before stepping through the door into Brant's cell. The guard didn't leave right away, though.

"How come you're here every day? Is he family?" he asked, making conversation.

Faith shook her head. "My father knows him, and asked me to visit. One last act of kindness, you know?"

The guard nodded. "Your father sent you to nurse him back to health too?"

"Couldn't have him dying before he got to trial."

Brant waited patiently as they talked about him as if he wasn't there. He hated seeing the guard fawn over Faith. He didn't seem to want to leave her alone now that she'd finally given him some notice, after months of vying for her attention.

Conversation had turned from why she was at the prison to his life. Did he like being a guard, did he have family, a girl of his own…? Brant's stomach churned as Faith giggled at something the boy said—and really, that was what he was; a boy. Wasn't he missed at his post by now?

Finally, *finally* a shout came from down the hall, and the guard sighed. "I best be getting back to my post. Just call when you're done and I'll come back."

Faith gave a nod, still playing the part, but as the guard walked away she dropped all pretenses and turned to Brant. She looked tired, her eyes drooped, and her shoulders sagged.

"Please tell me you found him as dull as I did," she said, walking over and sitting down on the foot of Brant's cot

"Oh, I don't know, he seemed like a nice boy. I wouldn't be so quick to write him off."

Faith scowled. "Just eat your breakfast. We're getting you out today."

Brant nodded, not even bothering to argue with her about her involvement. She had more than proven that she wasn't going to listen to him, and it was too late now anyway. So he ate his porridge, which was more of a slop than anything. She opened the book she had been reading but he paused his meal and shook his head, his mouth full of food. He pointed to the Bible sitting beside his cot.

"Can you read from that today?" he asked after swallowing his food.

She looked at him, eyes wide, and he could swear he saw hope, or some kind of joy there. She nodded and picked up the book slowly, reverently, and turned to a section near the beginning.

"This is one of my favorite stories," she said. "It's about a woman named Ruth."

She started to read and Brant sat, eating his food, engrossed by the story, completely forgetting about what the day had in store for them.

When an hour had passed Faith closed the book and set it back down beside him. "Take this with you," she said, getting up. "My father would want you to keep it."

She walked over to the door and called for the guard, then turned back to Brant while she waited for him. "Matt will be here soon. Be ready."

When the guard walked up she stood patiently by the door. "I was hoping you'd come for me," she said with a shy grin, her eyes hooded as she played the part of the shy, interested girl.

Brant hated seeing her subject herself to the boy's attention; making herself appear like a silly, flirtatious girl when she was so much more than that. And to make it worse; she was doing it all for him.

True to her word, Brant heard footsteps approaching mere minutes after Faith left.

"Quick," said Matt, unlocking the door. "We don't have much time. Caton is creating a distraction."

Brant grabbed the Bible, holding it tightly against his chest as he slipped out of the open door. He and Matt walked brusquely down the hall towards the exit, the keys still hanging from the lock of the open cell door. As they stepped out into the bright daylight, sights and sounds bombarded Brant. After months in the cell, cut off from the world, it overwhelmed him and stopped him in his tracks.

"We have to keep going. Caton's little brawl will only be a distraction for a few minutes."

Brant's feet moved again, falling in step with Matt as they walked towards the docks. He chuckled at the thought of Caton in a brawl. In the year he'd known him he'd never seen him lose his temper—the closest he'd come was on Brant–much less fight.

"Halt!" came a shout from behind, ripping Brant away from his private amusement. His feet stopped on their own accord and he looked at Matt, silently asking him what to do.

"Run!" he hissed, taking off down the street, Brant right on his heels.

* * *

Johnny waited impatiently after the soldiers ran past. Matt should have been here by now. The soldiers would have been running either because they discovered Brant missing, or for Caton's distraction. Either way, it only took minutes to walk from the prison to where the ships were docked, and Matt hadn't arrived, nor had Johnny seen Caton's ship sail away.

All Johnny could think was that something had gone wrong. They'd been caught.

When Johnny saw Faith approaching his heart sunk.

The only reason she'd have to be here was to tell him their plan had failed. He watched her as she walked up the gangway and approached him, his heart hammering in his chest the whole time. She looked nervous, agitated, only solidifying in Johnny's mind their failure.

"What happened?" asked Johnny before she could even open her mouth.

She frowned. "What do you mean? Nothing happened. Not that I know of, anyway."

"Then why are you here?" The whole situation was becoming even more confusing. First Matt and Brant are running late, now

Faith was where she wasn't supposed to be and not because she had news.

She shuffled nervously from foot to foot and dropped a bag on the wood deck with a muffled thump, a bag that had previously slipped Johnny's notice.

"I'm coming with," she said, obviously trying to sound firm, but her eyes were downcast and Johnny could see a slight tremor in her hands.

He smiled slightly, but his chest was tight and aching for her.

"He's only going to break your heart," he said, placing a hand on her shoulder.

She looked up then, a sad smile on her face. "I know, but I have to try. I can't just let him sail out of my life, you know? And he's changed, Johnny. He's a different man."

"He's not sailing yet, though. I'm getting worried."

"He'll be fine. He and Matt are more than capable of taking care of themselves. We'll just keep waiting."

* * *

James waited at the gangway when Caton walked up.

"Brant here?" he asked. His lip swollen and split, and he had the beginning of what would surely be a dark purple and yellow black eye by tomorrow morning.

James shook his head. "Not yet. I hope the other guy looks worse," he said, indicating Caton's beat up face.

He shrugged and offered half a smile. "I think I got the worst of it. Turned out okay—the guards hauled the other man away for assaulting me. Brant should be here, though. You haven't heard anything?"

"Nothing."

"And Matt?"

"Haven't seen him either."

Caton frowned. "Do you want to go see if Johnny has heard anything?"

James nodded and trotted down the gangway towards his brother's ship where Johnny was waiting. It didn't take long to find out that Johnny hadn't seen or heard from Brant or Matt either.

"We could send Faith down to the prison."

James shook his head. "No, she's too involved as it is. We'll wait until morning, but be ready to sail at a moment's notice if things start going south, or if they show up."

"And if they don't show up by morning?"

"We leave. That was the plan all along, and we stick to the plan."

James left the *BlackFox* and walked back to Caton's ship. With things so close, reality that he might actually lose his brother came crashing down. He'd gone through a series of emotions in the past few months, from betrayal, to abandonment, to anger. But now he just felt scared. He was still angry with Brant, and he didn't really want to be in his life, but if their plan didn't work Brant would die, and quite possibly Matt as well. No matter how bad of a person Brant was, or how much wrong he'd done, James didn't want him to die. He wanted to know that Brant was off somewhere safe and living a happy life.

CHAPTER TWENTY-TWO

Brant's muscles screamed in protest. He crouched behind a pile of crates, too afraid to move even a muscle.

He and Matt hadn't had an easy time losing the guards. They'd run through the streets, zigzagging into back alleys and through houses. It seemed everywhere they turned there were men in uniform looking for them. Eventually they managed to make a few twists and turns without running in to anyone, and had been able to hide near the docks.

Now, after the running, and what was now probably nearing three hours of hiding behind crates, Brant's muscles had cramped and stiffened, threatening to give out and topple him right into what provided him cover.

Matt was hidden behind another pile just a short distance away but he had yet to emerge. They didn't dare come out. Not yet. Every few minutes Brant heard the distinct marching footfall of a soldier, guard, or group of them. They were still on the lookout, still searching. Brant didn't expect to be able to move from his position until well after nightfall. At least then they could blend into the shadows as they made their journey towards the *BlackFox*.

He shifted slightly, taking some of the weight off of his left leg. Had they searched the *BlackFox* yet? Had Johnny been questioned? Or James? Or Faith?

Brant's stomach lurched at the thought of Faith being interrogated. It was terrifying enough to consider any of his friends in that situation, but for some reason the idea of Faith was so much worse. She was strong, but she was also innocent, naïve, and fragile—though she would probably protest that vehemently—and she'd never experienced the fear of being imprisoned or sat in a cold dark room and questioned. Would she be able to withstand the questions? To feign innocence?

He wasn't worried about himself; he was worried about what would happen to her. The noose didn't discriminate between male and female, young and old. If she admitted to helping a convicted criminal she would hang.

Brant almost wanted to get up and turn himself in, just to protect her. But he didn't move. He crouched, and through a space between the crates, watched people walk by. The sun moved slowly across the sky as the day wore on into evening, and eventually his limbs grew numb to the cramping and pain. He lost track of how many times and how often he shifted his weight from one leg to the other.

Finally, as the sun disappeared and night took over, Matt emerged from his hiding place. He took a cautious look around, and signaled Brant to follow.

They walked silently beside each other, keeping to the shadows as much as they could. It was only a short walk to their destination, but it would only take one guard to notice them. Brant's heart hammered in his chest, and he could swear anyone who passed by could hear it.

Matt led him up to a gangway. This wasn't the *BlackFox*, but he recognized the ship from somewhere. He paused and waited until Matt turned to see why. Brant didn't even need to say anything, immediately Matt smiled as if in understanding.

"Caton's ship. We can't risk them searching the *BlackFox* and having you aboard."

Brant nodded and started walking up the gangway, but paused when he passed Matt, who didn't make any move to follow.

"Aren't you coming?"

Matt shook his head. "I'm going to the *BlackFox*. Johnny and I are going to sail her to Tortuga before we meet up with you in

Spain."

Brant walked back down the gangway and embraced his quartermaster. "Safe travels, my friend," he said, stepping back. "Thank you for not giving up on me."

Matt smiled. "I can't leave my Cap'n behind. Now you best get out of sight before someone spots you."

Brant turned and walked up the gangway, onto the ship that would sail him away from his prison and to freedom. But the thought of being out to sea, of going back to Spain, didn't comfort him. Instead he felt more lost than ever.

* * *

Catherine walked the perimeter of the ballroom. No one stopped her to make conversation. Not a single gentleman requested a dance. She was alone, completely shunned, and she didn't even mind. She found quiet strength and contentment in observing, rather than participating. There was no pressure on her to put on a show or converse with people she didn't even like. She didn't have to keep a painfully fake smile plastered on her face. The only disappointment she had was that she wasn't dancing.

She loved to dance, and to see so many couples twirling about the center of the room, and not have a single invitation, was disappointing, to say the least. She watched with silent longing as a waltz was performed. Her lips upturned, ever so slightly, as she imagined her feet moving to the music.

Watching the dancers, she saw many familiar faces. Men she had danced with before, women she had spent many an afternoon with. And then she saw a face that held pain more than familiarity; Charles. He had a woman in his arms, and he was smiling at something she said. They moved effortlessly across the dance floor, completely in sync. A stab of jealousy shot through her, surprising her at the emotional reaction she felt towards the sight.

It's too late, you ruined any chance you had with him, she silently berated herself.

Forcing herself to avert her eyes, she continued her journey around the room until she found the door to the garden and exited into the cool night air—soon it would begin to warm up as summer took over. A slight shiver went through Catherine as the air hit the bare skin of her arms and neck. The glass doors shut behind her, blocking out much of the sounds from inside the ballroom, and she felt a sense of relief pass over her.

How had she turned from content and strong, to hurting and weak, just from the sight of one person? If anything, Charles should be the one hurting. She was the one who had done him wrong. He was the one who had invested his whole heart in her only to have her stomp it underfoot, like a horse would a snake. But the pain was there, nevertheless. Pain that shouldn't exist.

She strolled the garden. Flowers that would begin to bloom in a month lay wilted and dormant. The leaves, which would be vibrant green in the summer, were a sick sort of grey. She looked at the sad sight and frowned, and her mind returned to the ballroom. Her thoughts still focused on Charles holding another woman in his arms, smiling at her the way he had smiled at Catherine only a few weeks ago.

I've made a mistake, she thought. *I could have made a life with him.*

She walked back into the ballroom, her destination being the grand entrance, so that she could call for her carriage and make an escape. Her steps were hurried and her eyes focused on only one thing: the exit. She didn't feel the quiet strength that she had possessed earlier. Instead she felt panicked and alone.

"Catherine."

The voice stopped her dead in her tracks, and left her standing with her back towards the speaker as she collected her nerves about her. Slowly she turned, her smile in place like a shield.

"I didn't realize you were here," said Charles, the woman he had been dancing with still hanging from his arm like she owned him.

"It seems I still warrant an invitation to these events."

She knew her voice was bitter and biting and wished she could retract her words and try them again with a more amiable tone. But Charles didn't seem to notice.

"I'm glad. I wouldn't have wanted our… situation to have hurt you."

He was standing there being courteous and kind. He should be wishing social death on her for what she'd done to him. Why did he have to be such a good man?

Catherine opened her mouth to reply, but closed it again. She didn't even know what to say to him. I'm sorry? That seemed a little redundant. Thank you? For what? Not hating her?

"You're not leaving, are you?" he asked, pushing the one-sided conversation further.

"I am."

"But the night has barely begun. Don't leave."

"I'm tired, and quite frankly no one wishes to speak to me. There is no point in my staying."

At Catherine's words, the woman on Charles' arm scoffed. "I wonder why that is."

Catherine shot a crippling glare at the woman. "I don't see how this is any of your business. Why don't you go find yourself a drink? You must be quite parched after all that dancing."

Her face paled in anger and she looked up at Charles, as if asking him if he was going to allow Catherine to speak to her like that. But he gave her a slight smile that even Catherine could tell held an apology, and patted her hand, removing it from his arm. The conversation between the two of them was silent, but its meaning was loud and clear. The woman turned on her heel and left in a rustle of skirts and a huff of exhaled air.

"I wish you'd stay. Learn to fight your battles rather than hide."

His words stung more than the disdain from everyone around, or the barbed comments from his female companion. His gentle rebuke only accentuated her disappointment in herself. Why couldn't he just be angry? Why couldn't he ignore her, hate her?

"Maybe I'm just not that strong."

"You are. You know how to look after yourself, Catherine."

She smiled sadly. "Because I did that so well with you."

"You had the right idea."

"When are you leaving?" she asked, bringing up the reason that had ended things between them.

"Next week."

"You'll love it there. It truly is beautiful in Jamaica."

Charles' face fell. "But I'll be going alone."

Her heart began thudding in her chest, and the blood thundered in her ears. If she didn't know better it sounded as if Charles still loved her—that he still wished she had said yes when he had asked her to come with him.

But Jamaica... she couldn't go back there. Not now, maybe not ever. It held too many bad memories, too much hurt and pain. Too much Brant Foxton.

"You'll meet new people there. Create a new life."

"It's just another adventure, right?"

Catherine nodded, offering him a smile of encouragement. "I really should be going, though." She couldn't take much more standing here and conversing as if nothing was wrong, and she was certain he couldn't either—he was just being a gentleman and making conversation with her, trying to show the world that he wasn't angry. He was still trying to protect her.

"Have a good evening, Catherine. I'm not sure I'll see you again before I leave, so I just want you to know that I'm not angry. I wish you all the best in your life—maybe one day your scars will heal and you'll be able to trust your heart to someone again."

Tears sprang unbidden to Catherine's eyes, and she quickly swept them away with her hand. Turning, she walked brusquely towards the exit without saying another word to him, fleeing the man who was much too good for her, who had her heart wrenching.

She cried the entire way home. What happened to strength and contentment? One conversation with Charles and she was reduced to the weak woman who was sitting in her carriage, a woman that at one time she never would have recognized as herself. How had she made such a mess of her life? If she could go back, she never would have allowed herself to fall in love with Brant, not the first time, not the second time... she never would have given him the chance to hurt her.

The thought of Brant made her stomach churn again. Was he dead? Would she ever know his fate?

She wiped angrily at her tears as the carriage drew to a stop in front of her house. The driver opened the door for her, and she climbed out. No, if Brant was dead she would know it—she'd sense it somehow, a piece of her heart dying. He was alive—Brant Foxton was a survivor.

Catherine, however, seemed to be destroyed by men at every turn. Brant, Charles… *Maybe I should just join a convent*, she thought to herself as she ascended the steps into her empty house. Her parents were still at the ball, and likely wouldn't be back for hours.

Catherine retreated to her room and called her hand-maid to help her out of her gown and into her nightgown.

But she was unable to sleep. It wasn't yet midnight and her emotions and thoughts plagued her. So she wandered around the empty house from room to room, straightening pillows, flipping through books, anything to distract herself until she was tired enough to sleep.

But nothing chased away the pain she felt, or the thought of Charles and the wrong she'd done to him. And underlying it all was self-pity. She wanted him back, because he made her forget her pain. He made her laugh, made her feel strong and in control, and if she were completely honest with herself, she had been jealous tonight. She did care about him, more than she had thought. More than she was willing to admit out loud. And now he was leaving, sailing out of her life, just like she had done to Brant. It was divine retribution.

CHAPTER TWENTY-THREE

James looked up as Brant climbed down the ladder and into the crew's quarters. He got up from his bunk and walked over, embracing his brother. Tears escaped down his cheeks as weeks of pent up emotions were released in a moment of relief.

"I'm sorry," said Brant, returning his brother's embrace.

James released him and wiped angrily at the unbidden tears. "You're a first class pillock, you know that?" he laughed through his tears.

"Yeah, I do."

James sighed, turning away from Brant. He had come to his decision a few hours ago, but now that the time was here he didn't know how to break the news to Brant. The noise from above deck told him that they would be casting off any minute now, though, so he couldn't afford to wait.

"What's wrong?"

Was he that transparent that Brant could tell something was troubling him without him saying or doing anything?

"Brant—" he started, then stopped. He looked around the ship, down at his feet, anywhere but at his brother. With a sigh, he started again. "Brant, I'm leaving."

Looking up, he met Brant's eyes. They had a sad, confused look to them. The look James had seen when Catherine had left, when Senona had left. Now he was responsible for that look—the look that told James he was destroying a little piece of Brant.

Brant nodded slowly, as if trying to make sense of the information before replying. James didn't give him a chance, though.

"I can't live this life that you've created, and I can't be involved with you on the run. I'm staying in Port Royale, and I'm going to start fresh, maybe go work for Sam on Foxton Estate until I can get my feet under me."

"Okay."

The single word stopped him dead. He frowned and looked at Brant, surprised at his lack of argument.

"Okay?"

"You're right, this life isn't for you, and I can't ask you to continue following me into an uncertain future. If you want to make your life here, rather than in Spain, I won't argue with you."

"Foxton Estate is the closest place to home…"

"Senona will understand," offered Brant, as if he was reading his mind.

"I'll write to her."

"But not to me," said Brant with a chuckle, but his eyes didn't reflect that sound of amusement. They looked lost.

James shook his head. "Not for a while. I know you're trying to change, but it's time for me to make a life for myself, and that means I need some time away from you. I hope you figure things out, Brant, I really do. When you get your life in order, you know where to find me."

"You know I can't come back here."

"Write me."

Tears filled Brant's eyes and spilled over onto his cheeks. James couldn't remember ever seeing him cry, and for a moment he wondered if he was making the wrong decision. Maybe Brant needed him.

"Well, you best be going then. The ship is going to leave soon."

James nodded, his resolve returned by his brother's words. He grabbed his small bag of belongings off the floor and went to climb the ladder up to the deck, but Brant grabbed his arm and pulled him into another embrace.

"Take care, okay?"

James nodded against his brother's shoulder, willing himself not to cry.

"I love you, James. I may not have been the best brother or father figure ever and I'm sorry for that, but I do love you."

"I know."

He pulled away and climbed up the ladder, not willing to delay his departure any longer, knowing that if he kept talking he might not leave.

"James! Where are you going?" asked Caton as he walked by, but he didn't stop, didn't even acknowledge him. Even a single pause and he knew he'd turn back and stay.

"James! We're leaving port *now.*"

As he walked down the gangway, he heard Brant say to Caton in a calm voice, "He's staying behind. He's chosen his own path."

That's when the sobs broke free, and James walked away from the ship knowing that he'd never see Brant again. His shoulders shook and his breath came in hitched gasps, but he didn't pause in his journey, he pushed forward, thankful for the nearly abandoned streets so that no one would see his distress.

His brother may have survived, may have escaped death, but James walked out of his life regardless. Not out of anger or hatred, but out of necessity. He loved his brother. All the bitterness and anger he had was just fear. He'd realized that when he thought that the escape had failed. That was also when he realized that despite his love for Brant, he couldn't live this life anymore.

For the first time in James' life he was on his own, and despite the heartache this decision brought, he was excited to follow this new path before him. The future was brand new and unknown. Once the initial mourning period of losing all those he held dear was over, he would embrace this new life and adventure with enthusiasm. But right now he was going to mourn the loss of Brant, Johnny, Caton, Senona, Matt, Catherine... Everyone he called his family, all the people that had been brought together by their journeys across the ocean.

* * *

Brant watched James as he walked away until he was out of sight.

"What do you mean he's staying?" asked Caton, the shock evident in his voice.

"He's going to go live his own life." Brant could hardly believe the words he was saying—it was almost as if a stranger had spoken them. They felt foreign and wrong.

"Good for him."

Brant nodded. Yes, he was proud of his brother for finding the strength to take this step, but what he couldn't say aloud, what he couldn't admit to Caton, was that they would never see James again. Because if he admitted it out loud, he wasn't sure he'd be able to hold himself together. So instead he just nodded.

"Let's get this ship out to sea," he said, changing the subject. "I feel uneasy sitting in port."

Caton smiled. "Just a few minutes and we'll be home free."

"We won't be free until I have nothing but water surrounding me," muttered Brant.

Caton's chuckle sounded nervous. The night was far from over. Port Royale's guards knew that Brant had escaped hours ago, and were on alert. All it would take would be for them to decide to search every ship, or chase theirs down.

The ship didn't take long to cast off, and they sailed slowly away from the island of Jamaica and towards Spain. As land slowly disappeared into the curtain of the dark night sky, Brant breathed a sigh of relief, feeling comfortable to walk around the deck and climb to the crow's nest.

He was exhausted, and still out of shape from the months in a prison cell and recovering from his stomach wound, so the climb was longer and harder than he had expected, or hoped. But as he leaned against the mast, he let out a long sigh, and smiled at the feeling of the breeze caressing his skin. It was as if the ocean was welcoming him home. Despite her betrayal, Brant still loved her, and it felt good to be accepted back.

"Thank you, Lord, for delivering me," he prayed, his eyes

directed upwards to the sky. "And please, watch over James."

Peace washed over him with his simple prayer. His escape was nothing short of a miracle, and he firmly believed the hand of God had been there. Why He had been bothered to save someone like Brant, he'd never know. But he could never say he didn't believe. Not now. Not after everything he'd been through.

He sat up there until he could barely keep his eyes open. The position of the moon told him it was past midnight now, so he climbed down and into his bunk. Sleep welcomed him quickly, and for the first time in months, he wasn't plagued by nightmares.

CHAPTER TWENTY-FOUR

Johnny couldn't describe the relief he felt when Matt walked aboard the *BlackFox* and announced that Brant had made it to Caton's ship, and they would be leaving port within the hour. His body ached from the hours of holding himself tense, as if he were a cat ready to spring at the slightest sign of trouble.

"So we're casting off?"

Matt nodded. "The sooner the better. We want the navy to be suspicious of us, not them."

The *BlackFox* had been prepped to go since late morning, so it took a matter of minutes to cast off and begin their journey away from Port Royale and towards Tortuga. Faith had fallen asleep earlier that night, but as they began to sail, she appeared bleary eyed from the captain's cabin—which Johnny had given to her for the journey. He had hoped she would have stayed inside longer, not wanting to explain himself to Matt.

"Brant?" she asked, walking up to Johnny and Matt, her voice still heavy with sleep.

"He's safely aboard Caton's ship and should be on his way to Spain by now," replied Johnny, hoping that if he acted as if all was normal, Matt would just let Faith's presence slide.

She sighed and opened her mouth to reply, but before she could get a word out Matt interrupted.

"What are you doing here?" he asked, looking first to Faith and then to Johnny for answers.

Faith blushed and looked away, as if looking for someone else to explain. The fact that she clasped her skirt, rubbing the fabric furiously between her fingers did not go unnoticed.

If Johnny hadn't been so exhausted, he would have teased her about it. Instead, he spoke up for her. "She wanted to come with."

Matt raised an eyebrow and turned back to Faith. Johnny could see she was preparing for a fight, her shoulders squaring up.

"Brant doesn't know what he has in you."

Johnny looked over at Matt. He could feel his eyes widen, and he was fairly certain his jaw hit the wooden deck. Looking over at Faith, he could see she was growing redder than before.

"He doesn't have me," she replied, but she smiled.

"If you're here, then you're as good as his. You know you're throwing away your entire life for him. You'll never be free, and there will always be the risk that he'll be found and executed."

"I know."

"Does your father know you're here?"

She nodded. "He wasn't overly happy, but gave his blessing when he realized I wasn't going to take no for an answer."

"Then I won't argue with you. It's too late for that now anyway." Then he turned to Johnny. "I wish you would have told me about this before we left port, though."

Johnny shuffled uncomfortably. He knew he should have, and it had crossed his mind briefly, but he liked Faith, and he respected her choice. Not only that, but he refused to be the one to break her heart. He'd leave that to Brant when the time came.

"It slipped my mind," he lied, offering a shrug of his shoulders.

"I'm sure."

"Is there anything else I should know before I go to bed?" asked Matt, looking pointedly at Johnny. "Anymore stowaways?"

Johnny shook his head.

"Good."

Matt walked away, towards the small cabin below deck that was reserved for the quartermaster, leaving Johnny and Faith alone on deck.

Sleep had left her face, and she looked to Johnny, letting out a giggle that sounded more like an escape of emotions than true happiness.

"I thought he might turn the ship around and take me home."

"I think he might have if you were anyone else. Though I'm sure I'll be receiving some choice words in the near future when you aren't around."

"I'm sorry to put you in this situation."

Johnny shrugged. "I could have sent you home hours ago. It was my choice. Besides, Matt is soft—and a few harsh words never hurt anyone."

"Nevertheless, I'm grateful. You've been a true friend."

Johnny placed his arm protectively around her and led her towards the captain's cabin. "And as your friend, I'm telling you to get some sleep. We're by no means out of danger yet, and things could get interesting. Get some rest while things are quiet."

Faith didn't move away from his arm and allowed him to guide her, but when they paused at the door to the cabin, she turned around and embraced him. "Please tell me I'm not making a huge mistake, Johnny. Please tell me he won't break my heart like I think he will."

He closed his eyes, searching for an answer. Inside his heart was breaking for her. "I wish I could tell you that, but the truth is, I really don't know. I have no idea what Brant feels towards you, and even if I did, he has his own code he lives by. I don't know if you fit into it."

She let go and looked at him, her eyes shining with unshed tears. He wished he could tell her Brant would return her love and sail off into the horizon with her, like some romantic story, but he couldn't lie to her. She needed to know what she was getting into.

"At least you're honest. I suppose that counts for something, even if it isn't what I want to hear."

She planted a kiss on Johnny's cheek and quickly retreated into the confines of her cabin before he could say another word to her. He stood outside the door, listening for a time. He could hear sniffles as she cried. He could now understand the anger James had harbored towards Brant.

If Brant breaks her heart, I'll fight for her honor myself, thought Johnny as he walked away.

* * *

The next few weeks were tense aboard the *BlackFox*. Every sail they saw had the crew jumping in anticipation of a boarding by the royal navy. But each ship sailed past, ignoring them.

Why aren't we being chased? Johnny wondered as he took a watch up in the crow's nest. It made absolutely no sense that they wouldn't pursue Brant, and the fact that *his* ship had left Port Royale the very day he had escaped prison should have been enough to have the navy in hot pursuit. But they sailed without an issue, and that made Johnny all the more nervous. Matt and Faith seemed content with the idea that they had gotten away, but he couldn't help but feel everything had gone too easily. Had they seen through their plan and chased Caton's ship instead? For a brief moment Johnny entertained the idea that James had betrayed them. He had been so angry, so adamant that Brant didn't deserve rescue that maybe, just maybe he had turned Brant in.

Johnny shook his head to dislodge the accusatory thought. No, James may have been angry, but he would never turn in Brant. They were brothers, despite everything they had been through.

Faith's head peeked up over the edge of the crow's nest. "May I join you?" she asked.

"Sure." Johnny offered his hand to help her up. She grasped it and tumbled up onto the platform in a very unladylike fashion, feet and skirts all tangled in a heap with petticoats showing. She blushed a deep crimson red, and scrambled to her feet, straightening her skirts as she attempted to collect her dignity. Johnny smirked and sat down, leaning against the mast, and trying to hide his amusement. *I'm going to owe her an apology for this*, he thought, stifling a chuckle.

"You know that hardly matters after you've climbed up all this way, and given every sailor below a nice view of your petticoats."

It was as if his words were tearing down a physical sheet, he could almost see her dignity, that she had just managed to find, come crashing down again. He hadn't believed her face could get any redder than it had been a minute ago, but it did.

"Oh dear," she muttered, embarrassment seemingly stealing her voice away. "I didn't really think…"

"If anyone looked I'll have them walk the plank."

Faith frowned, her face still flushed with embarrassment. "They don't actually do that, do they?"

"Look? Or walk the plank?"

"Walk the plank."

Johnny could tell she was trying to change the subject so he obliged. "Not often. You're more likely to be set adrift in a boat. Honor among thieves and all."

Faith giggled. "It's beautiful up here. How far do you reckon we can see?"

He shrugged. "Not too sure, but from up here we'll be the first to spot anything out there," he said, indicating the horizon.

She grew silent and stared out. "Do you think they're following us? Waiting to *see* Brant before they move in?"

"I don't know. I doubt it. It's not as if they need a reason to board. They're the navy. If they want to search a vessel, they can."

"So you think we just got away with it?"

Johnny shook his head. "No. Can't you feel the storm in the air?"

She frowned. "What do you mean?"

"The storm… there's a tension in the air that's building up. This is just the calm before everything comes crashing down."

"I feel like I'm always looking over my shoulder, wondering when they're going to swoop in."

"Me too. But when they do come we just have to remain strong and stick to our story."

Faith didn't reply, and when Johnny looked over, he saw her face had become pale and her eyes wide. Her mouth was set in a firm line, her jaw clenched together as if forcibly holding in fear. He wrapped his arm around her shoulders and drew her close. He felt a sibling connection to her, protective, and he wanted to make her feel safe. The dynamic in their relationship was different than the one he shared with Catherine, though. Catherine was the older sibling, and their relationship had always reflected that. Faith was to

Johnny like a younger sister, despite her actually being older in age than he.

"Hey, don't worry. They can't hold us on anything. Brant isn't here and they have no proof we were involved."

"I've never broken the law before," she whispered, as if telling a secret.

Johnny chuckled. "As far as I'm concerned, you still haven't. All you did was talk to a guard. He's the one who allowed himself to be distracted while on duty. Did you take the key?"

She shook her head. "Matt did when he walked by."

"See. You broke no laws. The only person who broke a law would be Matt from where I stand."

"But if Brant was tried on the basis of piracy, couldn't the entire crew of the *BlackFox* be as well?"

Johnny shrugged. "If they were going to do that, they would have already." He grimaced when he realized that his voice didn't sound convincing, even to himself. The thought had crossed his mind. If they couldn't have Brant, would they take the entire crew instead? The sooner they got to Tortuga and then left for Spain, the better. Spanish waters were home free.

Faith sat with Johnny for the rest of his watch. Their conversation turned less serious after a while. Faith asked him about his life in England, what it was like to go to boarding school, and live in a house full of servants. She expressed disbelief that he had left all that behind by choice.

"When the ocean calls to you she's impossible to ignore. You don't feel that?"

Faith shrugged. "A little. I used to watch ships coming and going from port and wonder what adventures they were having. But that was because my father was out there, and home to me was nothing glamorous. You had the whole world at your feet and you left."

"We all sacrifice things for what we love. You left your life behind for Brant. I left mine behind for the ocean. It's a part of life."

When they climbed down, Johnny went first to ensure no one looked up her skirt—she trusted him not to, but had admitted that she didn't trust the rest of the crew; even though he insisted they were all perfect gentlemen. Johnny chuckled to himself as he climbed down. Truth was he didn't put it past the crew to look. They weren't gentlemen, they were sea dogs. They had very little in the ways of manners.

"You know," said Johnny once they were both standing on the deck. "If you plan on climbing anymore during the voyage you should probably borrow a pair of my breeches. I know I said the crew wouldn't peek, but—"

"I know you lied. I've been around sailors before, you know. There aren't many gentlemen among them."

"I think they'd resent that generalization."

"Well it's my dignity I'm protecting, so I'll generalize if I please."

Johnny laughed, there was that temper again. Her eyes flashed a bit in challenge, but her smile showed that she wasn't being *too* serious. Not enough to cause a fight anyway.

"I'll get you those breeches then. That way you don't have to go accusing my sailors of being scallywags."

"Your sailors? I thought Matt was acting captain."

Johnny shrugged. "Confidence will get you what you want. If I want to be captain I have to grasp the role."

"I think that's called usurping."

"Johnny, good, I was just looking for you," came Matt's call as he approached. It was as if he knew they were talking about him.

"How can I be of service?" asked Johnny, offering a mocking bow.

Faith stifled a laugh, making Johnny grin. He felt like he was getting back to his old self, the Johnny he had been back when he'd first met James—care free. Some of it was an act, a front to put Faith more at ease in a scary situation, but most of it was him acting on impulse.

Matt rolled his eyes but didn't rebuke him. "The cook needs help in the galley. Some pots need scrubbing."

Johnny groaned. Was Matt serious? Had he heard their conversation and decide to put him in his place? Apparently Faith had the same thought, because she started laughing uproariously.

"Your sailors? It seems like Matt has you right where you belong."

Johnny grumbled, "Yeah, yeah. Someday, Faith. Someday I'll be a captain."

"But today you're scrubbing pots," said Matt, his face impassive.

Johnny felt as if he was the brunt of a joke, so he didn't give them the satisfaction of a response, just walked towards the galley below deck. He was back to the bottom rung in the ship hierarchy, apparently. He'd hoped that being aboard the *BlackFox* would bring him above the rank of deck hand. But Matt wasn't letting him sidestep doing his time—he'd have to earn his place on the *BlackFox* if he wanted to move forward.

Fine, if it was going to take scrubbing pots without complaint, then he'd do it. For now.

CHAPTER TWENTY-FIVE

Catherine walked down the street, a large brimmed hat protecting her from the warm afternoon sun. She was alone, without an escort, but she didn't really mind. She was in a good area of town, the streets lined with town houses of the well-to-do. The people strolling the streets around here were mostly of the reputable sort, and the few that might be considered shady were outnumbered by guards keeping the streets of the higher members of society safe.

She looked around at the various houses and people wandering the streets. A man walking on the opposite side of the street caught her eye, his gait a familiar movement. It didn't take long for recognition to set in. Charles Henley was hard to mistake for anyone else. He always held himself with confidence and strength, as if the world lay at his feet—which, in a sense, it did.

Her heart quickened but she averted her eyes and continued walking, hoping he didn't notice. She wasn't sure she was able to face him again, so soon after the ball. She'd cried herself to sleep that night and she hated herself for letting a man reduce her to tears. She had promised herself she'd find her strength again after Brant, but had failed at that endeavor at every turn.

She snuck a glance up and realized her mistake when she saw him wave and start to cross the street.

"Catherine, I was hoping I'd see you before I left. May I walk with you?" he asked as he fell in step alongside her.

"Of course," she replied, smiling through her discomfort.

Charles did not offer her his arm, and instead walked comfortably with her. "I wanted to apologize for how I acted the other night. I didn't mean to upset you."

"Upset me? You were nothing but kind and courteous."

"You looked upset when you left. I thought perhaps it was something I said—"

"I don't deserve your kindness after how I treated you, Charles. I was surprised was all," she lied. Yes, she'd been upset, but not because of him. She was upset with herself, and probably would be for a while. At least until she stopped running into him everywhere she went. If she didn't know better she'd almost think he was *trying* to make an appearance every time she ventured into public.

"That's a relief. It has been bothering me all week."

Catherine smiled slightly. If the man had any fault it was that he was too kind and forgiving. Where was his righteous indignation?

"Who was the woman you were with the other night? She seemed nice."

"Lady Bridgette Gregory. She's a family friend. We grew up together. In fact, I'm on my way to her house now for some supper."

Catherine held back a frown. A long-time family friend who obviously had her eyes set on marrying the esteemed Charles Henley. There was no other reason for her to have her claws out and so protective the other night. But Catherine said nothing.

"She'll be coming to Port Royale with me actually."

Catherine choked, trying to hold in her shock. That had gone quickly. So she'd convinced him to marry her already? She hadn't thought Charles was on the market for a wife, but perhaps he was. He'd moved fast enough from her to Lady *Bridgette*.

"I, uh, I should be getting back home," she said, pausing their walk and turning back in the direction she'd come. "I wish you and Lady Bridgette all the happiness in this new chapter of your life."

For the second time in a week she found herself walking away, leaving a stunned Charles standing, staring after her in silence. For the second time in a week she fled from the man she could have called her own.

* * *

Brant paced the deck like a caged animal. He'd never felt trapped on a ship before, but here, running from the law, running into an uncertain future, he felt restless. He wanted to make it to Spain, apologize to Senona for his actions, for taking her husband away and putting him in danger. He wanted to figure out where he was going from here. But being aboard this ship in the middle of the ocean had things at a standstill, and he was left unable to take action.

Caton walked up, a smirk plastered on his face like one painted on a court jester, and he chuckled in some personal amusement. "You look positively distressed."

Brant raised an eyebrow in response. "Please tell me why I shouldn't be distressed. I've broken more laws in recent history than I can count, and if I get caught again there won't be any trial. I'll likely be shot on the spot."

Caton set his lips in a stern line. Brant could tell what he was thinking just from his expression, but Caton didn't speak. He remained silent and just offered Brant a look that was somehow both disapproving and sympathizing at the same time and let him read between the lines.

"Not even a word of sympathy for a friend?" asked Brant.

Caton smirked. "You know you'll get no sympathy from me, so don't ask for it."

It was enough to stop Brant's restless pacing and allow him to laugh a little. For some reason it relaxed him to know that Caton wasn't stressed, nor did he care about Brant's problems.

"How long until we reach Spain?"

"The captain told me another week or so. The *BlackFox* should have made it to Tortuga by now."

"Good."

"What are we going to tell Senona about James?"

Brant felt his heart ache at the mention of his brother. He had been avoiding any and all conversation about him, unable to deal with the fact that he had lost his brother—not from some sort of accident or illness, but because of his own poor choices.

"The truth."

Caton shook his head. "Can you imagine how that will go over?"

"It will go over a whole lot better than lying will. You should know that, she is your wife."

Brant knew he should have held back on that jab. And seeing Caton's face darken in anger only solidified that knowledge. *What is wrong with you*, he thought, trying to push back the less-than-kind thoughts. Caton had been nothing but a friend, and willing to put everything on the line for him. He had long ago come to terms with the fact that Senona was and will always be nothing more than a close friend. He sighed, and ran his hand through his hair to prepare for Caton's rebuttal.

"Watch yourself, Brant. You're a fugitive. It won't do any good to go making enemies right about now."

Caton's reaction was nothing more than he had expected and deserved. He would have said the same thing. He probably would have done worse, actually.

Caton watched Brant, as if waiting for something, but he said nothing, just shrugged an apology of sorts and walked away. Quite honestly he was in a foul mood, and had been since he had left Spain. Only a few things had managed to alleviate that; Faith and his escape. He had been trying to put his life together, and putting his trust in God, which helped enormously. But James' leaving had taken a toll on him, and when he dwelled on it too much it left him feeling depressed and alone. It certainly didn't help matters that he was restless and stuck aboard a ship.

His mind wandered to Faith as he climbed up to the crow's nest. He would have loved to show her this view, where there was nothing but the swell of the sea all around him as she welcomed him home. He leaned out from the mast, holding tight to the ladder, and let the breeze wash all around him. Yes, this was home. This was his love. Maybe if he could have shown Faith this, she would understand that he was married first to the sea, that the ocean would always be first in his heart. Of course, neither Senona nor Catherine had come to that realization when he showed them the same view. Instead, they'd fallen deeper in love with him, and it wasn't until hurt and betrayal threatened to tear their friendship apart, that they realized he'd never be able to reciprocate their love.

Of course, he'd never be able to stop loving them either.

But Senona was married, Catherine was gone, and Faith was left far behind, safe and out of his life.

A pang of longing shot through him. He'd been missing their mornings together, her reading to him, talking, conversing. Climbing up on to the crow's nest he was met with loneliness. Everyone left, moved on, or gone. Faith had been his connection, his anchor in the storm that was his life. He wished so desperately that he had been selfish enough to take her with him.

Feelings of being utterly alone washed over him—a feeling that had been all too familiar right after Catherine had left him, and had him spiraling out of control. He thought he had it under control, and maybe he did in the sense that he wouldn't let himself walk down that path again, searching for some kind of meaning—but he felt empty again, and he had hoped that was gone. It should be gone. He had people that cared about him and loved him. But instead of being able to dwell on the people he *had,* he could only think of the people he had lost.

CHAPTER TWENTY-SIX

The *BlackFox* sailed into Tortuga's port only a day or two behind their self-imposed schedule. The summer storms had started, and although they hadn't been slowed down too much, getting to Spain could get interesting. They were variably chased into Tortuga by storm clouds threatening to turn the sea into an angry, raging beast.

The threatening storms had Johnny worried. He wanted to make port for a month or two, at least until the worst of the storms were over, but Matt didn't seem too keen on that.

"Three days leave, then we head back to sea," he instructed as they approached the dock.

Johnny noticed a few worried glances, but no one argued. It wasn't unheard of to sail through the storms, but most sailors didn't take the risk. They respected the sea too much for that.

"Matt, are you sure?" he asked, pulling him aside where they wouldn't be overheard.

"We have to make it to Spain."

"Brant will still be there in a few months. It might be best not to try our luck. There's a storm following us in, and we just weathered a rather large one. I just think it might be best to remain in port."

"It would be best. Under normal circumstances I wouldn't risk it, but we're on the run ourselves. Don't forget that we broke Brant out of lock up."

"They can't prove it—"

"Think they'll care? If they're looking to blame someone they won't care much if we're guilty or not, they'll just hang us in the breeze on suspicion. Do you want to risk your neck, or Faith's, on that? I'll try my luck with the storms."

Johnny swallowed hard and nodded. Matt had become a lot stronger, a lot more sure of himself in recent months. There was no double guessing behind what he said. He had made his decision and he was sticking by it. He'd grown into the role of captain that had been thrust upon him.

"We'll spend a couple days in port, just long enough to really spread around that we were here. Then we'll head off to Spain."

"Yes, sir," replied Johnny, offering no more argument.

Matt skillfully directed the vessel alongside the dock, and crewmembers lashed it tightly to the posts. Docking was always a bustle of activity as things were stowed away, and it was no easy task navigating the harbor, but the crew worked well together and made quick work of it.

With the gangway dropped, Faith wrapped a shawl around her shoulders and prepared to leave the ship. Johnny watched her and smirked. She was out of her mind if she thought she was going to traverse the port city of Tortuga.

Tortuga was well known as the city of sin. It was a den of thieves, a haven for pirates and smugglers, and a place of business for prostitutes and pick pockets. Not a place for a nice girl like Faith.

"Where do you think you're going?" he asked, intercepting her at the top of the gangway.

"Off the ship."

Johnny shook his head. "Absolutely not. You aren't safe here."

"I'm not exactly upper class. I know how to handle myself."

"Not in Tortuga, you don't." Even Johnny was hesitant to leave the ship in this particular port.

"Port Royale isn't the nicest place either—"

"Tortuga makes the seediest areas of Port Royale look like the

King's court. You're staying safely aboard the *BlackFox* with me. I'm sorry, Faith, but Brant is already going to have my head for allowing you to come along. If I let you go into Tortuga, and something happens to you, he'll have me drawn and quartered."

Faith's face grew red—a sure sign that her temper was flaring up, and Johnny prepared himself for a barrage of angry words. He'd discovered that the girl could give a tongue lashing like no other, but at least she wouldn't sneak off. She'd express her feelings, rather loudly, and if he managed to stand his ground (which was no easy feat) she would stand down—or at least that's what he hoped would happen.

"Johnny Marshall, I am a grown woman and if I say I'm going off ship, then I'm going to do just that. What Brant will do to you doesn't really concern me, now does it? He can hang you, draw and quarter you, and then ship the pieces to the four corners of the earth for all I care. Now let me by."

Johnny raised an eyebrow, torn between nervousness and amusement, but stood his ground with his hands crossed over his chest. A part of him didn't doubt that in the heat of her temper she would do exactly as she threatened.

She breathed heavily, and her hands were planted on her hips. But it was her eyes, flashing in an anger that reminded Johnny of a summer storm of the worst sort. He'd be battered and bruised after this, he was sure, and he certainly didn't envy Brant dealing with her in the near future. She was going to be with him to stay, whether he liked it or not.

The thought almost brought a chuckle to Johnny's lips, but he pressed them together to smother the smile—it would only serve to fuel Faith's anger—and walked forward, taking her arm and forcefully wheeling her back around and towards her cabin.

"Look, I'm not even going off ship."

"I don't need a prison guard," she shot back.

"I wouldn't be going, even if you weren't here," he lied. Of course he would have been. He enjoyed a game of cards or dice as much as the next man, and a drink didn't go down too bad either. But Faith's safety, and in turn his avoidance of Brant's wrath, was a little higher on his list of priorities than a good time.

He could see her slowly settling down. Her breathing had

regulated anyway, and her color had returned to normal. Just her eyes continued to betray her anger. But she allowed him to escort her into her cabin, and she took a seat behind Brant's desk. "Good thing I like this ship," she muttered.

Now Johnny did chuckle. "I understand that you want to stretch your legs, see something besides this cabin and this ship— we all do. But your safety is important to me. Besides, you need Brant to be in a good enough mood to at least hear me out if you want me to speak on your behalf."

"I don't need you to speak on my behalf. I made the decision to follow him, I'll speak for myself. It's not really the situation for a mediator, now is it?"

"No, it's not."

"Now, how about you teach me how to play some cards, since we have nothing better to do?"

Johnny smiled, relieved that the storm that was Faith's temper had passed rather quickly. At least she'd keep Brant on his toes... if he reciprocated her feelings, that is.

"That I can do," he replied, pulling a deck of cards from his pocket and pulling another chair up to the desk.

* * *

Days passed by for Catherine, but she wasn't looking at the ones behind her, but instead her thoughts were firmly on one day in the very near future. Charles was leaving tomorrow. She would probably not see him again, and if she did he would likely be married to that *lovely* woman she had met at the ball last week.

It had been troubling her so much that she'd barely slept since their chance meeting on the street. But she refused to cry, even though her exhaustion threatened to bring the tears.

She knew it was for the best. She wasn't ready, not after

Brant, but she wanted to be ready because she wanted Charles. She kept telling herself that when she was ready there would be a nice, caring man for her, but all she could think was that he wouldn't be Charles Henley. He wouldn't be good enough.

Charles deserved to find his happiness now, not when she was ready. Yet she couldn't stop being angry with herself from letting him go. The idea that her and Brant could work had not been the biggest mistake of her life, the whole situation had brought her to Charles' attention. No, the biggest mistake she had ever made was letting him go. Not realizing the extent of her feelings before she had hurt him beyond repair, and for having too much pride to tell him the truth of it all.

The entire house was quiet at this time of night. The servants slept soundly in their quarters, the candles and lanterns had been extinguished, and she sat alone by the coals of a dying fire in her father's study. A glass of port sat in her hand untouched. She had poured it, thinking it would make her feel better, but once the blood red liquid was in her hand she felt no desire to drink it. Instead, she stared at it as her thoughts took over her entire being. With nothing to distract her, she was plagued with memories of her short time with Charles. She could hear his laughter, feel his gentle touch. Every memory was as clear as if he was sitting in the room with her.

"Catherine?" asked her father, banishing the images of Charles as if they were smoke swept away by the breeze. It was a welcome distraction, and she sighed in relief, thankful for the brief reprieve from her own mind.

Now she took a sip from her glass, and waited until her father sat beside her before responding. "I couldn't sleep."

"What's troubling you?"

"Charles leaves tomorrow," she said.

Her father nodded somberly. "Why don't you tell him how you feel, dear?"

Catherine scoffed. "That turned out so well the last time I tried that. No, it's best I let fate take its course."

"It's my experience that we create our own fate. If the thought of him leaving distresses you this much, you have to let him know how you feel. I don't care how improper it is. I want to see you happy. If Charles Henley makes you happy, then you should tell him that. Please, Catherine, it pains me to see you like this."

Catherine offered her father a smile, but he didn't seem to accept it. His eyes expressed sadness, backing up the words he said. "There is someone else..." she trailed off.

"Tell him anyway. What will it hurt?"

"My pride."

"I don't imagine you have much of that left after the Brant debacle."

Catherine looked at her father, surprised at how he spoke to her. Sure, he was blunt with Johnny like that, but she was his daughter, the apple of his eye. He had always been kind and gentle with her. "My pride is all I have left. It's all that is keeping me going."

"Perhaps it's time to let that go then, because your pride is what is getting in the way of you being happy. Quite frankly, I miss seeing your smile, my dear." He got up and walked over, taking the glass from her hand and putting it on an end table. Then, he offered his hand.

Catherine hesitated, then took the outstretched hand. She wasn't ready to leave her quiet den of solitude, but she knew there was never any sense in arguing with her father, so she allowed herself to be raised from the chair.

"Go to bed, Catherine. Get some sleep."

"And you, Father? Are you going to bed?"

He smiled, escorting her to the door. "It's my turn to be alone with my thoughts."

*　*　*

When Catherine awoke the next morning, she felt rested for the first time all week. She had fallen asleep almost as soon as her head had hit the pillow, and had been too exhausted to even dream—that she could remember anyway. Getting up, she washed her face and rang for her hand maid to come and help her dress and do her hair.

An hour later she was ready to face the day. She walked downstairs and into the dining room, where her father was sitting quietly, drinking tea and reading the morning paper. Her mother was nowhere to be seen.

"Good morning, Father."

He dropped the paper just low enough to see her over it. "Morning, dear. You best eat something quickly. I called a carriage for you not too long ago."

Catherine frowned. "Called a carriage?"

"Yes, to take you to see Charles. His ship leaves today, does it not?"

"No, Father."

"It doesn't?" he asked, raising an eyebrow.

"Yes, it does. I mean, no, I'm not going to see him."

"Yes, you are. I won't take no for an answer. I can't abide seeing you this miserable. If I thought it would do any good I'd go see him myself, but alas, I'm afraid what has to be said needs to come from you."

Catherine opened her mouth to argue, but the butler walked in, stopping her before the words could leave her mouth.

"The carriage you called is here, sir."

"Thank you. Well then, Catherine, you best be going. You wouldn't want to miss him."

Slowly, as if her slippers were made of lead, Catherine walked towards the front door and exited into the glaring sunlight. Of course it would be sunny today. It was never sunny in London and yet, on what was likely the dreariest day for her, it shone brightly.

Climbing into the carriage, she gave the driver directions and sat back as the vehicle lurched over the streets. She was thankful for the plush interior, for what would have surely been a rough ride without it. But her mind wasn't on the carriage ride. It was on what she was going to say to Charles when she got there.

What could she say? *I'm sorry, I made a mistake. I love you. Please leave that other woman for me.* Catherine snorted at the very thought of those words leaving her lips. No, this visit was useless. She would say her goodbyes and make no mention of her feelings. Her father didn't need to know. This way he would be content that she'd tried, even if she really hadn't.

The carriage pulled to a stop and the driver hopped down, opening the door for Catherine.

Her heart began to pound wildly as she stepped down, and forced herself to put one foot in front of the other as she climbed the steps to the front door of the Henley's town house.

Pulling on the rope that rang a bell somewhere inside, she

waited for the door to be answered. It took every bit of her self-control to keep from turning around and climbing right back into the carriage. Just as her strength and resolve was about to give way, the door opened, revealing Charles.

"Catherine?"

She stared at him, unspeaking. She was shocked that he had answered the door, and not a servant or butler. It took her a moment to collect her thoughts.

"Uh," she said, quite unladylike, "I came to say goodbye."

"Please, come in."

Charles led her through the house and into the parlor, offering her a seat.

"No, thank you. I won't be long. Like I said, I just wanted to say goodbye and wish you the best."

"Thank you."

His voice sounded hollow, empty, and maybe even a little sad. Catherine frowned, wondering what it meant.

"Is that all?"

Was it? She could say so much more. Could she live with him leaving, and not knowing the truth of how she felt? She nodded. "Yes, that's all."

She started walking back towards the door. As she reached for the handle she paused, her hand in mid-air. Charles was leaving, for good, and she was just going to walk out this door. She was getting good at walking out, maybe it was time she turned around and faced things.

Allowing her hand to fall by her side, she spun on her heel on her way back to the parlor, but Charles stood right behind her.

"Catherine—"

She held up her hand. "Let me speak, before I lose my nerve."

She took a deep breath and let it out slowly, her shoulders shaking in the process as her nerves found release. "I know you're leaving today, and with Bridgette, but I have to say this: I made a mistake when I told you I couldn't come with. I didn't realize the extent of my feelings for you Charles. I had been suppressing them, telling myself that you were nothing more than a shield for my reputation. But you had become so much more than that, and I didn't even realize it until you were gone.

"I hurt you, I know that. I don't expect you to forgive me, but I need you to know that our relationship may have started out with me using you, but it turned into so much more. I love you, Charles. I'm so sorry for the pain I caused you, and I wish you all the happiness in your new life. I'm sure she's much better for you than I am."

Tears were streaming down her face now, and she turned back towards the door, walking out before he could say anything. She didn't want to hear what he had to say, she couldn't.

"Catherine!" Came the shout from behind her, but she didn't stop. "Catherine, stop!" A hand grabbed her arm and spun her around, landing her directly into the surprisingly strong arms of Charles.

"Catherine, I love you, but who is this woman you think I'm going to be happy with?"

Catherine wiped her tears away. "The woman you were with at the ball; Bridgette."

A smile erupted on Charles' face. "I told you that she is just a family friend. She lives in Port Royale, and is happily married. She was just here for a visit."

Catherine stared at him. Married? As it slowly sank in, the tears started anew. Charles released his hold on her and cupped her face in his hands, making her look him straight in the eye.

"Catherine Marshall, you are the only woman I could be happy with."

She choked back a sob at his declaration.

"Come with me," he said in earnest. "Come with me to Port Royale. Make a life with me."

She nodded, smiling through her tears. "Yes, yes! But under one condition."

"Anything."

"You have to marry me first. I won't get on a ship with a man again without being married."

He chuckled and brushed his lips against her forehead. "I would have it no other way."

He let go of her face and drew her in close to him. They stood in the middle of the street, unaware of the traffic around. Catherine rested her head against his chest and slowly got control of her crying.

"Perhaps we should move inside," suggested Charles, moving her so that he had one arm wrapped around her waist to guide her to the door. "And let's see if we can do something about those tears."

Once inside Catherine was shown to a seat in the parlor, while Charles asked one of the servants to bring her a cup of tea.

With the steaming cup held in both hands, she breathed in the smell and willed her heart to stop pounding. The adrenaline and fear from her declaration still coursed through her, and her body hadn't quite caught up with the relief her mind felt.

"I still have to leave today," said Charles, taking a seat beside her.

"I know."

"But I'll be back. As soon as I can I'll return and I'll marry you, Catherine."

She smiled at him and placed her hand over his. "I'll be counting down the days."

His eyes shone with what Catherine could only describe as joy, and his grin was uncontainable. "I can't quite believe this is real. You have made me so happy."

She brushed away the tears of happiness that hadn't quite abated. What a fool she had been to almost let this man go. Here he was, nearly in tears from happiness because *she* loved him. She never moved Brant that way. This was the way love should be; you should need the person so badly it hurt. She had thought she had that with Brant, but instead she had heartache *because* she was with him. Things were better, easier when they were apart and that wasn't right.

"You do realize I'll be the talk of society… again," she said, looking up at him.

"You can handle it. At least this time it should be positive. As the future Lady Henley, you should have most of societies' ladies flocking to be in your good graces. I dare say you won't even miss me while I'm gone, you'll be so busy with social engagements."

"And planning the social event of the year, don't forget."

"Ah yes, the wedding."

"Oh no," said Catherine with a laugh. "Our engagement party will be the social event of the year. Up until our wedding, and then that will pale in comparison."

"Anything to make you happy, my dear."

"Sir," interrupted a servant.

Charles looked up, waiting for the man to continue.

"Your carriage has arrived and your trunks have been loaded."

"Thank you."

Charles turned back to Catherine, standing up, and he drew her in to his arms. "Our time together has been far too short."

"But we have our whole lives ahead of us. Just remember that when you're sailing hundreds of miles across the ocean."

He nodded, leaning down and brushing his lips ever so gently against hers. The kiss was so fleeting and soft, like a whisper of wind against her lips. Without another word, Charles left, walking out of his house and climbing into the waiting carriage.

Catherine followed him out, but stopped in the doorway and raised her hand in farewell. Charles stuck his head out the window and waved, blowing her a kiss. The simple gesture brought tears on anew, and Catherine wiped them away hastily. She knew she must look a frightful mess after all the crying she'd been doing.

As his carriage disappeared from view, turning a corner in the street, Catherine closed the door of the house and walked down into the street, making her way back home.

She could call a carriage, but the sun was still shining beautifully, and she had a newfound energy coursing through her.

As she walked, she brushed her fingers against her lips and smiled, remembering the gentle touch of Charles' lips against hers. Yes, their time apart would be hard, but she knew they could withstand the test of time. He wasn't Brant. He never would be. And for that she was thankful. She'd found her happily ever after.

CHAPTER TWENTY-SEVEN

Brant watched as the ship sailed into the harbor in Barcelona. It had been a long and tiresome few months. Every waking moment was spent wondering if they were being pursued, every night filled with dreams of being abandoned and alone. But he found an odd sort of comfort in the worn pages of Nathan's Bible. And despite the worry and fear that filled Brant, whenever he opened that book he felt a calm come over him.

When his feet finally hit the planks of the Barcelona docks, and no militia marched out to arrest him, he let out a sigh that took with it the tension he had been carrying for months. He was safe. Now he could have the reprieve he so desperately needed, before deciding his future.

"Come, my friend. Senona will be eager to see you are safe," said Caton, walking up beside him.

Brant nodded. "Though I'm sure she'll be happier to see I haven't gotten you in too much trouble."

"Don't fool yourself, Brant. She cares about you. Now come on, let's collect some horses and go home. I have a wife and child I miss dearly."

Brant followed Caton to the stables where his family kept their horses and they acquired a couple mounts, and then rode out to Caton's country home.

The ride relaxed Brant as he watched the countryside pass by. He was in no hurry to get anywhere, but he could see that Caton was anxious, and he didn't blame him. They kept the pace fast, cantering and galloping as much as they could, but never slowing beyond a steady trot. They covered the distance quickly, and what would have normally been over an hour's ride lasted a mere forty-five minutes.

Senona must have seen them coming, because she burst out of the front door running. Brant had to chuckle; she was wearing breeches and her hair hung loose, streaming behind her like a banner as she ran across the yard towards the still trotting horses.

"Looks like she missed you," said Brant, looking over to Caton. The man wore a grin that could compete with a jester's.

"Not half as much as I missed her, I assure you," he replied, then spurred his horse into a ground covering gallop.

Brant held back, giving the husband and wife a chance to be reunited without him, and slowed his horse down to a walk. He watched as Caton drew his horse to a halt, and jumped down before the animal had even come to a complete stop. Senona threw herself into his arms and they twirled for a moment before he set her down. Brant could imagine the words that passed between the two, Caton's forehead now pressed against hers. The joy and love between the two was so apparent that even if one couldn't see it, Brant was sure they would be able to feel it. It was a tangible energy in the air, crackling like lightning in a storm.

The two walked towards the house, hand in hand, and Caton handed his horse off to the groom, Brant seemingly forgotten. He didn't mind, though. He rode up a minute later, dismounting and leading his horse to the small stable where the groom was almost finished untacking Caton's mount.

Brant deposited the horse into an empty stall for the groom to look after once he was finished with the other one.

Walking into the house, he followed the sounds of laughter and voices into the parlor where he was greeted with the sight of Caton lifting a baby into the air, followed by delayed giggles and squeals of delight from the infant.

"He's so big!" exclaimed Brant. "It seems strange that the last time I saw you he wasn't born yet."

Caton and Senona turned to him and she walked over, embracing him. "I'm so very happy you're okay, Brant. You have no idea the worry you put me through."

He kissed the top of her head; much like a brother might, and broke the embrace. "I'm sorry, Senona. I truly am. I was selfish and stupid—"

"You were hurting."

"That's not an excuse."

She nodded. "Now come, you need to meet little Alvaro."

Caton walked over and handed the child to Brant. The action caught Brant by surprise, and he gingerly took the boy, holding him tightly against his chest for fear he might squirm right out of his arms. But as he looked down at the young boy, the child's face broke into a grin and Brant's heart jumped a beat in excitement.

"He likes his *Tio* Brant," he said, unable to contain the smile that had erupted on his face.

"Of course he does. We all love his *Tio* Brant."

He felt a warmth course through him as he held Alvaro and realized, suddenly, that *this* was what he wanted in life. Children weren't a trap; they were a joy and blessing.

"Where is James?" asked Senona, frowning as she looked around. "Is he still outside with the horses?"

"He stayed behind," replied Caton.

"At the ship?"

Brant shook his head, and tears that he thought had long ago gone dry, welled up again. Concern immediately crossed Senona's face and she looked from her husband to Brant and back again.

"Where is he?"

Brant opened his mouth to answer, but he couldn't bring himself to tell her. How could he? James was just as much her family as his own, she had adopted him as her own brother, and loved him the same. The news would hurt her as much as it pained Brant, and he couldn't utter the words. He couldn't hurt her.

"He stayed in Port Royale," said Caton for him.

Senona frowned, her forehead and nose crinkling. "Why?"

"He needed to create his own life. I guess Port Royale is the closest thing he has to a home."

Tears welled up in Senona's eyes, but much to her credit, she held it together, giving a curt nod of understanding. "I suppose it was only a matter of time. He wasn't cut from the same cloth as you or me," she said to Brant.

He chuckled and put Alvaro on the ground. He promptly crawled away towards a small pile of wooden blocks.

"And you, Brant?" she asked. "What's next for you?"

He shrugged. "I really don't know."

"You're welcome here as long as you need to figure things out."

"I'll stay tonight, but tomorrow I'm going to go back to Caton's townhome. You need to be a family without me around."

Senona gave him a sad little smile. Unspoken understanding passed between them with one look, and Brant could tell she knew it was for Caton's sake that he would keep his distance. For their friendship to work he had to know when to back away—after their history, it wasn't fair to subject him to their still close friendship.

Caton gave him a thankful smile that held understanding of words that would never be spoken between the three of them.

"Well, I need to lock myself in my study and go over the books—make sure everything has been running smoothly while I was away."

He dismissed himself, leaving Brant and Senona alone in the room.

"Are you going to be okay?" she asked, sitting down on the floor to play with her baby.

Brant nodded. "Eventually I will be. I'm on the right course now. It'll just take time."

* * *

Boots pounded on the dock behind Johnny as he ran. The steady cadence of marching overwhelmed the staccato of his own footfalls. His breath came sharp and heavy.

He'd left the ship this morning just for a brief walk through town before they set sail again. He wasn't sure if it was fortune or not to notice the soldiers searching tavern to tavern for crewmembers of the *BlackFox*. They wouldn't find anyone. Everyone was aboard the ship this morning to prepare for setting sail. Everyone but Johnny.

The soldiers had spotted him just as he'd turned to head back and warn Matt. He'd taken off running, hoping that he could keep far enough ahead of them to allow the ship's escape.

His feet pounded up the gangway. "Loose the boat! Cut the ropes!" he yelled through panting breaths.

Matt ran up from where he had been bent over a map at a table. "What's going on?"

"Set sail, now! Soldiers—"

Matt's face paled. It didn't take another word from Johnny, he was already shouting orders.

Johnny collapsed to his knees, his sides aching and his breath coming in short painful gasps. Would they make it? The marching boots came louder, and the *BlackFox* was only just beginning to pull away from the dock.

"Stop, in the name of the King!" came a shout.

Johnny looked up at Matt. "We stop now, we prove that Brant isn't here, we're safe. We clear our names."

Matt shook his head. "Remember what I said? They're looking for someone to pay, and they won't care who. We run."

The ship continued to pull away and Johnny watched as the soldiers started running. It was futile though. The gangway had fallen into the harbor as they pulled away, leaving them with no way to get aboard and put a stop to their flight.

Johnny regained his breath and stood up, walking towards the rail. He watched the men, milling about as their commander yelled at them, ordering them back to their own ship so that they could give pursuit. It didn't matter though, they'd never catch them. Not with the head start the *BlackFox* had.

He smirked, waving down at the soldiers who were now in order and marching back to their own ship. "Nice of you to see us off," he called down.

The commander paused and looked up, but didn't offer Johnny a response.

"You have a good day too," he shouted to the commander's

retreating back.

"You shouldn't tease them."

Johnny turned to face Faith. "What harm will it do? They won't catch us."

"It's rude."

"And you're no fun at all."

Faith smiled. "Someone has to keep you in line, Johnny Marshall."

The ship sailed out of Tortuga's harbor and into open sea. Johnny saw the men visibly relax the further they got from the dock and the King's men. It didn't take long to notice a white sail behind them, sporting the British colors. They would follow, but they wouldn't catch up.

Johnny didn't see Faith for the remainder of the day, and he assumed she was tucked away in her cabin, away from the hubbub of activity and the general sense of unease and nervousness that had come back with a vengeance. It had mostly faded away by the time they had docked in Tortuga, but the reminder that they were wanted men didn't sit well with Johnny, or the rest of the crew for that matter.

Watch was taken with diligence. Matt had told Johnny that he was concerned there might be more British navy in the area, and he didn't want to be taken by surprise. So, instead of the usual one or two man watch, there were three on at all times—one stationed permanently in the crow's nest for the duration of his shift.

Johnny's shift was midnight until three. Somehow he always managed to pull that watch. He stationed himself in the crow's nest, allowing the other two to take the fore and aft decks. At around 1 a.m. he heard the creaking of someone climbing the ladder, and he peeked down to see who was joining him.

The moonlight revealed the slim figure of Faith, her skirts and hair whipping about in the wind. It made Johnny nervous that she climbed the rigging in skirts, but she had refused to ditch them for the much more practical breeches. Instead, for proprieties sake, she wore them under her skirts.

"You're going to fall to your death in those skirts, my dear," he said as she stumbled up onto the platform, her toe catching the hem of her skirt and sending her sprawling—it wasn't the first time she had landed in a heap up here.

She looked up at Johnny with wide eyes. "At least I'll look good and proper," she spat back, but he could tell she was shaken up.

"What brings you up here at this time of night?" he asked, changing the subject.

"Couldn't sleep. Today was a close call, wasn't it?"

Johnny nodded. "If I hadn't been in town, hadn't spotted the soldiers, we probably would have been boarded before we even knew what was going on."

He didn't have to go into detail of what that would mean. She was there when he and Matt had discussed the importance of not being caught, and the pallor of her face told him she was envisioning how things *could* have turned out.

"I think we can give thanks that you went into town then."

"Thanks to whom?"

"God."

"You know I don't believe in that, Faith."

"You call it coincidence? I call it divine intervention."

Johnny shook his head and smirked. "Whatever helps you sleep at night."

A frown marred Faith's face when he looked over at her to see her reaction. "I won't preach at you, if that's what you're looking for," she said. "You let me find my strength in my way, and I'll let you find yours in your way."

"Fair enough," replied Johnny, letting the conversation come to an end.

CHAPTER TWENTY-EIGHT

Brant walked through the streets of Barcelona with Isidro. They weren't close by any means, but it was nice to have someone who wasn't attached to family, wasn't settling down, wasn't a constant reminder of what he didn't have.

"How does it feel to walk the streets a free man?" Isidro asked out of nowhere.

The words 'free man' seemed unreal to Brant, as though he'd wake up and realize he was still in prison, awaiting his death. But he had pinched himself more times than he cared to count, and still he remained free. "Good, great in fact. There is nothing to make you feel more alive than a death threat and a harrowing escape."

"But now you're a wanted man."

The words were an unneeded reminder for Brant. He'd been avoiding the question of what he was going to do now that he couldn't sail the seas a free man. He couldn't risk being caught, and that sentence would follow him until the day he died.

"Now I'm a wanted man…" he repeated quietly.

"You aren't going to stay in Spain, are you?" he asked. "You and Senona—"

Brant shook his head. "No, I won't stay here. This isn't my home, and you're right; it isn't healthy for me to be around Senona and Caton. Those feelings won't ever fade."

"Is that why Catherine left you?"

Brant looked over at Isidro, and he could feel his mouth hanging agape. He drew it shut. Well, Isidro certainly was blunt, and as unexpected as it was, Brant had to admit it was refreshing. No one else bothered to ask him *why* Catherine left, or if it was his fault. Maybe they should.

"I don't think it was so much my love for Senona. I think she could live with the fact that there would always be feelings there—I chose her. It's the ocean she couldn't share me with."

Isidro nodded and they walked in silence. Occasionally Brant glanced over at his companion, but he seemed to be deep in thought, so he too remained silent.

After a few minutes Isidro snapped his fingers and pointed at Brant. His eyes were alight with excitement. "You should go to the New World," he said, looking quite proud of himself.

"And do what?" Brant asked, followed by a chuckle.

"I don't know, what do they do out there?"

Brant thought of Corbin, the sailing master he had learned under all those years ago when he had joined the *BlackFox* crew. He had left, gone to the New World to map it out. Could that be something he could do? He knew maps, he knew how to use the tools, and he loved it.

"You look like you're actually considering it. I wasn't serious, Brant. The New World is—"

Brant smiled. "It could be a good place for me. It's new, open, and wild. They won't know who I am out there. I could start a new life."

Isidro shrugged. They had arrived back at Caton's townhouse where Brant was staying, so they stopped their journey.

"Wild being the key word there, Brant. It's not a safe place, nor comfortable. What about the parties and the luxuries?"

Brant smiled, walking up the steps to the door while Isidro remained in the street. "I think it could be the perfect place for me."

* * *

The *BlackFox* limped through the storm season as they sailed slowly but surely towards Spain. It worried Johnny how many storms they were weathering, and with each one the ship came out a little more damaged, and the men a lot more tired. They needed to make port for repairs, but couldn't. Not until they reached the Canary Isles where they were safe from the British grasp.

Johnny had been assigned to help Harold, the ship's carpenter, with as many repairs as they could manage while at sea. But even now Johnny could see a large storm was rising up and chasing them down. They were only a day, two at most, out from the nearest Spanish isle. They needed to make it before they were battered to pieces. The *BlackFox* was a good, faithful girl, but she could only stand so much before she gave in.

Faith walked up, her hair whipping in the angry wind. "Johnny, I'm scared," she said, her eyes not leaving the dark and foreboding clouds.

"It'll be fine," he replied, not believing it himself.

"That looks like a bad storm, and we've already been through a few—"

"We'll weather her alright, and we'll make port tomorrow. After that it's just a week to Barcelona. The *BlackFox* is a good, strong ship. She'll make it through."

Faith nodded.

"Just go inside your cabin and wait it out. You'll be safe there."

Matt approached and his eyes met Johnny's. The look that passed between them let Johnny know that Matt had the same bad feeling about this that he did, that he had heard what Johnny had said and he believed it about as much as Johnny did. But neither said anything until Faith walked away.

Even as she retreated, and Johnny stood stalwart by the rail with Matt, the sails began to whip about furiously.

"This isn't good."

Matt nodded. "I know. Maybe you should ask Faith to pray."

"I don't want to scare her."

"Then maybe we should pick up praying," he replied. "Because I'm not sure we're going to make it through this one."

Johnny's heart thudded in his chest, and as if on cue, the clouds released their heavy burden and rain began pouring down on them.

"Tie in those sails!" shouted Matt, walking, Johnny keeping step beside him as the deck began to roll and toss about, and the waves they rode became larger and rougher.

There was no time for talking now. The deck was alive with activity as the rain pelted down on the men and the wind battered them about. Already the swells were becoming monstrous, and the *BlackFox* rode over them only to crash down on the other side.

The men wrestled with the ship. Matt held on to the wheel trying to hold it on course. The wheel was tied, helping Matt fight the wind, but he still had to push his entire body into it.

Johnny looked up to the dark and boiling sky and for the first time in his life uttered a short prayer, "Please, God. Get us through this." They had been fighting the storm for over an hour and the men didn't have much more in them to give.

No sooner did he say the words did he see blue sky starting to peek through just ahead. Relief soared through him as his exhausted body realized that the end was close. They were going to make it.

A loud snap filled the air, ripping through Johnny's thoughts. His eyes strayed from the sign of hope and up to the source of the sound, which was now flapping and snapping in the wind.

"Johnny, get up there and secure that sail!" shouted Matt from his position at the helm.

Johnny ran up to the mast and began scaling the rigging. His arms and legs shook with fatigue and exertion, but steadily he climbed up, and shimmied across the spar towards where the sail had come free from its restraints.

The wind lashed out at him, screaming in his ears like an angry banshee as he struggled with the sail. The rain was starting to slow just enough that he could tell that the storm was coming to an end.

Finally, he managed to contain the sail and tie it in its place. He worked his way back to the mast, taking his time, allowing himself pause for the crashing of the ship over swells.

He could feel the ship moving up, riding a swell, and he prepared for the crash. He braced himself against whatever was at hand. But it didn't come. Frowning, he stood up to see why. The swell just grew larger and larger in front of his eyes and the ship kept riding up it, not yet reaching the crest of it. Johnny's heart stopped, and he reached for his waist to feel the reassuring touch of rough rope holding him securely to the ship—a rope that would drag him down if the ship crashed to pieces, which it surely would at the hands of this wave. She had been through too much. She was abused, battered, bruised, and broken. This would be the wave to end her, and she would take him and everyone on her to the depths of the ocean.

Untying the rope, he threw it aside just as the ship crested the wave and began its plummet down. Johnny closed his eyes, hearing nothing but the wind and the rain. As the ship landed he felt himself ripped from her embrace and flew through the air.

Then it stopped. Suddenly. He hit the water with such force that it felt more like a solid wall than the gentle embrace he expected; driving the breath from his lungs as pain ripped through his entire body, from his head to his toes. The last thing he saw before everything went black was the sun, peeking out through the clouds.

CHAPTER TWENTY-NINE

Brant rode next to Senona at a leisurely trot. He had been keeping his distance from her out of respect for Caton, but today she had invited him to go for a ride and he couldn't pass it by. He had missed her, and with James, Catherine, and Faith gone, he really needed time with a friend.

"Isidro tells me you're considering going to the New World," she said, opening the conversation that he had been toying with since their ride began.

"I think it could be a good place for me."

He waited for her argument. Waited for her to say that he should stay; that he was safe here and that he could retain his business partnership with Caton. Of course, any refuting she could do would be futile. He had already made up his mind that he couldn't stay here—largely because of her—and that he had no interest in being a business man.

"I agree," she replied.

Brant frowned. That wasn't exactly the response he had been expecting. "Come again?"

Senona laughed. "You want me to tell you to stay? I'm not going to do that, Brant. I know you aren't happy here and it's time you made a change in your life. Go to the New World. I hear it's a good place for men who have a hard time following the law."

"If I go it means goodbye."

She nodded, but Brant could see the pain in the way she held her shoulders and patted Naldo's neck, turning her attention away from him and their conversation, trying to mask her true feelings. But he could read her like a book.

"Maybe it's about time we said our goodbyes, don't you think, Brant? This relationship of ours... it's complicated. We're not friends, we never will be. We both know that. When you had Catherine at least we could stifle everything, but now that you're alone it isn't fair to you to be around me, and it isn't fair to Caton to allow this closeness to continue."

"I know."

"I'll always care about you, Brant. But I love Caton, and as much as it hurts me that you're leaving, I think it's for the best. Maybe a fresh start is just what you need."

They stopped their horses, having arrived back at Senona's estate. "Thank you."

"For what?"

"For understanding."

She dismounted, but Brant remained on his horse.

"Won't you stay for supper?"

He shook his head with a sad smile. "No, I think it's best that I remain distant as much as possible. It will make goodbye easier."

Tears filled her eyes, but he had to credit her for her strength. She refused to let them fall. Instead she pressed her lips into a firm, tight line, and nodded.

"I won't leave without saying goodbye this time, I promise."

He wheeled his horse around and kicked him into a gallop, running from the woman who would always own a piece of his heart.

* * *

A solid knock sounded on the front door of Caton's townhouse, resonating through the front hall and into the parlor where Brant was lounging on a couch. He looked up from the book he was reading. He was finally getting around to finishing

Paradise Lost. The butler was already making his way to the door, but his attention on the book had already been lost, so he sat up straight and set the book aside, waiting to see who was there.

Brant heard the door close, and footsteps approach.

"Señor, there is a Matthew here to see you," the manservant said in Spanish, stumbling over the English name.

Brant smiled at the fact that Matt hadn't given a last name, and he wondered if maybe Matt didn't even know what it was, since he'd never told it to anyone that Brant knew of.

"Show him in," he said, standing up.

Moments later, Matt walked in. He looked tired and aged. The last few months appeared to have been hard on him. Brant was used to seeing a robust, happy youth, but in front of him stood a tired, sad man.

Walking over to his friend, Brant shook his hand. "Matt, I'm so glad to see you."

"And you, Cap'n. Everything went well?"

Brant nodded. "As smooth as can be. And on your end?"

"There were a few tense moments, but we came out alright. Sailing through the storm season was the worst part."

"How did my girl hold up?"

"Admirably, Sir. She's a bit battered and bruised, but give it a couple weeks and she'll be ready to take back to sea."

"Perfect. Where's Johnny?"

Matt's face paled. "We..." he trailed off.

Brant's heart sank and settled somewhere deep in the pit of his stomach. "Where is Johnny, Matthew?"

"We lost him." His voice was dull and flat.

"What do you mean 'lost'?"

"The last storm we weathered, a week back, he went overboard. We searched but there was no sign of him. The storm was bad, who knows how far he was swept away..." he trailed off again. Then he seemed to pull himself together, raising his head high, his face impassive and strong. "We did everything we could, Sir."

Brant nodded, swallowing back the sorrow that threatened to take over. Yet another casualty because of his selfishness and stupidity. Would others ever stop paying for the error of *his* ways?

"First James, now Johnny..." he said to himself.

"What happened to James?"

"He stayed in Port Royale. It was his own choice, but I won't be seeing him again. I can't go back there."

Matt nodded, as if it didn't surprise him, but said nothing.

"I'll write to Catherine and let her know. You see to it that the *BlackFox* gets the repairs she needs. We're taking to sea as soon as she's ready."

"Sir, there is one other thing."

Brant sighed. He couldn't take any more bad news. "What is it?"

"It's Faith."

Brant closed his eyes and held his breath, waiting for Matt to finish what he was saying. James leaving, then the news of Johnny, those were hard enough. But if something had happened to Faith, he could never forgive himself. Never.

"She's... here..."

He stared at Matt, letting the words sink in. "Here?"

"She came with us."

"Why?"

"I think maybe that's something you have to hear from her. She's waiting on the ship."

Brant walked past Matt, towards the front door, but paused when he realized Matt was still standing in the parlor. "What are you waiting for? Let's go."

* * *

Brant couldn't walk fast enough. Faith is here, sang through his mind. Of course, that silly, stubborn girl was here. She didn't listen to a thing he said. Ever. If she had, he'd be dead a few months ago. And she certainly wouldn't have followed him here.

He practically ran aboard the *BlackFox*, stopping only to scan the deck. There she stood at the bow of the ship, wind blowing her hair and skirts about her, looking like the ship's figurehead.

She hadn't noticed him yet, too busy staring out at the city. He slowed his walk, willing his heart to stop pounding. *Please*, he prayed silently, *let her say she loves me.* Those were the words he needed to hear more than ever right now.

He walked up to her, resisting the urge to pull her into his arms and profess everything he felt for her but had been suppressing for months, since he had first met her in the jail cell and she had cleaned his wounds. He had thought she was an angel back then, now he *knew* she was.

"What are you doing here?" he asked.

She looked up, and he could see the nervousness in her eyes. "I couldn't stay behind. Not after everything—"

Brant smiled. "Faith," he said, reaching out and resting his hand on her cheek. "*Why* are you here?"

Her eyes focused on the deck beneath her feet, lowering her eyelids in such a way that showed her youth and innocence, the way that made Brant's heart pound uncontrollably. He waited for her to speak, but she remained silent. Then, her shoulders squared up and she looked him directly in the eye; all the fire and spunk she contained shining through in her eyes. "I came because I love you, Brant Foxton, and you don't just abandon love. If you want to send me home, then fine. But I couldn't live with the regret of not knowing how you felt."

"Faith. Oh, Faith," he said, dropping his hand from her face and pulling her against him. "I love you. I do. But—"

"Don't say 'but', Brant. You love me. That's enough."

"But I'm not good for you," he continued. "And you need to realize that a life with me will never be easy. I'm selfish by nature, and I have a past that will probably continue to haunt me. But if you'll give me a chance, if you'll be patient with me, I want you to be a part of my life. I want you beside me."

Tears filled Faith's eyes and spilled over onto her cheek, but the smile that erupted on her face told him that he couldn't have made her happier.

"You have no idea how many times I've dreamed of hearing those words."

"How do you feel about going to the New World, then? I hear it's full of opportunity and adventure for a man like me."

"Anywhere you go, Brant Foxton, whether it be the ocean,

America, or the other side of the world, it doesn't matter. I don't care where I am, just that I'm with you."

Brant lifted her chin with his index finger, staring her straight in the eyes. She had just said the words he had been longing to hear all his life. As his lips touched hers, he realized that for once in his life, he was at peace. He had found a belief in God, and now all he was missing was her. Not the ocean and all her triviality. Just Faith.

ABOUT THE AUTHOR

Christine Steendam is the award-winning romance author of the Foremost Chronicles and the Ocean Series. She also flirts with sci-fi and comic book writing and is a yearly participant in NaNoWriMo.

Christine makes her home in Manitoba, Canada on a sprawling 15 acre ranch with her husband, two young sons, and a brood of animals including Guinness, her beloved chocolate quarter horse, Beau, her St Bernard/Golden Retriever cross, and a gaggle of barn kittens.

www.christinesteendam.com
www.facebook.com/authorchristine.s
www.twitter.com/chrissteen1991